CLOSE KNIT

Also by Jenny Colgan

CLOSE KNIT

A NOVEL

JENNY COLGAN

AVON

An Imprint of HarperCollinsPublishers

HarperCollins books may be purchased for educational, business, or sales promotional use. For information, please email the Special Markets Department at SPsales@harpercollins.com.

Published in the U.K. by Hodder in 2024.

FIRST U.S. EDITION

Interior text design by Diahann Sturge-Campbell

Library of Congress Cataloging-in-Publication Data has been applied for.

ISBN 978-0-06-326056-6
ISBN 978-0-06-338666-2 (library hardcover)

24 25 26 27 28 LBC 6 5 4 3 2

In memory of my mother and grandmother,
who taught me to knit,
and always helped with the tricky bits.

"Knitting is one of the few times in your life where there are no bad consequences for making a mistake."

—STEPHANIE PEARL-MCPHEE

PREFACE

A Note on Scottish Schooling

Scottish schools start with primary schools—primary one, or P1, begins the year you turn five, and goes up to P7. After this is senior, or secondary school, which starts with S1 the year you turn twelve, known as "first year," and continues to S6, "sixth year," when you turn eighteen. Collectively, pupils are "primary ones" or "first years," etc.

PROLOGUE

The small community of Carso, in the very North of Scotland, would be straining at the seams to call itself a town, but wildly insulted if you referred to it as a village.

After all, it has a secondary school; tiny (and the next nearest is Kinlochbervie, 75 miles away, which makes it very inconvenient to date and/or fight other pupils) but it is a school nonetheless. It also has a ScotNorth SuperMiniMarket, which is absolutely almost a co-op (but not, alas, a fabled "Big Tesco").

It is a pretty town of long, low-roofed, whitewashed cottages, joined together up the cobbled main street; small pubs, and a very fine old kirk that is subsiding into the graveyard but everyone politely pretends not to notice.

The north side of Carso is entirely bounded by the sea. It is on the roof of Scotland, where the Arctic and Atlantic waters meet, and swirl and churn so it can look like the water is filled with whirlpools where the tides duke it out.

From the shoreline, there is an archipelago that dots its way up into the distance, its tiny eruptions—Cairn, Inchborn, Larbh, and Archland—like charms on a bracelet.

The light on the North Coast is flat and golden and wide; you can see, on the water, where the swirling seas all meet, from the west and the great Atlantic Ocean, to the east, which leads you to the Baltic Sea and the Scandinavian cousins of its residents. The weather changes dramatically fast; careering up from the northern tips of the Highlands to your back, pouring down fog, rain, or bright clear frosted sunlight at any time of more or less any day.

The wild sea grass waves, and the beach is bright, long and white, the water always dangerous and punishingly cold, but fine for paddling; the clear water of the rivers that open out there are perfect for bathing, if you don't mind occasionally being brushed by a large trout, or getting too close to the otters, who do not like you in the slightest. Seals pepper the coastline of course, with a lot to say to each other, and to you, if you go out to catch any of their fish. Fishing is the town's main industry—it was once the herring capital of the world—though tourists also stop on the North 500 to stare at the very tip of the country, and dairy farming stretches far across the flats.

The water and the air are clear, the people friendly and close-knit and it is considered by many who make their lives there as the friendliest, safest, best place in the world, particularly to raise a family (if you don't mind the odd wet day, and seriously, why would you, when you can watch kestrels lazily circle, or herons stalk the beach, or baby lambs hop spring puddles and all you need is a jacket and a bunnet).

There is a book van that comes round with your reading, and a tiny plane that goes up even further, to the islands of the north, or, if you are feeling intensely cosmopolitan, Glasgow, which connects you to the rest of the world "down below." It is a special and singular part of the world, with more animals than people, and even if it is not for everyone there are many who find it freeing. A place where you can't hurry the tractor on the road and, anyway, it's rather nice to look at the stocky Highland coos, with their absurdly luxuriant hair, or the shifting sands on the dunes, or the many many castles tucked away in every bay. Everywhere the evidence of centuries of kings and tribes and battles and fortifications; when this rough land was covered in blood. Now it is as peaceable as a place that still gets Amazon deliveries can be.

Plenty of people spent their lives there and had never been further south than Glasgow. Why would you?

ON THIS DAY, Gertie Mooney was walking home along the waterfront and, as usual, she had her head in a dream.

Gertie Mooney having her head in a dream was not a state of mind that would have surprised anyone; not her mum, Jean; not her teachers; not her boss, Mr. Wainwright, at the ScotNorth supermarket, of whom Gertie—whenever she popped her head out of a dream—was terrified because he was gruff, even though he was rarely gruff with her (apart from occasionally telling her off for daydreaming) and ran charity fun runs.

Gertie's tolerance for men being gruff with her was quite low. She had been raised more or less entirely by women. She lived with Jean and her grandmother, Elspeth, in one of the tiny whitewashed Shore Cottages, which look so small you can't believe people live in them instead of, say, hobbits. Today her daydream is of a new apartment, as currently her home is full of wool. It is not just home to her own family; it is also the base of Carso's Knitting Circle, also known as the KCs, a posse of women both feared and admired for their ways with a set of size 00s, a skein of angora, and an extremely strong side-eye game.

Jean and Elspeth had been everything to her, after her father had moved on when she was a baby and gone back to his other family a long way away, the existence of which came as rather a shock to Jean, who did not like talking about it one little bit. And the KCs had helped, every step of the way, from Gertie's first learning to walk (swathed in yellow wool, which would suggest the twins, Tara and Cara, had a hand in it as they loved yellow); first school uniform (knitted scratchy cardigans Gertie loathed with a fiery passion, but when trying to explain this was met with indulgent tuts that she was showing herself up); to her first time on a bike with Auntie Marian's strong hands to guide her.

But it was getting too much. And since the pandemic, the wool had begun a mission creep. Jean had stockpiled it, even though it was toilet roll—not Black Isle yarn—that had been in demand, and it was still stacked up in Gertie's tiny tiny bedroom like a soft reproof.

Today she was daydreaming about getting her own place. Let's see. *Some rich handsome millionaire moved to the town and decided to build ... some luxury penthouses along their cold and wild shore. It could happen. And the most beautiful one at the top had a hot tub and he was moving in there and was ever so lonely, having come to get away from it all, and said darling Gertrude ...*

Gertie sighed. She hated her name. It was not a sexy, romantic name. It was the kind of name, as she had often complained to Jean, designed to make sure she never met anyone. Jean thought Gertrude was wonderfully exotic, having been a Jean all her life, and anyway, it suited her, being quirky, and Gertie scowled and said, well, what did that mean, exactly, and Jean had said "nothing" very quickly, because the house really was too small to fight in more than was strictly necessary.

Gertie turned into her own street, the dusk falling, the spring lights just starting to show in the tiny windows. It was pretty, she thought. And back in those days ... she softened her gaze on the street; blurred her vision of the council wheelie bins and the Ford Fiestas ... and she lost herself in a dream suddenly, the modern world vanishing as she imagined herself back to the days when the handsome local fishermen would come join the knitters to mend their nets ...

In the summer they would sit outside and knit in the long light nights that stretched till midnight, and if the men were home they would join them, stitching up their sails, and they would toss compliments and barbs between them all and drink rough mugs of tea, a dram of whisky for special occasions, and look out on the waves just beyond the end of the gardens, and the aprons flapping in the fresh breeze, and watch young . . . maybe a handsome Iain, thought Gertie, in an open-necked ghillie shirt—oh yes. Flirting again with . . . let me see. A pretty name. Rosamund? No. You didn't get many of them in the Highlands back then. Let's see. Maggie, the horseman's daughter. Yes. Pretty Maggie. And Maggie laughing so with her head tilted back as they shared a hunk of rough cheese, and thought, all things considered, there were worse ways to pass an evening—to pass a life, maybe—than living in the Shore Close cottages, knitting in the garden, as smoke passed over from the pipes of the men, and someone would start up a fiddle in the corner because, well, running your needles is always easier when you're on a rhythm, isn't it so.

And as the herons took off across the bay, Gertie could almost see them, dancing and circling in the smoky haze of the evening, new grass sweet in the air, the laughter, and the click of needles, and handsome young Iain has grasped Maggie round the waist, now, of her rough linen dress, with its Tuesday-clean apron tied around her, small and neat as a pin, and he has her turning in a circle and some of the older ladies look up to watch, because it's a happy place to be on a night like this with the birds coming back, huge flights of swifts and sparras above their heads, the water so thick with fish you could walk on their backs to the New Found Land, and Maggie and Iain would be in the kirk before the weather turned again, Maggie with a coronet of late summer roses in her hair . . .

And Gertie found herself thinking, well, times were tough then, as indeed they were, but then people will think that about us one day: "Well, it must have been awful in the 2020s; it took a day to get to Australia and people used to die in car accidents!"

And, thought Gertie, drawing close to their little front door, which opened right onto the street, it must have been easier in those days to meet someone down the road you quite liked at seventeen, and to just decide to get married and stick with it. Hard, but compared to her life of endless crushes, awful online apps, Instagram, and modern dating . . . but Gertie wouldn't, she told herself quite often, rather die exhausted in childbirth than deal with the hellish modern dating scene. But you could buy a house for less than a zillion pounds back then, and actually live in it, rather than do what people did now: pay a fortune for anywhere remotely nice, then come up and visit it once a year for a fortnight, complain about the weather, and act surprised that local people weren't happier to see them.

After all, pondered Gertie, still dreaming of another time in the same place, in those days the air was clean and the seasons were more or less predictable, and they ate good fresh clean food from the land and not only had they never heard of Instagram, or celebrities, many had never seen their own faces in a mirror. They had a saying we still have today: "*Èist ri gaoth nam beann gus an traogh na h-uisgeachan*," which means: "Listen to the wind upon the hill until the water abates," which means: "This too shall pass," which means: "It is what it is."

PART ONE

CHAPTER 1

I t is what it is," was what Jean Mooney said as Gertie, still with her head in romantic Highlanders of many years ago, came through the low front door, went upstairs to change out of her work tabard, and came face to face with thirty-two new flecked mohair mixed-color packs.

"Mum!" Gertie had yelled down in outrage. "I'm going to have to sleep on a bed of wool!" The cottage had a front room, with a large fireplace—the room itself was small, and the floor sloped, but the fireplace was lined with big logs purloined some time back from the shipyards. There had been a push a few years ago to get on the gas, but the urge had passed, and Gertie was glad. She liked to gaze into the dancing flames.

"That sounds nice!" returned Jean.

"You're hoarding."

Jean sniffed. "I'm just being careful! Wool is getting expensive."

She glanced out of the back window, where several fields of sheep were cheerfully grazing the springing emerald grass, full and rich after several weeks of heavy rainfall.

"Although I swear I cannot tell why as it only goes from over there to over here."

"You're hedging wool?"

"I'm sure I don't know what you mean."

"You're going to sell it on to the wool shop if the price keeps going up."

Jean and the Woman in the Wool Shop had a fabled enmity, lost to the mists of time.

"Again, I don't know what you're talking about."

Gertie looked at it mutinously, closed the door to her bedroom, and came back downstairs.

"I'd almost think you were trying to get rid of me. Whilst also turning a tidy profit."

"You think I want my beloved only child to move out and see a bit of the world and spread her wings and build a life for herself beyond a very small town? That's ridiculous," said Jean, as the kettle boiled.

"Huh," said Gertie, frowning, even as the bell rang and the KCs hastened into the tiny hall, festooned with incremental school pictures of Gertie, her black soft curly hair wrestled into bunches or plaits, trussed up in wool.

"Hey, Gertie," said Cara (or Tara, it was hard to tell when they had identically knitted bunnets on). Cara and Tara were twins who hated each other and yet had somehow dealt with this lifelong animosity by choosing to spend vast amounts of time together, including most of their evenings. They both worked in the local council office and were elders at the kirk, where they bitched each other up nonstop to the minister, who considered it a mark of his own penance and saintly patience that he would let this endure, so it worked out pretty well for everyone. They knitted a lot of bright yellow bonnets for "the babies in Africa," nobody ever daring to tell them that perhaps wooly hats weren't currently top of the priority list for the booming countries of that continent; and if they were sad they had never had their own babies to knit for, they never said.

"What's been going on in that big head of yours today?"

They were convinced Gertie's tendency to drift off was a mark of her supreme intelligence rather than, as it had actually been, a terrible hindrance in her exams. Not that she minded the Scot-North particularly; the work wasn't hard and the people were nice and she had plenty of time to vanish into her own dreams.

"Mostly how I'm going to build a nest in what used to be my room," said Gertie.

Next through the door was Marian. Marian was a terrible knitter, because she had very large hands, and she wasn't particularly good at doing her makeup either, being newer to it and everything, having been on the fishing boats for a very long time before coming to a certain realization about her true self, so nobody minded, and everyone had a mouthful for anyone in town who remarked, or seemed to indicate that they did mind, or had something to say about it, or even looked like they might. That worked out perfectly well for everyone apart from the occasional distracted passerby who hadn't realized they were staring until it was too late, and they had Jean in their face, which was extremely unnerving at the best of times.

"Hey," Marian said. "I heard there's that new man in town again."

Everyone's ears pricked up and they turned and stared at Gertie, except for Majabeen who had just turned up. Majabeen had a fondness for beautiful Kaffe Fassett work, meticulously done. Everyone would have admired it more if she ever stopped talking about how wonderful her children and grandchildren were and how well they were doing. Whilst a certain amount of bragging was respectable, indeed expected—Marian's daughter getting a promotion; the twins' cousin getting his early parole—Majabeen's children were always winning scholarships and awards and whilst it was amazing it was also very slightly exhausting. Majabeen pretended it was all a terrible burden, talking about how awful it would be if one of her grandchildren only became an orthodon-tist rather than a cardiologist. Majabeen thought Jean indulging Gertie's fantasy life was ridiculous.

"Stop it, please," said Gertie, burying her face in her knitting.

Whilst Jean favored mohair and extravagant tops with large knitted flowers stitched on "for interest," Elspeth was Fair Isle all the way, in murky greens and blues; the twins stuck to yellow and Majabeen loved the vibrant jewel colors, all mixed together. Marian was more of a beginner, was also color-blind, and was valiantly opposed to girls in pink and boys in blue, so her choices tended toward the eccentric. The faces of the family who'd received as a moving-in gift an entirely black baby layette remained etched in everyone's memories.

Gertie, on the other hand, loved subtle shades; palest blues and grays that matched the ever-changing sky; sometimes with a thin line of bright color—a gold, or a pale pink—that mimicked dawn on the horizon; earthy, soft tones that reflected the water and the countryside that had surrounded her whole life. In her deep fantasy world, she dreamed of her designs being feted, worn around the globe. In her actual world, it was mostly Jean complaining that she should "jazz things up a bit."

Because knitting for Gertie was not just a way to produce things. It was so much more than that. It was how she self-soothed after a difficult day, when the boss was grumpy or the customers impatient. It was the way she indulged her creative side, which couldn't happen when she was stacking shelves (although she was always the go-to for holiday displays); choosing the colors with infinite care; the weight of the wool, often light as thistledown; experimenting with, e.g., a 1940s shoulder, or a pillbox hat.

It was the joy of feeling something growing from her hands, entirely of her own creation. And the comfort of the familiar motion, learned at her grandmother's knee; in/round/through and off.

If worried or stressed, opening her knitting bag and setting the weight of her needles in her hands, and launching into the soothing click-clicking rhythm always slowed her racing thoughts or quelled her agitation, leaving her imagination free to soar, to go where it would. Even, she occasionally thought, a little ruefully, if the agitation was caused by the other KCs, particularly when they were in the middle of one of their "Let's Sort out Gertie's Love Life!" phases.

"What new man?" asked Jean fussily. There were long discussions of every man who passed through their small town.

"Calum Frost is back," said Marian, smug with knowledge. "He's hanging round the airport again."

"OOH!" said Jean to Gertie. "You should get down there. Brush your hair."

"Don't be stupid, Mum," said Gertie. Calum Frost was a Norwegian aviation magnate who owned—amongst many other things—the tiny airline that ran out of Carso to the islands. He was funding MacIntyre Air after they'd lost a plane the previous summer, much to the displeasure of Morag MacIntyre, local pilot. Technically she—and Ranald, her grandfather—worked for Calum Frost, but she pretended she didn't, and Calum was pretty good about it.

"Anyway, when would I need to get on a plane?"

"You could get on a plane!" said Jean.

"It literally goes up the archipelago," said Gertie. "To places where there is even less to do than there is here."

"You could go to Glasgow!"

"I will, Mum," Gertie replied, knowing this was the fastest way to get her mother to drop it and, sure enough, Majabeen soon launched into a long story about scholarships, which was extremely difficult to follow, and Gertie could stare into the fire, accompanied only by the clack of needles, and lose herself . . .

It would be someone to make cozy socks for—nice and large, without presumptions; it's nice to have a roomy sock. She dreamed of someone—someone whose face was fuzzy. They didn't have to be terribly glamorous; she certainly wasn't. But someone nice, just coming home at night, coming in out of the cold, into the cottage—no, nix that. SURELY she wouldn't still be living in the cottage. Okay, well, maybe another cottage then, but all for them, with a nice layout and one of those nice glass extensions at the back she'd seen people get. And he'd come in from a freezing day, the wind flicking his nice hair sideways, into the cozy sitting room and there'd be some nice cock-a-leekie soup on the stove, and he'd just be so happy to see her and so happy to be home, and he'd put his arms around her waist whilst she was at the stove and say, "Honestly, I don't know what I'd have done without that hat today," and she would feel the cold coming off him, and turn round to welcome him home . . .

It didn't feel like so much to ask. It felt a million miles away.

CHAPTER 2

In contrast, Morag MacIntyre, the town's pilot, along with her grandfather, Ranald (and Calum's money, which she didn't like being brought up) couldn't be happier with her boyfriend, Gregor. Everything about this curious, clever, understated man just obsessed her more and more. It felt like they would never and could never get to the end of each other; rubbing off each other's foibles, the push and pull of early courtship; the sex, the wonder, the fights about washing up methods.

But his location was, to say the least, a problem; Gregor lived on Inchborn, a mostly uninhabited island with a ferry once a day in the summertime. It wasn't practical or remotely affordable for her to commute via plane, so she was stuck with days off, when she could get a lift, and using the radio when she couldn't, which wasn't ideal as half of the village (the male half, generally) could tune in at will.

It would have been all right if she hadn't had to spend the rest of the time bunking with her grandfather, Ranald. She had cash, she could have rented somewhere herself, but everywhere in town was expensive holiday lets; and buying places was pricey too. So many local houses were empty second homes, which drove everyone absolutely crazy with the unfairness of it. Just because they were born in a beautiful place, it meant they were never going to be able to afford to live there.

And she did love her Gramps, and she had her own room; the room she and her brother always used to share on their summer holidays, where Morag would be so excited to sit in the plane, and

Jamie would be happier down on the sand, staring at the shell-fish or chasing crabs. He was now a renowned wildlife photographer and illustrator, having broken the family's hearts by getting a scholarship to an incredibly illustrious art school and becoming extremely well-respected and successful in his chosen field (which, unfortunately, wasn't piloting a plane). He normally started conversations with Morag by asking her cheerfully how many ducks she'd killed that month.

The room was still stocked with her old, slightly weatherbeaten, dog-eared paperbacks; Harry Potter, of course; Garth Nix; and a complete set of Biggles books. The single-paned Victorian glass looked out to the wild sea and, to the left, the airfield. The house was kind of falling apart, but its rambling, homely nature had always been a balm to Morag.

There was one fly in the ointment, however, and it was round and stern and came with a flatulent hound. Peigi.

When Morag had lived down south she hadn't given Peigi a second thought, beyond the fact that she was quite pleased Ranald had someone looking after him. Peigi had moved in as a "house-keeper" not long after Ranald's beloved wife, Morag's grand-mother, had died. Ranald, like many men of his generation, had stoically battled on and refused to discuss it, something that worried everyone. Peigi had arrived to help out with cleaning and providing dinner, once the supply of sympathetic lasagnas from the neighbors had dried up, and that had seemed a reasonable solution; she was a widow too. It would be company, Morag had thought.

When Morag had had to come up and help out the previous summer, Peigi had been annoying, but she hadn't had much to do with her.

Now, however, Morag was living there long-term, paying board (nominal; Ranald didn't want to accept anything at all but Morag had insisted. The rest she put into a savings account for . . . well, one day. Maybe.). And Peigi didn't like it one little bit. She scowled if Morag came into the kitchen to make a cup of tea. She slammed around when Ranald and Morag sat down in the evening to discuss routes and weather patterns and got even more furious when Morag bought Ranald a fabulous flight simulator for Christmas and they spent hours making up complex routes for each other and trying to land on the roofs of skyscrapers.

She wouldn't let Morag cook. Morag wasn't a great cook—that was very much Gregor's department—but she craved some variance to the bland stringy stews and pies Peigi turned out. Ranald didn't really care: he was a proper "food as fuel" man. Morag, though, found it all stodgy and uninspiring and not what you wanted to come home to after a set of tricky landings or some swift turnarounds or a mechanical fault that wouldn't wait for an engineer and required her to get grease up to her elbow, outside the plane in the rain.

"So how long are you staying?" Peigi would ask with a sniff every so often.

On the other hand, when Morag escaped gladly at the weekends for Gregor's, or zipped over to her parents, Peigi would then make a big deal out of her not treating the house like a hotel. The last time she had gone, Peigi had pulled her aside, her dog Skellington following her, farting with every step of his short legs. He had conjunctivitis again, something Peigi never seemed to bother getting cleared up, so kept pawing at his pus-filled red eyes whilst hacking like a sixty-a-day smoker. The whole house smelled of wet dog.

"I just need to know," said Peigi. "Because your grandfather is too polite to tell you. But I can do it for him. Just so he knows. When will he get his house back?"

And Morag had mentioned the predicament to Gregor in the hopes that he *would* perhaps suggest them getting a place together, except he had very gently pointed out that it was very early days and they probably shouldn't shack up together just because of sub-par stew, and Gregor being a careful man was one of the things Morag loved about him, but it was still very annoying.

So that needed sorting out, as well as the lovely but also slightly tricky news that Nalitha, who ran check-in for the airline, was pregnant again. This was great, of course it was, but Nalitha had been with the company for a long time and did absolutely everything, and Morag was going to have to find a replacement sooner rather than later. Jobs were abundant in the Highlands so she wasn't sure how, exactly, she was going to find someone happy to come and check in, haul luggage, and handle everything at their little kiosk in the breezy tin shed Carso proudly called its airport. And her boss, Calum Frost, who she had rather hoped would be quite hands-off when he had taken over, was proving quite the opposite. He was rather taken with the place.

But finding a place to live. That was the real problem.

CHAPTER 3

Sir! Sir! Moss has got a clarsach in his mouth! Again!"

Struan McGhie put down his guitar carefully, with a sigh, looking round the large room, with its climbing bars and terrible acoustics. Music lessons took place in the gym hall. As did gym, lunch, assembly, performances, and . . . basically it was the only free space in the school. They tried to keep the windows open all year round.

"Moss, unhook," he ordered, and the little boy removed his jaw from the small ancient harp that was missing its top E string, but was otherwise tuned beautifully.

"All right," Struan said, slowly so they'd understand. "Now we're going to try again. I just want clapping, and if we can, the left of the room and the right of the room are going to sing your different tunes, but AT THE SAME TIME."

The faces were wide-eyed with concentration. There was a general belief that kids under twelve who weren't particularly gifted couldn't sing in harmony. Struan thought this was nonsense and had spent much of his last eight years as a music teacher attempting to disprove it.

"Chaidh mo lothag air chall.
O hù gur h-oil leam."

Half of the children started to sing, on his left-hand side, sweet and quiet and low. He nodded. Now they had to sing the next section whilst his right-hand side came in.

"Chaidh mo lothag air chall . . ."

He made sure that the strong singers were equally divided to help the less sure on each side, and let both rip. Annabel O'Faoilan was right up there with the girls on the right, bang in, straight on the note, no bother. Okay, the timbre of her voice tended toward the tortured cat end of the register, rather than the soft gentle melody he was aiming for, the one that made all the parents cry at the end of term when the voices separated, but she was too good an anchor for him to ask her to pipe down.

On the left, Moss, the usual trail of snot from his nose forming a permanent furrow to his lip, had his eyes tight shut behind his thick glasses, desperately trying to force the other tune out of his head and stick to the first one. Struan joined in with whichever side was struggling.

"mo lothag dhan fhèithidh 's mòr am beud dhi dhol ann . . ."

If it were up to him he would keep dividing the voices into four, even five, but he knew when not to push his limits with St. John's Primary 6s. And it still sounded rather lovely; any gaps in technique more than made up for by the purity of the voices.

Even Hugh McSticks, who had started off as a consummate grunter when he sung, unable to lift his voice off one single note at a time and sounding not entirely like a ship passing in foggy water, had managed to soften down and relax enough to follow the tune, and if he wavered in and out of the thirds for his group or the others, well, that didn't matter at all. Just as Struan was cheerfully thinking this, Hugh McSticks suffered a drop of about an octave mid-note, which he personally didn't seem to have noticed at all, which meant the lovely soft song sounded like it was finishing by crashing into an elephant.

Even with Hugh, they all finished roughly at the same time, some of them even remembering to look at him conducting and quieting their voices at the end, and he grinned at them broadly. He glanced quickly over at Oksana, their guest child from Ukraine.

He didn't ever call her out. But it didn't escape his notice that she never sung a word.

"This is going to be great!" he said. "We've got the Easter concert tied up. We're going to embarrass the heck out of the Primary 7s—they're done for."

The children liked that, and beamed.

"What about the Primary 2s?" said Khalid, who had an unbearable sister in Primary 2 and as such was concerned about the outcome.

"I'm not sure about the Primary 2s," said Struan sympathetically. "I think they're dressing up as rabbits and hopping about a bit to look cute with their teeth out to a Disney song."

There was a collective groan.

"Well, that's not fair!" said Khalid.

"I agree with you," said Struan. "I would like to tell you life is not a competition."

"But it is," said Khalid, unhappily.

"But musically we're going to be the best. And I was thinking . . ."

He pulled out a leaflet that said: "Wick Musical Festival." "You guys are getting so good, we might enter the music festival!"

There was a bit of an ooh, and a clamor to look at the leaflet.

"Well, as long as you keep at it. Remember, *Chaidh MO* is the emphasis . . ."

The bell rang and they instantly jumped up to charge for the door.

". . . and, a bunch of other things, but you're no longer listening," said Struan, as they charged out, school bags flying. He managed to catch the clarsach as Moss knocked it over en route. He was theoretically responsible for making them line up and walk quietly back to class, but he never quite seemed to manage it.

He rubbed his eyes. He'd been out late the night before playing in a pub with his band, and it had gone on late, and he'd got home to find his girlfriend Saskia fast asleep, or at least pretending to be fast asleep, and her suitcase pulled out of the cheap broken cupboard he'd been promising to fix for months.

Struan knew she hated him doing gigs and staying out late, even though when they'd first met she had basically loved the fact that he was a musician in a band, and now she couldn't bear it. His music career wasn't enough to live off, therefore he also had his teaching career, which he also loved, and which paid the bills, but it wasn't enough to keep him creatively satisfied, which meant he was always doing slightly too much, and then drinking a few too many beers. It was starting to show (when he was young he was so skinny he couldn't keep weight on, so he wasn't exactly sure how this had happened) and he was absolutely exhausted all the time. And Saskia also didn't like coming to gigs and hanging out at the side listening to the same songs with an adoring smile on her face anymore. This was a familiar pattern.

She was still the prettiest girl in town, but he saw that smile less and less, alongside lots of remarks about how they should get out of this hole maybe? (He wasn't entirely sure if she meant the flat or Carso.) He was rather proud of his flat, a lovely two-bedroom near the newsagent, so he was always handy for *Viz* magazine and Irn-Bru, and with no neighbors after the shop closed he could practice all night and play his records and not bother anybody. Struan liked Carso and had his regular gigs, so he wasn't sure what she meant by that either. The hinting was getting more and more fervent.

Struan was thirty-two; he'd been down this road before. Girls thought the idea of going out with a musician was dreamy, until the fourth time they stumbled over the accordion coming back from the bathroom in the dark, and couldn't plan any weekend events all summer because he was booked solid for ceilidhs, weddings, and dances. Then of course she wasn't nuts about the teaching—he kept bringing home the kids' colds for starters and, once, their nits, when he was trying to show Wee Shugs how to play the drums and must have got within hopping distance, a mistake he had done his best never to repeat. Anyway, there would be lots of hints coming his way about auditions for bigger bands and bigger tours in cities with which his family would fervently agree.

The suitcase was probably a sign, he had thought, and gone and opened a solitary beer in the kitchen, even though he knew he was up for school in the morning. Saskia was gone by the time he woke up, at twenty to nine, throwing himself in the shower and into an old T-shirt, which was far too cold for the weather, for a morning wrestling with his Primary 6s.

Ach. Maybe when everyone kept telling you your life was a failure, you should listen to them? Maybe he should do what Saskia was telling him and just move?

He glanced round the flat as he got home that evening. Saskia was nowhere to be seen. He sighed. The flat *was* nice. But maybe she was right this time. Maybe he should have one more shot at the big time, before it was too late?

CHAPTER 4

I've told you about this before," said Mr. Wainwright, as Gertie sat behind the till, her fingers—which had been clicking her needles under the register—now fallen silent.

"When we're quiet, you dust."

Gertie bit her lip.

"But!" said one of her co-workers. "Remember when you turned the heating down because it was too expensive? Gertie knitted us all vests!"

"Yes," said one of the other women, Barb. "I mean, it was a kind of nothing color . . ."

"It was sandstone," said Gertie quietly. "I thought it was a beautiful color."

". . . but it worked perfectly."

"And I'd have had a lot more days off with my arthritis if it wasn't for the gloves," chipped in Kel, who did the boxes out the back. "Although, yeah, what about a nice blue once in a while?"

Mr. Wainwright scowled. This was not in the manual.

"Gertie, go clean the windows."

This was clearly punishment, and Gertie sloped off. She'd been offered a job in the wool shop that Jean had said she couldn't take unless she wanted to dance on her grave as quick, and she'd absolutely meant to apply to a crafting course at college—she had, for ages—but the pandemic had got in the way and it had suddenly got so hard to motivate herself to go and do something . . . She didn't like, sometimes, the number of years she'd been working at the supermarket.

She glanced at the local messages board as she passed with her bucket. It must have been updated since she'd last looked. Dog walking, dog trimming, dog minding; quite a lot of dog stuff. The ScotNorth was now officially the last shop in the town you couldn't take your dog into, as everyone informed them, crossly, when they stopped them coming in. In vain Gertie would explain they had bread rolls on the bottom shelf and it wasn't fair to ask a dog not to accidentally eat a roll at dog height, but the owners were still cross with them, and it wasn't much fun for the staff either when the local Irish wolfhound, Finn MacDrool, had to be tied up and howled so loudly up and down the street for his owner that it set off car alarms.

There were a couple of yoga/aromatherapist/homeopathic/crystal/tarot types. It was not a very big town, so if you were into that kind of thing, it helped to be able to do a bit of everything. And there was, heavens to Betsy, was that . . . an advert for a *flat*? Those never came up these days. *Perhaps one of the people who taught yoga also had a beautiful home. Maybe it was a really lithe beautiful man who looked a little like Joe Wicks, who didn't really need to advertise on the classified noticeboard of a small-town supermarket, but wanted someone really down to earth, someone who maybe had always wanted to try yoga but had always been too shy to join a class, and in the bright beautiful sunny sitting room started carefully showing her some moves that would make her all lovely and toned and . . .*

Suddenly Gertie caught sight of two people out of the corner of her eye. And ice water ran down her back. The two figures approached, laughing and chatting. She remembered them well from school and shuddered. It was Morag MacIntyre and Nalitha Khan.

CHAPTER 5

Morag, not long back in Carso, hardly shopped for herself at all and if she did she went to the fancy Post & Pantry, where they did sourdough bread and taramasalata and small jars of pickled artichokes, because she had, according to Peigi, "fancy London ways"; Nalitha didn't live in town. So neither of them ever came into the ScotNorth, but today they were making an exception.

It was so strange, thought Gertie, that she still felt it. It had been so long ago. Why did the stings of adolescence stay so fresh when she couldn't remember what she'd had for lunch yesterday? She could immediately smell the weird ham smell of the school canteen, mixed with Lynx Africa and hairspray and trainers and dust and textbooks. She could see them, Morag with her black curly hair straightened to within an inch of its life; Nalitha wearing big gold hoops in defiance of the dress code, all tall and confident and laughing with the boys. Well. One boy in particular. And all these years later she still couldn't bear to think of it.

Now the two of them were waltzing by, looking better than ever, and obviously, Gertie realized with some bitterness, still great friends. Nalitha was clearly pregnant, with huge wedding and engagement rings on.

"I don't want to eat here," Morag was saying. "It's all Scotch eggs and Ringos."

"What's wrong with that?"

"Can't we find a nice bistro or something? Sit down?"

"But I have to eat NOW. I mean, NOW. This is one of the weird things about being pregnant."

Gertie found she was furiously eavesdropping, even as she stared at her bucket and prayed for them to go straight past without noticing her.

"Hey," said Nalitha to Morag, "oh my God, look at that."

She was indicating the little handwritten for sale/wanted board.

"Oh, someone's selling kittens," said Morag, frowning as she studied it. "Gosh, that would be nice, though, wouldn't it? Mind you, Gregor and cats is a whole big other issue I don't really like getting into. Ornithologists and cats are, like, massive enemies."

"Do cats know that though?"

"Well, no," replied Morag. "The best way to have a sworn enemy is to not even care whether they're your enemy or not." She reflected. "Plus, it might be a bit, 'WE HAVE A PET NOW!'"

"Huh," said Nalitha. "Anyway, not that, no. Look."

"What?"

"I thought you had 20/20 vision!"

"Better than actually," said Morag, proudly.

Nalitha leaned over her own bump and rapped her knuckles against the newest ad, in scrawled blue ballpoint pen.

TWO-BED FLAT TO RENT OFF HIGH STREET

With a telephone number.

Morag stared at it.

"You could take it short-term!" pointed out Nalitha. "While you and Gregor sort out what to do."

"I doubt it takes goats, though."

Gregor was perfect, but also had a pet goat. So. Almost perfect.

Nalitha rolled her eyes. "Come on. Look. It says it's not on Airbnb!"

"Yet," replied Morag.

Nalitha took a picture of the ad on her phone. "This could be just right for you. Now hurry up—I have to eat."

And they rushed past Gertie without noticing her. Which was slightly a relief and slightly reminded Gertie of school all over again.

A two-bedroomed flat, thought Gertie, dreamily, finishing off the windows. All to herself. Imagine. You probably didn't even have to bend down to get through the door. It might even have a bath. The little Shore Road house didn't have enough room for a bath. There was a tin one they'd kept in the shed that Elspeth used to get washed in as a baby in front of the fire and was now . . . well, it was full of wool, thought Gertie, somewhat crossly.

Imagine . . .

And she took her phone out and quickly snapped a photo of the ad too.

Back inside, Gertie had rather hoped they would be getting their whatever and going. She didn't like reliving it. That first time her dreamworld had ever come up hard against reality. Very hard.

ELEVEN-YEAR-OLD Gertie—all black cloudy hair and snub nose, legs so long she constantly looked like her knees were knocking; freckles over every part of her that no amount of "oh, look at your lovely freckles" from Jean could stop her longing for creamy skin—had walked slowly toward the large metal gates of Carso Secondary. It looked huge to her, then. She stood outside it, staring up. Her best friend at primary, Amna, had just moved to the bright lights of Stornoway and she felt very alone amongst the hordes of new kids.

As she did so, a lanky teenage boy in baseball boots bounded up behind her. A guitar bounced off his back and he nearly tripped as she came to a sudden halt.

"Hey yah!" he yelled, backing up. Gertie immediately started apologizing, but he grinned broadly.

"It's not so bad," he said, immediately twigging her for a first year, the sleeves of her blazer hanging halfway down her too-long skirt. "Don't worry about it."

And he grinned, blue eyes sparkling, and just like that, Gertie forgot instantly all the terrifying advice from the KCs about men, as the first crush of her life walked through the open gates. And his name was Struan McGhie.

There would be others, of course, many, many others. Zac Efron. Mr. Brewster, the young, bequiffed rock-star-looking and patently-unsuitable-for-teaching-geography teacher (who lasted eight months before going off to make cheese and leading a much easier, quieter existence without everyone—teachers, pupils and parents alike—falling in love with him every ten minutes); a variety of Jonas brothers; and Usher, whom she could never quite successfully maneuver in her imagination into a situation where his private plane would have to perform a forced emergency landing at the town's tiny airstrip, and he would somehow have to stay at the smallest cottage in town with her, her mum, and her gran. But she knitted him a couple of lovely tight beanies, just in case. She never mentioned it at home. All men were anathema to the KCs (except Rod Stewart, obviously).

Struan, though, was a different matter to pop stars. Because he was right there. He was a third year, and played in a ceilidh band already and hung out with girls and boys; Gertie, still in the full gender apartheid of being twelve, found this astonishingly cool. She learned his timetable by heart and somehow contrived to be at every entrance and exit more or less at the same time. Struan, being fifteen, and chock-full of hormones that rather distracted his gaze in the direction of girls who had actually been through puberty, was completely incapable of noticing.

Gertie, very bravely and unusually, came up with a bold plan.

So bold it kept her awake at night. She couldn't share it with the KCs, who would pooh-pooh it immediately and then one of the twins would tell her to change her hair and let her long fringe grow out and stop hiding her face behind it (something, she discovered, years later, the twins were actually correct about).

But Struan was a musician, people even said he might be famous one day—he was so popular—and he'd played the Christmas concert, even though it was normally just the big scary fifth and sixth years.

So carefully, painstakingly, with many mistakes and unpickings, in her favorite pale soft colors—a variety of grays with a dusty rose edge and a thin stripe of yellow in the fingers—she made a set of fingerless gloves, which is very difficult to do; ideal, she thought, for someone who practiced the guitar all the time. He would be so surprised and delighted that surely he would notice her, and smile and . . .

She told the KCs they were for her, so they would help with the tricky bits, which of course they did, whilst making many helpful suggestions about adding brighter colors or perhaps some adorable buttons, as they could not help themselves; until finally they were ready (sans buttons) and they were the first thing Gertie had ever finished that she was completely and utterly proud of. She wrapped them carefully in a leftover box from Christmas, and a bit of stray ribbon, and tied it as neatly as she could. Then on Valentine's Day she'd written a card, chosen after much agonizing and at great length, and left it near the bottom of his locker.

She spent the rest of the day in absolute agony, unable to focus on a single lesson, desperately waiting for lunchtime where, if she was lucky, she would catch a glimpse as he hung out with his wide circle of acquaintances, grabbing a sandwich before heading off to the music department.

She wasn't hungry and let her friends go ahead. Struan was with his friends Morag and Nalitha. Nalitha was incredibly beautiful and exotic-looking in an area without much diversity, and if she was annoyed by standing out, well, she didn't let it show. Always beautifully dressed and made up, her shiny long black hair swinging to her waist. She was utterly breathtaking. And Morag; well, everyone knew the MacIntyres. They lived in a huge rambling house by the sea—much bigger than the cottages—and not only that, her grandfather ran an airline! He had his own plane, which took people from Carso to the islands of the archipelago. Not only *that*, but Morag was learning to fly too, which meant all the boys found her totally fascinating, even as she ignored most of them to concentrate on coming top in maths, physics, design, and technology and geography.

The pair of them were inseparable; not party girls, just friends, with their own private jokes and jaunts to the islands on the weekends. Gertie would have loved to have been their friend, but doubted she'd be able to, even without the chasm of two years separating them—they were clever and popular already, and she was the dreamy girl whose entire wardrobe was homemade.

They were nice without being swots, and weren't intimidatingly cool, and, of course, they got to be friends with Struan. A bolt of jealousy went through her as he bounded up to them, in a jolly mood.

Suddenly turning hot and cold all at once, Gertie realized what he was jolly about. He took out the card, and showed them: the gloves. Nalitha burst out laughing. Morag was obviously telling her off and actually admiring them, whilst Struan screwed up his face, laughed again, and shook his head in disbelief. Then Morag hushed him and looked around the room, obviously in case the culprit was lurking. Cheeks burning, grateful beyond belief she hadn't told anyone what she was doing, Gertie had turned away from her friends, muttered something about "girls' problems," and bolted for the door, resolving once and for all that the KCs were right: men were awful, not to be trusted, and she was better off without them. Because he had laughed. And the girls had too.

GERTIE HID BEHIND the till now. The girls were still chatting in front of the biscuit display.

"I really need to find someone," Morag was saying. "You are having this baby. It's happening."

Nalitha nodded.

Gertie couldn't help overhearing. Anyway, it was the supermarket. Conversations were generally held to be communal there, she told herself. She rang up Perry Albert's nine bananas and huge bag of chicken breasts. He was on a new bodybuilding program that was doomed to fail, as it did every time he hooked up with all his mates at the pub and then they ended up at the chippie having battered haggis suppers. But she admired him for trying.

"I'm looking," said Nalitha. "The CVs are . . ." She made a face.

"They don't need to be *you*! They don't need to be brilliant. Just get me someone nice, and polite, who can check in passengers and doesn't mind occasionally lifting stuff."

"By 'stuff' you mean farm animals, though," pointed out Nalitha.

"Well, don't put that in the ad."

"I didn't," Nalitha replied.

"So what's wrong with the CVs?"

"There aren't any."

"What do you mean?"

"Nobody's applied. Come on, Morag. Antisocial hours. Standing about in the cold. Grumpy passengers. Miles away from anywhere."

Morag rolled her eyes.

"I mean it. And the pay is terrible. Why would anyone want to go miles away from home and work really early mornings and late nights when they can, say, sit nice and comfortably here in this supermarket from nine to five, then walk home?"

"I just . . . we just need someone nice."

"Well, you don't actually," said Nalitha tartly. "You need someone who can handle quite a lot. Drunks and people who are terrified of flying and safety issues and angry people and people who've missed flights and have the wrong tickets and are weird about their baggage and all sorts of things. Not just anyone can do this job."

"Well, I know that," said Morag, affectionately. She loved working with her best friend.

"Yes, but you pay buttons."

"We make buttons! We profit-share in anything that comes in!"

"I know," said Nalitha. "And I care about the company. I love my job. I'm just saying. For the money. I'm not sure we're going to get anyone."

"We have to get *someone*," said Morag in exasperation. "Summer's coming!"

Summer was the big busy season in the Highlands and islands of Scotland, right through to the beautiful orange and brown soft smoky autumn. The nights were short; it was light until midnight, and although the weather was invariably changeable, you sometimes did get lucky. There would always be a handful of the beautiful days when you could travel through turquoise seas—never warm, but stunningly clear and fresh—and golden beaches; huge wide fresh skies, with the mountains reflecting perfectly in the lochs below; the forests teeming with birds and wildlife; salmon leaping from the streams. It was a glorious time of year when the air was sweet with abundant gorse and heather that chased the bluebells, that chased the daffodils, that chased the snowdrops; and the deer (far too many deer, muttered locals, eating suspiciously sourced venison for supper again) scampering with their tails bobbing; rabbits ducking in every hedgerow; lambs hopping fences; squirrels bounding joyfully through the trees.

Few people enjoyed the summer as much as the Scots themselves and people came from all over the world to walk and hike and rest at cozy stone pubs and drink Irn-Bru and take ferries and little planes to islands with sand so white it looked photoshopped; to sit up at night and watch the sky barely darken, the stars only just visible. Children got muddy in streams and burns or built dams on beaches; lit bonfires and ran wild and carefree. Adults visited beautiful remote castles set deep in forests or on the tops of rocky crags staring out to sea; sipped peaty whisky in front of fires lit even in July as the evenings were still chilly; read books and listened to fiddle bands and forgot all the stresses of their lives, beyond having to go slowly behind the stupid big RVs on the North 500 road.

The Highlands and islands of Scotland were, Morag was convinced—and, as a commercial pilot she had traveled far and wide, so had done her research—amongst the most beautiful places on Earth.

Unfortunately, one of the reasons for that was they didn't have a lot of people in them—Scottish people lived along a line in the south of the country, just as Egyptians lived down the Nile—which was mostly lovely, having the landscape to yourself, but now, when she was trying to hire staff, a bit tricky. The youngsters would rather go down and make money in Glasgow and Edinburgh, where you didn't need a car, and you could find a place to live that wasn't an Airbnb, rather than stay up in Carso with its two pubs and no nightclubs.

Nalitha grabbed the first slice of plastic-wrapped Dundee cake she came across.

"Don't eat that," moaned Morag. "I'll get Gregor to make you one."

Gregor had many qualities but one of her favorites was what a good cook he was.

"He's forty miles away and at work. On a mostly uninhabited island," said Nalitha. "I don't think you realize this baby needs to eat now."

"And the baby wants Dundee cake that doesn't expire for another two years?" said Morag, examining the packet.

"Yes!"

"Well, it's got whisky in it, so the baby can't have it."

"Nnnn!" said Nalitha. She looked over for something else, and suddenly saw Gertie, and her smooth forehead wrinkled slightly as if in vague recognition, but then her eyes slid off her again.

Nalitha had a think about the girl she'd just seen. Pregnancy brain was not very useful.

"Mor, who's that quiet girl we went to school with who lived with loads of women?" she whispered.

Morag racked her brains. That was the problem about living in an isolated area; you ended up really far away from people you went to school with because you were all so scattered.

"Skinny legs. Black hair. Never looked where she was going, always trailing knitting needles and stuff."

"Gertrude Mooney?" came to her eventually.

"Gertie, of course! I think she's over there," said Nalitha.

"Okay," said Morag. "She was nice. I think. Didn't say much."

"Well, at least she wasn't one of the racists," said Nalitha grimly, who had those names carved on her heart.

Gertie stiffened. She had felt their eyes on her. This wasn't school, she told herself. Anyway, they hadn't been bullies. Gertie had been lucky with dodging outright bullies, or so she'd thought. She figured it was because she was so often daydreaming that she was the despair of the teachers and the really mean kids couldn't be bothered. But this was not at all true. None of the kids wanted to come up against Jean, Marian, Majabeen, and the twins in a bad mood. It wasn't nicknamed "the coven" for no reason.

But even so, they reminded her of her real humiliation, particularly for the months afterward when the KCs had loudly asked her why she didn't wear those lovely gloves and then she'd had to knit a pair in bright yellow and pretend it was the wrong color so they got all the satisfaction of being right, and she had to wear a pair of stupid yellow mittens for the next two years.

"Yellow mittens, remember?"

"Oh yeah. Goodness. I'm so used to everyone moving away."

"Except for us losers," said Nalitha.

Morag was just preparing her hello smile, when suddenly the door slid open and a loud voice could be heard.

"Aye hiyas!"

Someone was shouting at someone outside.

"GETIFA YA BASSAS AYE YIZ ALL O YIZ."

And a huge, filthy man lurched into the shop.

CHAPTER 6

Nalitha instinctively covered her bump, and Morag stood in front of her. They didn't want to draw attention to themselves. Nobody did; everyone looked away as the man, who was huge, with a straggly beard and several random jumpers on, stumbled in out of the weather. He smelled terrible.

"AYE YOUZ KIN A WATCH AYE ARIGHT BASTARDS," he yelled, arms flailing, as he fell against the magazine rack. Everyone immediately found a reason to move to the back of the shop and stare very hard at the cheese slices. Morag would have taken Nalitha out but the man was between them and the door.

"AY GIE US . . ." He stumbled around. "A WEE BOTTLE O BUCKIE AYE? A WEE BOTTLE?"

It's fine, thought Morag, just ignore him.

But it was too late. He'd seen them.

"OCH AYE YOU GOT A BABBIE IN THERE THEN AYE?" he shouted.

Nalitha colored immediately and Morag put a hand on her arm.

"NO TALKIN'? YOU NO TALKIN' TO ME? AHM JUST BEING FRIENDLY LIKE. JUST BEING FRIENDLY HEN. OR DOES YOU NAE SPEAK ENGLISH AYE?"

There was a horrible silence in the shop as everyone stood, on edge and very nervous.

"Come on," said Morag, quietly. They could just walk out. But he was so big, and unpredictable, and frightening. Nalitha, who normally wasn't scared of much, was shaking beside her. Pregnancy made you so vulnerable. She couldn't help it.

Morag straightened up, to pull Nalitha out with their heads up before he had a chance to do anything, but just as she thought about doing this, he knocked the display stand the Dundee cake had been on and it went absolutely everywhere.

"AYE FUCK THAT!" said the man.

Suddenly a lanky dark-haired person stepped forward.

"John Paul McGowan," Gertie said, in a quiet, gentle voice. "Now you know you canny come in here, don't you! You've been telt! And now I'm having to tell you again."

The man's face focused and turned to the woman talking.

"AH just want a wee . . ."

"It doesn't matter what you want, John Paul," she went on, inexorably. "I'm very sorry. You know you're not allowed. But you know, let me walk you across the road to the Project, and they'll give you some soup, yeah? And I made you a new hat."

"I don't want . . ."

"You do want a new hat," Gertie carried on. She was scared of some things, and many men, but she wasn't scared of John Paul, who was a poor soul right enough, had grown up with half the KCs who knew his backstory and had nothing but pity for him.

"You know you can't come in here scaring nice customers, John Paul, don't you?"

The wind had completely gone out of the man's sails, and he stared at the floor like a little boy.

"Aye."

"Come on," Gertie said, softness in her voice. "Come on, John Paul, let's get you sorted out, eh? They'll sort you across the road, can't they?"

She stepped forward, and to Morag and Nalitha's amazement, she offered the man her arm. And, even more surprising, he took it, and shuffled off, head down, as she marched him toward the door.

As he reached it, he turned his head back.

"Sorry, lassie," he mumbled in Nalitha's direction. "Ah didnae mean any harm."

Nalitha swallowed and nodded, still a bit freaked out.

Out on the street, they could hear him shouting at a parked car as he crossed the road. Inside the shop, the relief was palpable, and everyone started talking at once.

"Are you all right?" said Morag to Nalitha, who looked about to cry. Someone brought her over a chair.

"Oh no, I'm fine," she said, her eyes filling. "It's so stupid. If it was just me, I wouldn't give a toss. But it's the baby . . . it makes me weird and emotional."

"That's what it should be doing," said Morag. "But you shouldn't have had to go through that. Here."

She picked up the wrapped Dundee cake from the floor, read the ingredients, tore open the covering, and handed her a bit. "It says no alcohol stays in after cooking," she said. "I think you'll be okay."

Nalitha looked about to refuse, then grabbed it and gobbled it up. "I feel so stupid."

Gertie came back in, rubbing her hands with hand sanitizer. The other staff gathered round her, and Morag went straight up to say thank you.

"Thanks," she said. "Excuse me, are you Gertrude Mooney?"

Gertie immediately reverted to the twelve-year-old she had once been, scared to be confronted by the older girls. John Paul was one thing; she knew what she was doing there. The big girls, not so much.

And Morag looked really good; Gertie had thought that as soon as they'd walked in. Nalitha of course was gorgeous; Morag looked so healthy and bonny, with roses in her cheeks and lovely hair.

"Yeah," she said, trying to sound casual but just coming across a bit off. "Hi. I know you're Morag."

"What you did there was brilliant," said Morag. "Do you remember Nalitha?"

Gertie thought, *well, of course she did; they'd just left school*, as Nalitha waved weakly. Then she thought about it some more. Even if you took off a couple of years for the pandemic like it didn't count, actually she'd left school ten years ago. It was AGES ago. Even thinking that gave her a sudden spurt of panic. She couldn't. She couldn't have been working there for ten years. She couldn't have watched half her entire twenties go past her whilst she was restocking the coffee shelf. Whereas these two . . .

"Oh yes, of course," she said, coloring. "And I saw you and your plane in the paper."

"Right," said Morag, and Gertie assumed it didn't mean anything to her and she was brushing it off because Gertie was obviously some weird fan. Quite the opposite, in fact; Morag found it completely embarrassing, being very slightly famous in the paper just for doing her job, and hated it being brought up. Gregor found it hilarious but tried not to tease her about it more than was strictly necessary to be very, very funny.

"Well, nice to see you," said Morag. "Do you . . ." She looked around the supermarket, trying to make conversation. "Is it nice working here?"

Nalitha elbowed her suddenly in the ribs.

"What?" said Morag. It had been more painful than Nalitha had intended.

"Uh, it's all right," said Gertie, staring at the floor.

"Thanks," said Nalitha. "He gave me a fright."

"He's harmless, John Paul," said Gertie. "But I get you wouldn't realize that straight off."

AFTER THEY GOT back outside, checking the street in case John Paul was lurking, which he wasn't because he had been telt, Morag turned on Nalitha.

"What were you nudging me for?"

"Oh my God, you are so dense. Don't you think she'd be brilliant?"

"What? I'm worried about you!"

Nalitha heaved a sigh. "She's in there, keeping the place tidy, dealing with the John Pauls of this world, checking the stock, cashing up, turning up on time every day, presumably for years, doesn't ask for much . . . Don't you think she'd be perfect?"

"For . . . for what, your maternity cover?"

"Yes!" said Nalitha. "You have to be tough to do the job."

Morag frowned as they headed down past the quaint Mercat Cross. "Don't you remember her being all kind of . . . dreamy and quiet? Doesn't she moon a bit? Like her name?"

The mooning bit was undeniably true, as they had been friendly with Struan and Gertie had somehow magicked herself to almost anywhere he was in the school for about nine months.

"I don't want to sound harsh, but what if she's too tongue-tied to give the safety announcement?"

"You can learn how to give the safety announcement," said Nalitha sagely. "You can't learn how to deal with someone behaving erratically. You have to be a natural at that. Some people can just never do it. But she obviously can."

"Plus she'd need training."

"No, she doesn't," said Nalitha. "She's not actually flying, is she? You do all that—she'd just be working the desk. I could get a monkey to do it. Actually, I probably should. Better upper body strength for loading."

It was true, there was no stewardessing on Morag's flights; she and her co-pilot Erno did it all. There was no inflight service, no drinks. Dolly was a tiny sixteen-seater bus of a plane that hopped the route between Carso and the islands of the very north of Scotland, from Larbh to Archland and back again, often stopping off at Inchborn where Gregor lived.

Nalitha was right, Morag thought.

"Maybe she wouldn't want it," said Morag. They watched as a host of youths, clad in huge puffa jackets, went banging into the shop, yelling and catcalling at one another, filming their exchanges. The boys were making wisecracks; the girls were screaming with laughter. Morag found herself following them, glancing through the window. Gertie was handling it all seamlessly, serving them at double quick time, remonstrating with some of them to keep their hands off the sweetie shelf—but not meanly or crossly; always with a smile. Gertie in her comfort zone was more impressive than she realized.

Nalitha was sitting down on a bench. Obviously she was tired just heaving her bump about. It wasn't fair making her haul that about all day, standing up, Morag knew. But so far the Job Center had sent them two people who had asked if they could work from home. They used to get a steady influx of young people from Europe in the summer season. But of course, since Brexit all of that had gone.

Nalitha stroked her large bump meaningfully.

"Hmm," said Morag.

After another short walk, they found a nice little café and ordered some cheese scones. Nalitha pulled out her phone.

"What are you doing?" asked Morag suspiciously.

"Having a look." Nalitha pulled up Facebook.

"Oh my God, you are very 2012," teased Morag.

"Yeah, all right," replied Nalitha. Morag spent a lot of time on Inchborn, which didn't have a Wi-Fi connection and so she had managed to more or less wean herself off social media. She behaved as if she'd done some excellent moral duty with this instead of being forced into it by pure necessity. Also, all her old friends were pilots in Dubai and constantly posting pictures of themselves in hot tubs or at foam parties. It hadn't been, in the end, the life Morag had wanted and she was truly much happier where she was. But all the same it wasn't helpful to see those photos on the minus-4-degree days.

"I reckon Gertie is probably more of a Facebook person," said Nalitha. "I don't think she's very Instagram."

"That's insulting," said Morag. "Is it? Can't tell."

"I don't mean it to be insulting!" said Nalitha, who was always posting pouty pictures of herself on the 'gram looking fabulous but never used Facebook at all.

They found Gertie's Facebook page. Sure enough there was almost nothing on it except lots and lots and lots of knitting, and pictures of knitted items and free knitting patterns.

"There we are," said Nalitha. "Perfect. She's not going to turn up hungover after being on an all-night bender in Aberdeen with this kind of hobby, is she?"

Morag studied it more closely. "Yes, but she might just knit all the time?"

"That's fine." Nalitha was known to file her nails when the counter was quiet, after all.

"Pfft, I don't know," said Morag. "Maybe she loves her current job."

"Manhandling tramps in the freezing cold? Yeah, all right."

"Yes, but, Nalitha: the hangar is also freezing cold."

"There you go," said Nalitha, undeterred. "She'll be used to it, plus she can knit."

"Uh, excuse me," came a voice and they turned around in shock. Standing right there, staring at her own profile on Nalitha's phone screen, was Gertrude.

CHAPTER 7

Gertie had felt even more back at school when she walked into the coffee shop on her break to get something to eat. She liked to sit with her needles, or a book she could lose herself in, and the café was nice and not too busy. It was a cozy spot and a treat after she'd been standing up all day, and often if it was quiet in the salon her mum would pop in too.

The last thing she'd expected was the two girls she knew from school, heads together and, to her utter horror, discussing her.

Gertie wondered, sometimes, how other people felt about their senior school. Whether it struck so deep in everyone, or whether she was the only person who really cared about it, who even noticed or remembered what it was like. Maybe everyone else just shrugged school and puberty off like a jacket and got on with their lives completely unencumbered. Maybe if you moved away, you didn't notice it anymore.

For her, though, it remained, stronger in her memories than many of the years since. All she could remember from lockdown was the tape they had to put on the floor of the ScotNorth, reminding people to stand one cow length apart. But school—she could remember everything. The smell of the whiteboard pens. The dusty library. The art rooms, covered in splatter, and indifferently rendered bunches of flowers on the walls, as well as deeply emo self-portraits. The anxiousness at lunchtime about who she'd sit with: Jeannie McClure, normally, who didn't really care if she talked about Struan all day. Morag and Nalitha would be together, often mixing with the boys, who were drawn to Nalitha because she was gorgeous and Morag because they liked to talk about engines. (It would have surprised Morag very much to know that Gertie thought she was popular: she and Nalitha thought Amelia Mackie was the popular one because she was blonde and vivacious and all the boys fancied her.)

Gertie remembered acutely what it was like to be the last to be picked at the Scottish country dance classes they did in PE at Christmas time; to be left to dance with Banjo Alexander, who picked his nose and ate it in full view or, almost worse, Jeannie McClure and they couldn't decide who was leading.

She remembered the crazy teachers, the lazy teachers, the teachers so kind, in retrospect, that it was astonishing. She remembered the smell of the girls' showers, where nobody wanted to strip down, except those with big boobs who'd developed early, who liked to show off; the tiny skirts and gym shorts that didn't stop the boys trying to look up them. She remembered the cheap beans in the dinner line; how everyone brought packed lunches because the school lunch was so bogging, except for her, and Jeannie, and a few others, because they were on free school meals, and everybody knew.

She remembered pretending she didn't want to go to the sixth-year dance. Then Jean made her by saying if she didn't go, she would dress up as her and go herself. Then Jean slipped her a bottle of vodka and Irn-Bru in case it would help and Jeannie drank it and Jeannie ended up doing it with Banjo Alexander down the playground and everyone was so tainted by this horror they could never speak about it ever again. Gertie remembered it all.

Seeing these two cool, successful girls sitting there, talking about her; looking her up on Facebook (to laugh, she assumed automatically; of course they just wanted to laugh at her) had filled her with a kind of strange fury. Plus she'd had a difficult morning.

She wasn't a little girl anymore. Her life was perfectly fine, thank you. She didn't have to put up with this crap.

"Can I help you?"

BOTH GIRLS LOOKED incredibly guilty, but Nalitha recovered first.

"Aha!" she said. "We just wanted to see what you'd been up to!"

"Why?" said Gertie.

"Because you were so amazing in the supermarket there. You saved me!"

"From John Paul?" said Gertie. "Not really."

"Uhm," said Morag. "Do you want to sit down and have coffee?"

Bee, the young waiter, trotted by and clocked Gertie. "Oh, your mum was by looking for you," they said. "I said you might be in later."

Bee had taken it for granted that she was going to be sitting there. Suddenly Gertie found she was in fact sitting down in the chair Morag had pushed out for her, not quite sure why.

"Do you want your usual?" Bee continued, cheerily.

Gertie found herself shaking her head suddenly. Her usual was egg and chips and she didn't want to make herself look even more unsophisticated.

"Uhm, ham salad, please," she said quickly. Bee looked puzzled, but shrugged and carried on.

Morag looked at Nalitha, who made a tiny nod. Well, no harm in trying.

"The reason we were looking you up," said Nalitha, boldly, "was that . . . we wanted to offer you a job."

This was absolutely the last thing Gertie had been expecting to hear. She had expected them to insincerely pretend they were delighted to see her and ask after other kids and the teachers from school just because they happened to be in town. And actually because of where she worked, she did see everyone that passed through as it happened, so she did in fact know what everyone was up to, although she wasn't naturally nosy by nature. Jean was, though, and she got all the gossip through the salon and rechewed every morsel with the KCs, so there wasn't much Gertie didn't know.

Gertie frowned. "What do you mean?" she said.

"Obviously Nalitha's pregnant and I was looking for some help out at the airfield."

"And you thought of *me*?" said Gertie. Something did a little jump inside her. Had they remembered her, all the way back from school? *Had they been thinking, do you know who's brilliant? Gertrude Mooney. Let's find out where she's working and go down and ask her. All these years we've wanted her to work alongside us . . .*

This little fantasy, however, was rudely punctured a second later as the girls exchanged glances.

"Yes!" said Nalitha, just a fraction of a second too late.

"Oh okay," said Gertie, flushing. "Well, I've got a job, thanks. I'm a supervisor."

The girls nodded.

"I just thought . . . it's only for a few months," said Morag. "Wouldn't the supermarket let you take a sabbatical?"

Gertie laughed at the very idea, even though, despite the faff, the supermarket absolutely would have let her go and come back; in fact they encouraged good employees to go to university or traveling and held their jobs open for them. They were kind of trying to be a good employer but also it meant they didn't have to pay their staff any more money by simply never paying them when they weren't there.

Gertrude shrugged. "What would the job be?" she asked, tentatively.

"Well, you'd be checking in passengers, loading luggage, check-ing rosters, updating the website . . ." began Morag.

"But I wouldn't be on the plane?" said Gertie, looking worried.

"Oh no, we do all that," Morag replied. "The plane isn't big enough for stewardess service. Nal sometimes comes along for fun or if we need a bit of extra help. You can do that, only if you like."

Gertie's heart quickened a little. They sounded so casual about it. No constant spot checks for stealing, she guessed. No double signing in of alcohol and tobacco. No clocking on. No scary boss always grumbling about wastage.

"You're ground staff," confirmed Morag. "There's some train-ing, but not much. Don't walk under the wings, basically, and don't be a foreign spy. Nalitha will tell you everything else."

"I will!" said Nalitha, trying to look encouraging.

"The hours can be a bit antisocial . . ." said Morag.

"Like all night?" said Gertie, who'd recently been up till four doing the inventory.

"Oh God, no. I mean, you start at six a lot of days but you're done by two; that's our last run."

Gertie frowned. "I start at six now," she said. "But I don't get off till five."

They seemed to be at something of an awkward lull, as Gertie tried to think about it, and the waiter set down two coffees, one decaf, two cheese scones, one "ham salad," they announced, dis-playing a plate with limp lettuce, some sweaty-looking tomatoes, one slice of flabby ham, and a huge dollop of salad cream. This was a café that clearly resented having to make anyone a salad. After all, if you make the decision to come and sit down somewhere lovely with—normally—people you liked, and have a little treat, you might as well commit. The cheese scones on the other hand were bountiful; huge, striped with Orkney cheddar, scented and delicious. Gertie suddenly found herself regretting a lot of things, including her lunch choice.

"There you are!" said Jean, bearing down. She was wearing one of her own creations that day; a very fluffy black mohair jumper with gold knitted into a repeating cross pattern. This week her hair was dark red. Gertie loved her mum very much but she had a particular concept of "making the best of yourself," which involved huge spidery false lashes and a style of lipstick—outlined on the *outside* of your mouth—which had last been in fashion in 1994. Normally Gertie didn't mind it, but today, Morag looked neat and scrubbed clean and Nalitha had perfect black eyeliner in little wings by the sides of her eyes and her mum looked . . . well, she looked old.

Jean sat down, beaming, clearly delighted to see Gertie out with friends. She recognized Morag.

"Not getting your egg and chips?" she said to Gertrude. "That's not like you!"

Gertie shrugged. "Just thought I'd try something different," she whispered, going pink.

"Looks bogging," said Jean, with some accuracy. Gertie pushed a dismal lettuce leaf around with her fork.

"So, hello, Morag!" said Jean. "How's your gramps? Still single?"

Morag smiled. "Hello," she said. "He's totally fine. But I think Peigi has first dibs on him."

"That woman," tutted Jean. "Got her claws in good and proper."

Morag didn't disagree with her, but it was a little disconcerting to hear family news being related back to her by this total stranger. She smiled a little tightly as Jean introduced herself to Nalitha, who smiled politely.

"So are you just having a girls' catch-up?" said Jean, nodding at Bee to get them to bring over some egg and chips.

"Actually," said Nalitha, "we were offering Gertie a job. At the airline."

Jean was gobsmacked.

At first she'd just been pleased to see Gertie had someone to eat lunch with; usually she was on her own. But a job! With an airline! This was even better. She was proud of her sweet-natured daughter, but she did feel a pang every time someone else got a new grandchild, or announced their child was off to university or Australia or even Inverness for God's sake, whilst Gertie didn't ever seem to want to go anywhere.

"Well, this is fantastic!" said Jean. "Is this for the bairn?"

Nalitha nodded.

"So there's no point giving up the job I have," chipped in Gertie.

Jean snorted. "In a supermarket? You could get one of those any day of the week. She's overqualified. I'm always telling her."

She was. The problem also was, it never seemed to occur to Jean to envisage a life without her. Jean looked at confident, happy Morag and Nalitha and then at Gertie, staring miserably into her horrible-looking ham salad, and felt an uncomfortable twinge. She had, she knew, been too happy to have her daughter around. She liked them all being a little gang. But it didn't stop her conscience pricking that there should maybe be more to Gertie's life than knitting and *Britain's Got Talent* and a pizza on a Friday night.

"Yeah! Do it! It'll be brilliant!"

"Great," said Nalitha, who was feeling very in need of a nap and wanted to wind things up.

"Hang on!" said Morag, who'd kept a rather sharper eye on

proceedings. "I think Gertie will need to make up her mind, won't you?"

Gertie looked at her with some gratitude. Often, she wanted to say something and her mother would get in there first and then she'd feel it was pointless to add her side.

"Well, there's only one thing..." she said nervously. Jean looked at her and read her mind.

"Don't tell them that!" she said, knowing immediately what she was about to say and trying to turn it into a joke. "They don't need to hear it."

"... I've never been on a plane," finished Gertie, red as a tomato.

CHAPTER 8

Well it was a good idea," said Morag again, as Nalitha stomped back to the car, her ankles swollen and giving her grief.

"I just thought . . . I thought we'd solved it," said Nalitha. "I mean, you'll just fly about. I'm the one that will come back to a total mess and all the computer stuff messed up and people running a full drug-smuggling operation without you even noticing because you just love flying planes."

Morag did love flying planes, it was true. Ever since she'd been a child the idea that you could just take off; that you could be on solid ground, just like everybody else, beetling around on the surface, slow and heavy; and suddenly, with a long run-up you could burst from the earth; break the bonds of gravity and take off toward the sun and the light above, the entire sky your own; she thought it was the most wonderfully freeing experience in the world. She never tired of it. Even when she used to fly long-haul for a large airline, she had always loved take-off the best: the roar of the engines, the racing gray concrete beneath their wheels, the lackluster dull shapes of the airport and the outbuildings all around them until suddenly, the great machine lifting, lifting and finally free as a bird, the world and all its problems falling away behind you. And you could revel in the knowledge that, for the next few hours, all your senses would be filled with keeping this glorious creature on track; watching for cloud formations and weather patterns, glimpsing the linked lights of the world below; marveling at how busy it seemed when you were down there, but when you were up in the air, how relatively little space humans and their cities took up, compared to great stretches of shimmering water, or pink-lit desert, or dense canopies and forests.

The full glory of the planet whizzing steadily beneath your feet; what could be better? And Gertie had never even tried it?

People occasionally asked her if she found her job dull, because they found flying dull, and as well as this being an exceptionally rude question to ask anybody, it was completely incomprehensible to Morag. Did you find sunrises dull at 10,000 feet? Did you find descending over cliffs full of flapping seabirds dull; or landing, as she did at Inchborn, onto the long rolling beach when the tide was in the right spot? Was that dull? Was banking over cities, looking down on offices where people spent their days gazing at spreadsheets, nailed to the ground. That was what Morag thought was dull. Soaring to the avents—no. She didn't think that was dull.

"Maybe I'll try the Job Center again," she mused.

"They keep sending us people who want to be Instagram influencers," said Nalitha. "Remember that girl who just wanted a bikini shot of her draped over the plane? Mind you I'm still not sure we shouldn't have just done it."

"We're not quite that desperate," said Morag, even as Nalitha winced as the baby kicked her hard.

"Ugh. We are that desperate. I really thought she might consider it."

"She's never even checked in for a flight before," said Nalitha. "What if she wants to give them all bus tickets and punch a hole in them?"

"Might not be a bad idea," said Morag, considering how dodgy the Wi-Fi was in the hangar and how often the QR code scanner broke down. "Anyway, surely it's something you can learn? She's nice, Nalitha."

"She is," said Nalitha. "Is that enough?"

They approached Morag's home, the big rackety house on the seafront, buffeted by the wind. Peigi was standing on the doorstep with her arms folded, frowning mutinously—Morag was back and late for her tea, evidently, even though it was about ten minutes after lunchtime.

"Well, at least go and look at the flat," said Nalitha.

"I just might," said Morag.

MEANWHILE GERTIE WAS staring at the Crispy Pancakes her mother had rustled up for tea. They had been her favorites when she was ten. Ten. Her mother only did it when she thought she needed a special treat, or cheering up. It was a stupid tradition that normally made her smile, but tonight it was making her cross.

Why had she never been on a plane? Well they hadn't had enough money for starters. They went to the caravan park at Kinghorn every year, and went to the Burntisland shows and walked on the big beach and if it was warm enough got in the water, or if it wasn't warm enough they got in the water too and ate chips in the evenings and went to the amusements when it rained, which was often, and that was their holiday. Always had been. And it was lovely.

It shook her, the way things had been the same for so long. She should have gone abroad of course but Jean hadn't fancied it, Elspeth had never had a passport nor considered having one and had no interest in going anywhere as she thought Carso was heaven on earth, and had tried Glasgow once and hadn't liked it a bit.

Then the pandemic. Then she'd meant to but she didn't really have anyone to go with. Not friends that were close enough to go on holiday with. Then her friends moved away, or had families of their own they went on holiday with, so that was that.

She stared at the TV that was showing *A Place in the Sun*. It was looking at somewhere lovely in France. They were eating baguettes and drinking wine in the sunshine. She looked out of the window. It was pouring with rain that was banging against the single-glazed window of their little house.

"So I told her she should," Jean was saying in the kitchen, which was a bit rich all told, given that Jean had been abroad once and complained bitterly about how hot it was and how there was no use for a good cardigan. And you couldn't take your knitting needles on a plane, so really what was the point?

"Do they fly to the continent?" asked Elspeth, as if "the continent" was a terrifying, undiscovered region.

"No, they only fly to the islands and stuff," said Gertie, quickly. "They don't go out of the UK at all."

"Och no, she's better off at home," said Elspeth, drinking her tea from her special mug. They all had special mugs. Maybe, Gertie found herself thinking, there was more to life than special mugs.

Jean frowned.

"What?" said Gertie.

"Well, nothing," said Jean. All of a sudden, Gertie's phone started pinging with messages of congratulations.

"What? What is this?"

They were all from the other KCs. Jean had the grace to at least go a little pink.

"Well, I might have told people that you had been offered a job with a major international airline."

Gertie stared, her mouth hanging open.

"They don't even go to the continent," said Elspeth, looking confused.

"They're owned by that nice-looking Norwegian man though," said Jean, as if this sealed the matter.

"MUM!" said Gertie, furious. "MUM, what did you do? It's all round town! It'll get back to them. And they didn't even offer it to me in the end!"

"That's not true," said Jean. "You just shuffled off. They were surprised. I'm sure you could ask for it. Anyway," she added, lying, "I'm sure it won't get back to them."

Gertie thought of Morag and Nalitha, laughing in the common room once more, looking at her gloves.

"I don't believe you," she said, and looked around, desperate to storm off. Except, of course, the house being so tiny, she couldn't.

CHAPTER 9

Struan had cleaned up the flat best he could, then Saskia had come in and done it all over again to her standards, so you couldn't deny it looked clean. This was such a good quality she had, he thought. She got a plan, and she saw it through. It was admirable.

The flat was airy, bright, and plain, with windows facing over the top of the high street out to the sea beyond; you could see the airfield in the left corner of one. She was very excited about him moving to the new place she'd found for them (after he had properly groveled for being out late the other night). It was going to be a pretty long commute until the end of the school year, and it seemed she really thought he had a chance of getting this new job and . . . well, maybe it was time. He glanced around. Saskia had found a nice new build in a modern block with a pool, which was so fancy he wasn't quite sure what to make of it, but he knew the walls were thin so who knew when he was going to get to practice his guitar. Whereas here, Struan could sit and play at the open window facing the sea and nobody would bother him.

He had left a message on his outgoing voicemail that there would be an open house on Sunday morning, rather than bother trying to fix appointments with people, so either lots of people might come or nobody would. When his grandfather had left his only grandson this flat at the top of the world, it had been worth barely anything. Since then, rather a lot of people had decided that they would like to live, or holiday, exactly there, and he had found himself incredibly lucky. He would miss it. Maybe nobody would come over, he thought cheerily. Then he remembered he'd just have to post it on-line like Saskia had told him to do from the beginning, and his heart sank. He'd thought putting a physical ad in a local shop was a better way to get local people in, rather than random folk from all over the place, but she might be right. She normally was.

GERTRUDE WAS STILL furious with her mum, and had taken the early shift at the supermarket to prove it, even though it was quite a lot of getting your hands really dirty on the papers and bringing in the milk from the teeny wee lad on the tractor.

Mr. Scobie was waiting at the door as they opened, as usual, and had bought his daily essentials: a tin of soup, half a loaf of white bread, the cheapest brand of rolling tobacco, and the most expensive brand of fine dog food, for his stupid huge mutt Car-nation, who got tied up outside and woofed until he re-emerged, even though he came here every day at the same time and did the same thing. Evidently Carnation thought her woofing was the only thing that made Mr. Scobie come back. New customers got a bit surprised by the cacophony; regulars weren't fussed. On a tiny pension, Mr. Scobie could occasionally be tempted by a KitKat if they were on offer—Gertie would keep one back for him if they were—and on pension day he'd buy fresh free-range chicken, the most expensive they had. Gertie knew it wasn't for him.

The next person through the door was someone Gertie had never seen before, which was unusual. She frowned. He was me-dium height, with dark blonde hair, striking blue eyes, and an ex-pensive all-weather jacket. He was quite the best-looking person to walk into the ScotNorth since they'd been filming *Outlander* nearby and all the production assistants had popped in for bridies. That had been quite a couple of days. Everyone had used up their staff discounts on hair masks and mascara.

The man looked up at her with his ice-blue eyes and said, "Wow. *You are an absolute vision, I can't believe you're working in a supermarket. And who knitted that beautiful ghost-colored scarf you're wearing?*"

"Thank you," she said. The blue eyes looked confused.

"Sorry?"

Gertie mentally gave herself a shake. It was, after all, early in the morning.

"Oh, no, I'm sorry I didn't quite hear you . . ."

"I asked if you had any cold-pressed green juice?"

Gertie almost missed it again, looking deep into his eyes, but caught it just in time. Unfortunately it was not a question most highland ScotNorths were very equipped to answer.

"I have . . . Tizer?" she replied.

"Is that the same?"

"Well, one of the flavors is 'blue,'" she said quietly.

He looked at her.

"Blue, huh?" He had a curious accent, kind of American mixed with something else.

"I think it means raspberry."

"I try and avoid blue food on the whole." He frowned. "Except for blueberries. Got any of those?"

Gertie shook her head. "I've got some spring onions though," she said, indicating a large pile, which had just come in fresh from the farm. "I could jump up and down on them for you?"

For a moment the man's eyes twinkled. "That *does* sound great," he said. "But I think . . . perhaps a decaf coffee?"

"It's quite early," said Gertie, desperate to talk to him as long as possible whilst the shop was quiet. "Are you *sure* you don't want caff?"

He shook his head. "My nutritional therapist would have a fit."

"Well perhaps they should eat a more calming diet," Gertie said, and to her gratification, he laughed.

"Just the decaf, thanks," he confirmed. "I'm going to go out and enjoy this beautiful morning."

Maybe he would say to her, "When's your break? You could caffeine it up and come sit with me and . . ."

Or perhaps she would spill the coffee on him and he'd have to take off his . . . well, his perfectly serviceable waterproof jacket. And spilling very hot drinks on customers was generally discouraged. It was in the handbook.

So of course Gertie just made the coffee, whilst the stranger picked up lots of snacks, read the list of ingredients, shook his head sorrowfully, and put them back down again. Careful about what he eats, thought Gertie. Good for him!

"Well, enjoy," she said eventually, as he bleeped his card. She caught a flash of it as he did so and read the name printed on the gold background. Calum Frost.

MAYBE IT WAS fate, she thought, as the electronic bell dinged his exit through the sliding doors. Maybe it was meant to be. The KCs always liked to talk about how "what's for you won't go by you." Gertie wasn't sure about this at all. Rather a lot of things seemed to be going by her, quite frankly. And by the KCs, for that matter.

She followed him to the door and watched as he walked down the street. That was who owned the whole airline? Wow. He was . . . yeah. Wow.

Looking down, her eyes caught the ad again, for the flat, and she remembered how cross she'd been at her mum telling everyone she'd taken the job. On the other hand, if the job came with him . . .

A new job, a new start . . .

Suddenly Gertie's heart began to beat faster. What if she did have her own room? *And one night there was lots of snow, or something, and the Carso hotel was . . . fully booked or something and well maybe he would just have to come and stay somewhere and there was nowhere to stay and she'd say, "Come stay in my lovely apartment . . ."*

Okay, lovely apartments weren't often advertised by messily handwritten index cards posted up in local minimarts, but who knew? And at least it might shut her mum up for five minutes. Before she could even stop herself; before Calum Frost had even fully vanished down on to the seashore to, Gertie assumed, stare manfully out at the waves and contemplate how all the money in the world had still left him a lonely man, she had dialed the number.

CHAPTER 10

Morag turned up early at the flat viewing because Peigi was fussing around trying to make her go to church and she couldn't bear it anymore, plus she needed to catch the Inchborn ferry. Gertie turned up early because the timing of breaks was very strictly regulated after the whole staff night-surfing incident of 2022.

It was an old red sandstone building, common around these parts. The downstairs held a little antique shop, which was open at frankly impossible to predict times of the day and month. Gertie had rarely glanced upstairs, her gaze normally fixed to the ground as she wandered familiar streets in a dream. But the upper floor was solid Victorian architecture, and the rooms were surprisingly large and bright. There was a sitting room, with not much in it except for a working fireplace and a couple of old sofas; a small kitchen, two nice-sized bedrooms overlooking a communal garden with washing lines flapping in the wind, and a tiny box room.

It was the box room that Struan had used to store his guitars in. It was modest, but it was home and had been for a little while, and Struan found himself uncharacteristically reflective as he did what Saskia had told him and brewed coffee for the smell. Saskia's new flat had double glazing and underfloor heating and all sorts of things like that, but it overlooked lots of other places that were all exactly the same. Whereas from here, you could sit and tinker with your guitar of an evening and look down the street and see everyone coming and going, and sometimes you'd see your mates going into the pub and in fact sometimes they'd look up to the window and wave if they saw you and you could just take yourself off for a pint. It was great.

And you could see the holidaymakers traipsing up and down and buying fudge, and if you fancied a bit of fishing, which sometimes Struan did, having the enviable job of being a teacher who never had any marking, you could follow the cunning fishermen who knew where the good spots were and when the fish were biting, even as they tried to skulk up the road in secret.

And whilst the sitting room faced northeast, the window in his bedroom faced southwest, which meant you could watch the sunsets if you wanted, from bed in the summer, when the sun didn't set until after 11 p.m. He ran his fingers through his unruly hair. Yeah. He was going to miss this place.

The bell rang. He glanced at his watch, yawning. It was only quarter to ten. He'd been playing a wedding the previous night and hadn't got home till late. Which was fine as he didn't have neighbors to speak of so he could come in, heat up some food and put the TV on. He probably wouldn't be able to do that at Saskia's, he thought, slightly glumly. There were people all around and lots of passive-aggressive notes up in the hallways about removing shoes and not using washing machines after 8 p.m.

Oh well. Better get on with it.

GERTIE HAD BEEN, as usual, staring at her shoes as she approached the address, and Morag hadn't noticed her until they were both more or less there.

"Oh!" said Morag, surprised. She'd been so annoyed with Peigi on the way down and now seeing someone else—who might get the flat before her—at the door so early too was extremely annoying. Then she realized it was Gertie. "Hey again!" she said.

Gertie looked up at Morag, feeling intimidated as usual.

"Oh hello," she said. "Uh."

They both looked at the front door.

"Did you want the flat?" said Gertie. "It doesn't matter. I just . . . I was just looking."

"Well, come and have a look," said Morag, encouragingly, wondering just why this girl was so timid. She had bolted after lunch the other day, whilst she and Nalitha were still trying to get their heads around whether someone who'd never been in a plane before could work for an airline.

"Well, you were first," said Gertie. Morag looked at her hand, which had just about gone out to press the doorbell.

"I . . . I don't think that's how it works," Morag replied and Gertie looked even more embarrassed, as she'd never been flat-hunting before and in fact had, as Jean told everyone all the time, been born in the sitting room of the house she now lived in—"the last time Gertie was in a hurry to do anything." She didn't mean it to be cruel; she thought it was funny.

"Okay," said Gertie, face pink.

Morag rang and they stood back.

"Did you . . . did you find anyone for the job?" asked Gertie, timidly.

Morag turned to her. "Not yet."

There was an uncomfortable silence. Then the door opened. And both the girls' mouths dropped open.

"STRUAN?!" YELLED MORAG. "Oh my God!"

"Mores! I heard you were back in town."

They hugged.

"Oh my God, you haven't changed at all," said Morag, smiling. "You're still dressing like a student."

"I thought you were a fancy-pants pilot now, far too important to remember your old mates?"

"That's not true. I see Nalitha all the time. And she phones you and you're always playing a gig."

"I am," said Struan with a grimace. "Guilty as charged. Why do you need a flat?"

"Long story," said Morag. Then she wrinkled her nose. "A scary witch moved in with Gramps. Oh, there you go, not that long."

"Coffee?"

"Yes! Do you still take nine sugars?"

Gradually, Struan realized there was somebody else on the doorstep.

Gertie stood there, trembling. It had been so long since she'd seen him—which seemed strange in a tiny town with one supermarket, where she worked, but Struan was always on the road, shopping from the garage or eating school dinners; he simply never went there.

Struan caught her eye, and everything came rushing back to her: how obsessive she'd been over every single thing about him; how she had memorized his timetable and drawn his name over and over again in the back of her jotters, surrounded in hearts and outlines and stars; how she had dreamed of him night after night, watched him perform at school shows like she was watching a young Elvis.

"Oh, hi," he said casually. "I'm Struan."

"Struan!" Morag admonished him. "You remember Gertie! She was a first year when we were third years."

Struan blinked a couple of times. "Uh, sure?" he said.

"It's okay." Gertie's voice sounded twisted and hysterical. "I was in a different year."

"Can you remember your kids' names now?" said Morag, following him inside and up the narrow stairwell.

"Yeah," he said. "But I think I'm giving it up. Teaching, I mean."

"Nalitha told me you really liked it."

"I do! It's just . . . my girlfriend thinks I should give the music another shot . . . I have a big audition for a touring show and I'll probably get it so . . ."

Gertie's heart dropped at the term "girlfriend," although she didn't know what she'd been expecting. She had tried for a very long time not to think about him at all; it felt very odd, like she was in a room with her thirteen-year-old self. She almost smiled when she thought how excited she would have been back then to be walking into *Struan McGhie's* apartment.

"Ooh," Morag murmured as they reached the top of the stairs. A cold sun came through the landing window and filled the apartment with light. "This is nice."

"I don't know why you're sounding so surprised." Struan laughed. Then he paused. "Hang on, I heard you got with that weirdo hermit Gregor who lives on Inchborn. God, no wonder this looks nice."

"He's not a hermit! That's just his job."

"So, just weird then."

"He's not . . . so anyway what's your rule on pets?" said Morag. Struan shrugged. "What kind of pets?"

"Uh. Goats?" said Morag in a very quiet voice. "And possibly the occasional chicken."

"Oh man, he totally is weird." Struan went over and pushed the plunger down on the cafetiere. "So, are you girls looking for a place together?"

Morag was already busying herself through the place. "You're renting out the whole flat?"

"Yeah, it's got two bedrooms . . . I was going to pick two people, I suppose . . . hadn't really thought it through."

Morag rolled her eyes indulgently. "The ad was really unclear. You have not changed *at all*."

"Neither have you. You're still a bossy pot."

"I am not a bossy pot! Stop plunging that coffee, it'll be a disaster . . ."

Struan looked at her.

"Oh, come on. Yes, what you want in a pilot is people who don't know their own mind . . . Where are you headed?"

"I'm moving in with my girlfriend in Inverness."

Morag winced. "That's a heck of a commute."

"A pretty one, though."

"What if it doesn't work out and you have to move back five minutes later?"

"Thank you for your exceptional faith in me," he said, laughing. His mother had said exactly the same.

MEANWHILE, GERTIE WAS wandering around the two bedrooms. They were both big. She was so used to the cramped little cottage. Not that she didn't love it, she did, but it was so teeny and so full of stuff: wool and old crockery and, well, the entire town's knitting circle and the bags and needles and bottles of prosecco they generally traveled with.

The room at the back, where the afternoon sun would pour in, with its view over the greens behind the flats, was so quiet, and clean, and empty. Even as Morag and Struan caught up next door, she wanted to lie down on the bed, and just enjoy the headspace and peace. It was strange; suddenly she wished she'd brought her needles with her. Knitting helped her think about things, freeing up her brain to drift, or to focus. She looked at the bed. It could use a lovely patchwork bedspread—or perhaps something classy in her beloved stripes, cozy but soft, like a gigantic baby blanket . . .

Could she really just move here? She had money saved; Jean wouldn't take board money. Gertie had just never really considered it. But . . . could she?

She went to the door of the sitting room. The sofas looked comfortable and there was a little table where Morag and Struan were sitting drinking coffee. She beamed.

"It's nice!"

Struan smiled back. "Thank you! Do you have any really disgusting habits?"

"I knit a lot," said Gertie.

Struan blinked. "Do you knit . . . like, spiders and turds and things?"

Gertie laughed. "No."

"Well, then that should probably be okay. Why do you knit so much?"

"Why do you have six guitars?" retorted Gertie, gesturing around the room.

Struan shrugged. "Well," he said. "Sometimes I like to play something different . . . it depends on my mood. I find it . . ."

His voice grew more reflective.

"Music takes me away from myself . . . does that sound super lame?"

Gertie shook her head. "No," she said. "That's it exactly."

"What do you do like that, Morag?" asked Struan.

Morag frowned. "I never relax," she said. "You two are weird."

"Come on," said Struan.

Morag thought about it.

"Flying over snow," she said finally. "And I like watching Gregor with his birds."

Struan raised his eyebrows at Gertie and she stifled a giggle.

"Well, each to their own," said Struan. "If I did let you this place though . . . I mean, Nalitha says that his goat is in love with him."

"She's exaggerating."

"He doesn't have a goat?"

"No, he does, but she's more . . . in lust?"

Struan pursed his lips. "Okay. Well. Could we have a no-goat rule?"

"I wouldn't mind," said Gertie.

"You've obviously never lived with a goat," said Morag darkly.

There was a sudden loud buzzing to the door, repeatedly. They went to the front room to peer down and see who was there.

A huge line of people snaked all the way down the street, some with large dogs or children or, in a couple of places, with full suitcases.

"Oh my God," said Morag. "The housing crisis is . . . bloody hell."

"Yeah," Struan said. He turned to them. "Look, can you guys just take it? I don't think I can deal."

Morag and Gertie looked at each other. Gertie suddenly felt a bolt of excitement. Her own place?

"Sure," said Morag.

CHAPTER 11

Gertie's excellent mood lasted five seconds after she told her mother, and saw her face.

"Is it because I told people you were taking the airline job?" Jean said, tears threatening to overspill her thick black eyelashes.

"No," said Gertie. "No. Honestly. It's time. You know it is. I thought you'd be happy."

"I know I *said* it was," Jean replied glumly. She looked down. She had meant to be more encouraging to Gertie, of course she had. It was just, with Gertie not getting her exams . . . then the job had been so nice, just being down the road from the salon . . . and everyone said, ah kids, they mature later these days, then the pandemic had come along, and . . .

"Plus," said Gertie. "Don't you think it's time for *you* to be getting out there again too? You don't need your grown-up daughter cramping your style."

"All men are dickheads though. Have we all taught you nothing?" Jean bit her trembly lip.

"Oh, Mum," Gertie sighed. "Oh, you're right. You know, I should stay. Absolutely loads of people wanted the room."

She glanced into the cozy yellow sitting room where the fire was crackling. Elspeth looked up from where she was watching *EastEnders* with the subtitles on, and knitting a huge orange open-stitch scarf on giant needles, which meant she didn't need a different pair of glasses for seeing her knitting and reading the TV.

"What are you saying?" Elspeth called out.

Jean and Gertie looked at each other.

"I'll tell her," said Gertie.

"She'll be fine about it." Jean nodded.

But suddenly Elspeth froze.

"What . . . what?"

Her needles fell from her hands. The women darted forward.

"Mum?" said Jean, leaping over. "Mum, are you all right?"

"I . . ." Elspeth looked around as if she wasn't exactly sure where she was. Her leg started to tremble and Gertie carefully walked her over to the sofa, laid her down, and grabbed one of their home-knitted blankets to keep her warm.

"Mum?"

"Grandma?"

Gertie picked up her phone and dialed 999; her grandmother's mouth had fallen weirdly to one side and her eyes still weren't focused. Her hand was shaking so much she could barely dial the number.

THE PARAMEDICS, ALTHOUGH they took a while to come, were completely and utterly brilliant. They were jolly, if anything; certainly practical. A man and a woman, dressed in green, they bustled in as if this was quite normal, which of course to them it was.

Gertie had calmed herself down then googled what to do and had done it, to the letter. She had made her grandmother lie down on her side on the sofa, with a bowl to her right in case she vomited; had refused to let Elspeth have anything to drink even though Jean thought she should attempt some tea. Gertie sat next to her grandmother, checked her breathing, and kept her talking. She took her grandmother's hand. Their hands were exactly the same shape: small palms, longer fingers. Gertie's nails were neat and rounded and short; Elspeth's were polished with hard burgundy nail polish chipping at the corners. The backs of Elspeth's were a network of raised veins, soft pastry skin, brown spots. Gertie stared at her grandmother's hand for a long time. Her own hand would look like that one day, she thought. Her hand would turn into that hand. Although without another hand to squeeze it further down the line.

She always thought she had so much time to do what she wanted to do. Now she was holding a hand that was trembling and terrified and must, once, have looked exactly like her own . . . It must have happened so fast. In the blink of an eye. Just as she had felt when she saw Morag and Nalitha; ten years from school had flashed past. Did it all flash past then? And one day your hands were coiled, and there was fear in your eyes and you were waiting for an ambulance.

"Okay, let's be having you," said the handsome male paramedic. "What do you prefer: Mrs. Mooney or Elspeth?"

Elspeth blinked, but seemed to focus. "Elspeth."

"That's great! Good girl!"

His companion rolled her eyes. "You won't believe," she said, "how many female patients show remarkable powers of recuperation when *he* turns up. Some of them go and put their nighties *on*."

"Is he single?" asked Jean in a voice not quite quiet enough, as the male paramedic took Elspeth's pulse. Gertie had had to extricate her hand. She could feel her grandmother's cool imprint still.

"Muuuuum," whined Gertie. "How is *this* the time?"

"Good job—paramedic," Jean cooed.

"Excuse me," the male paramedic spoke without looking up from his stopwatch. "I'm gay as a window *and* married, thank you."

"You should just get a badge that says that," muttered the female paramedic. "Meanwhile I am single, actually. And every man I meet is 106 or is dangerously bleeding out."

"I can see how that would be difficult," said Jean. The male paramedic stood up and the women all looked at him expectantly.

"Strong as an ox, you are, Elspeth," he said. "I don't think I want to take you in. Unless you want to go in?"

Elspeth shook her head firmly. She was sitting up now and didn't look nearly as dreadful as she had a moment or two before. Gertie pulled the blanket closer round her.

"Hospitals are cathedrals of death," she mumbled. "Everyone knows that."

"Well, they're . . ." The female paramedic screwed up her face.

"Well, they're not holiday camps." The man took out a syringe.

"I'm going to give you this injection," he said. "Which should stop it happening again, or another event like that damaging you long-term. I'm not a doctor so I can't say for sure, but this looks like a very mild ischemic event. Like a small stroke, but don't get scared by that word—they're very common. You'll need to go and get checked out and let the GP run some tests in the morning— but honestly if we took you in now, the hospital couldn't do the tests till then anyway."

"And *Love Island* is coming on," said Elspeth.

"Well, exactly," replied the paramedic. "And it's Casa Amor."

He rolled down her sleeve as Gertie took the female paramedic aside.

"Is she going to be okay?"

"I can't say," replied the woman. "But if we were seriously worried we would take her in. I mean, I *can* take her in but she might be waiting for a bed for a really long time, and there's still Covid about and, honestly, I think she'd be a lot better off here at home until the morning. If it was my grandmother, you know?"

Gertie nodded. "Okay, good."

"You did everything right," said the woman, approvingly. "We'll write it up and phone your GP first thing in the morning. They'll get her up for tests."

Gertie bit her lip. "When this kind of thing starts happening though . . ."

The woman smiled, sadly, and Gertie could see in her eyes how tired she was. "She's . . . she's not young."

"No," said Gertie. "I suppose she isn't."

"But," added the woman, "honestly—well done. You'd be amazed at how many people go to pieces when something like this happens. But you were completely calm."

AFTER THE PARAMEDICS had gone, Jean made them tea and put a little bit of whisky in for shock. Gertie protested and remade Elspeth another one without any whisky in it at all, then Elspeth protested so she ended up with a tiny dash and, by this time, stone-cold tea.

The KCs arrived in force by 9 p.m. Gertie hadn't even told anyone; possibly someone had spotted the sirens and word had got around, or possibly there were deeper, older signals to a powerful coven of women feeling the pull of one of their number being in trouble.

"It's like the bat signal," said Gertie as she opened the door. "Only with crochet hooks."

Between them all, they put Elspeth to bed, making sure they checked on her every five minutes, until she told them, in a voice that started off querulous but now had an air of command to it, that they had to stop it or she wasn't going to get a wink of sleep. Then they convened an emergency council, organizing who was going to take her in the morning, and who was going to sit when and who was going to handle making all the shepherd's pie Elspeth was going to need to convalesce.

Gertie removed herself from the room—the whisky was being shared around again—and went and sat with Elspeth, who although fed up of seeing everyone else was perfectly happy to see her darling granddaughter. In fact, she tried to sit up as Gertie entered with an extra cup of tea, just in case. Elspeth waved it away; she absolutely didn't want to be getting up to go to the toilet in the pitch-black middle of the night more than was absolutely necessary. Her biggest relief was that she hadn't wet herself when that nice ambulance man had turned up. Old age was even less fun than everyone had warned her it was going to be.

"Hey, *mo grabh*," she said. Gertie sat down, enjoying the silence. Next door the rabble were rather leaning into the fuss and drawing up a night rota.

"It's all gone a bit dramatic next door," Gertie said.

"I know," replied Elspeth. "Well, good. I'm glad everyone is flying into action and having a lovely time."

"Was it scary?"

The old hand clasped at her.

"So scary," her grandmother whispered, a tear dropping from her eye onto the pillow. Gertie grabbed a tissue from the box by the bed, and tenderly wiped Elspeth's eyes with her other hand.

"I felt . . . so small," said Elspeth. "As if . . . as if . . ." She took a loud shuddering breath. "I don't feel . . ." she started again.

"Don't talk, Gran. Not if you're tired."

Elspeth shook her head. "No. I'm fine. This is important. You have to know . . . when it happened . . ."

"Uh-huh."

"I thought that might be it. I thought that was it. For me."

"Well, you're in your own bed now, so the medical people obviously don't think so."

"No," said Elspeth. "Not this time. But what I have to tell you is important."

Gertie tilted her head. "What's that?"

"You have to know," Elspeth said carefully, her pale skin creased with the effort, "that I don't feel eighty-four. I don't feel it at all. I feel your age. Inside. You never get any older. You can't believe it's all gone, and all those years have gone past. You think *it can't possibly be me.* Getting old happens to other people, but it won't happen to *me*. But it does. Suddenly you turn around and all the summers and Christmases have smooshed all the gither, and some days I'll see a woman holding her new babby, and I'll feel strange because Jeanette isn't still in my arms, and you aren't either. Because two minutes ago, you were." She sighed. "And now it feels like . . . I'm being asked to leave the stage. Like my turn is over. Even if it's not over quite yet, there's nothing *new* coming. No new act, or bit where I get to start over, make different choices.

"And it doesn't feel fair. It isn't the least bit fair, even if you don't die young, and I'm old. But it still doesn't feel anything like enough. For all the things you want to do and all the places you want to go and . . . I never went anywhere. And I never thought I wanted to. I have absolutely loved my life. I was happy here. I just want more of it, that's all.

"And what I would say to you is, don't wait. Go places. I think . . . I don't know. Jean never wanted to go anywhere. But I think you might like it. Who knows? But you should. Get away. Travel. Have fun. Because in a blink of an eye . . . you will be very very old, like me, and you won't be quite sure how you got here."

This was a very long speech from her grandmother. But it felt like exactly what she had thought the first time she'd picked up her grandmother's hand. Gertie nodded fervently.

"Now, go and let an old lady sleep," Elspeth said. "I promise not to die on you quite yet. And anyway it'll be a day out, going up the big hospital. They've got a nice restaurant."

Gertie kissed her on top of her head and went back to the still fairly lively group next door, thoughtfully. She had to check though.

"Mum," she said. "Do you want me to stay for Grandma?"

Jean shook her head vehemently. "Exactly the opposite," she said. "You have to go. You really have to go. I'm being selfish."

Gertie nodded. "Then I am going to go. And I am going to think seriously about the job."

And Jean kissed her daughter full on the forehead.

"Good. Plus, I have a new consignment of mohair showing up and I'm going to need the entirety of that room."

CHAPTER 12

So did you tell him?"

Morag was lying on Gregor's bed trying to pretend there wasn't also a goat in the room, which wasn't as easy as you might think.

"Yes."

"But did you tell him why?"

Morag had not, in fact, told her grandfather the two reasons that she was moving out—one, his housekeeper was evil; and two, she wanted to bring her boyfriend over and have sex with him quite a lot. She'd just said it was something she wanted to do and Ranald, being of an understanding turn of mind, had guessed the second reason, if not the first, and given her his immediate blessing. Peigi had practically stood on the doorstep grinning and watching her leave, as if she'd won, and Morag was trying to be sanguine about it. She'd dumped her stuff in the flat, said hi to Gertie, who it seemed spent a lot of time in her room. After years of living in a very overcrowded, stuffed little house she wanted absolutely nothing on view and was therefore spectacularly tidy—which suited neat-minded Morag down to the ground. Gertie was mostly on the phone to her mum or the GP, checking Elspeth was okay, but Morag didn't know that.

On Inchborn, where the early cool light was hitting the fresh sprouting hills full of daffodils, it had been a truly lovely weekend. Gregor was the kind of person who lost himself. He had exceptional powers of concentration—which was useful, as he was an ornithologist and ethnobiologist, charged with preserving and monitoring the wildlife on Inchborn, a tiny isolated island in the middle of the sea, dominated by its ruined abbey. When Gregor was busy doing something, he took his time, got totally immersed in the flow of it and the hours would fly by. This made him rather astonishingly good in bed, which you would not necessarily guess by looking at him, and a sensational cook, which you probably would.

Morag got up, put the goat out, and moved to the dilapidated sofa in the sitting room in front of the fire. It was proving to be an unusually cold spring but she didn't actually mind, as she was wearing four jumpers and the fire was making the room cozy enough to take one of them off. Plus the view beyond the window of the sitting room was of the small garden, fiercely guarded by Karen the chicken, who roamed it pecking furiously at things, and her best friend, Barbara the goat, who had always rather liked Morag until Morag had more or less started spending all her time there holding hands with Gregor, and worse. Barbara was now furiously jealous and would instantly boot Morag's hand out of Gregor's if she saw them together. Morag absolutely understood the instinct, as she would feel the same if she ever saw another female with her hand in Gregor's, but she found it easy to forget and sometimes had to move incredibly fast if they rounded a corner and Barbara was there. Right now she had moved back, and had her head ominously close to the window, eyeing them both up.

"Yeah . . . Erno's picking me up. That goat wants to kill me," said Morag.

Gregor smiled ruefully.

"Now you're meant to say don't be stupid, goats never kill anyone," she went on.

"Yeah, well . . ."

"She used to love me!"

"She's a very nice goat."

"Well, she's not now," said Morag. "She's following me around with her devil eyes."

"She's just jealous," Gregor reminded her.

"Animals can't feel jealousy!"

"*You're* an animal. Of course they do. Have you ever petted one dog and not another?"

"Yes, but . . . I mean, bees don't get jealous of other bees, do they? The ones that make, like, yellower honey and stuff."

"It's entirely possible that they do," said Gregor. Morag knew everything there was to know about mechanical engines, how to fix cars, boats, planes, anything you wanted. She was brilliant with a wrench or a welding iron and had made numerous improvements to his tumbledown house. She was, however, absolutely ignorant of the natural world, particularly for someone born in the Highlands of Scotland. "Can I let Barbara back in? Let her get used to you."

"No! She smells and she just wants to cuddle up to you on the sofa, and then you smell."

"Well, only of goat. What's wrong with that?"

Morag smiled at him benevolently. "I must," she said, "really love you quite a lot."

He looked up from where he'd been sketching some apparently unusually large daisies he'd found off the northernmost cliff face.

"Yeah?" he said, looking straight at her in a way that Morag found it necessary to put the book down immediately. It was only some time afterward that he remembered to ask about her new housemate.

Morag wrinkled her nose. "Uh," she said. "I hope she's going to be okay. I don't suppose I'm going to be there very much. She's *really* quiet."

Gregor frowned briefly, tracing a finger on her shoulder, still pink as they lay in front of the fire.

"Maybe she's scared of you."

Morag snorted. "Don't be daft."

"I've seen you strip a tractor," said Gregor.

"How's that scary?"

"Actually I found it a truly tremendous turn-on," he admitted. "But you are quite intimidating."

"I am not!" said Morag, then, seeing his face, sighed. "Am I?"

"You're competent," said Gregor. "That shouldn't be seen as threatening in this world, in this day and age. But people are weird."

"But she knew me at school," chipped in Morag. "They used to call me Morag the Gro-bag!"

Gregor laughed. "That's really stupid."

"It *was*. And horrible. I was shy."

"What did they call Gertie?"

"Moony Mooney. It didn't really stick, but that's what she was like."

"Your school sounds awful."

"Huh," said Morag.

"What did they call Nalitha?"

"They didn't. All the boys were in love with her and all the girls wanted her hair or were a bit scared of *her*."

Gregor smiled.

"Anyway, Gertie's never even been in a plane."

"Really?"

"Really! I know!"

"Well, you should fix that then. Have you found anyone else for Nalitha's maternity cover yet?"

"No. And Gertie doesn't want to do it."

"Maybe after a quick spin in Dolly she will?"

"And maybe she really really won't."

"Well, have you even had any more applicants?"

"Yes," said Morag. "Two who didn't turn up to the interview because they weren't feeling it and one was Extinction Rebellion. Took ages to clean off the graffiti."

Gregor smiled. "You know," he said. "There are introverts in this world . . ."

Morag looked at his dear face. "You think I should be more encouraging?"

Gregor shrugged, as Barbara butted the window frame.

"Oh, she really wants in. Can I have her in the kitchen whilst I'm cooking?"

"Are you cooking goat?"

"Mor!"

"I'm kidding, I'm kidding. Okay, just wash your hands."

A square of bright sunlight hit the sofa. Sunshine, the fire, a good book, a Saturday afternoon on an island that had no internet, no shops, no other people, no distractions and nothing to do except take long walks—which they had already done that morning—eat good food, watch the sun set or rise depending on which way you were facing, with coffee or wine—depending on which end of the day it was—make love, and try and read through the thousand-odd old books that lined the old house. It was very, very hard not to be happy there; the only downside—that she ever had to leave.

CHAPTER 13

Gertie was a bit worried she might not have the right flatmate etiquette, so she dealt with moving in the only way she knew how—she knitted Morag a beautiful pair of super-warm socks in the colors of the company uniform. It worked brilliantly. Morag's feet were always cold in the cockpit, just a skein of metal between her boots and the freezing sky. She was genuinely delighted, and then felt terrible about not getting Gertie anything so nipped to the ScotNorth and got her some moving-in prosecco and of course Gertie politely opened it at once.

She asked Morag lots of questions about MacIntyre Air, which pleased Morag, who felt she was inching toward the job but was actually a way for Gertie to gather more intel on Calum, particularly now she was following his Instagram. Just to see what kind of knitwear he favored. It wasn't creepy.

"He seems nice," ventured Gertie.

Morag snorted. "We thought he'd be a lot worse. Gramps—that's Ranald. He only works part-time now, so he mostly leaves it to me and I try and keep him in line."

"Well I did think he was nice," said Gertie.

"He won't seem so nice if you take one of his other flights and get stranded at 3 a.m. one hundred kilometers from your destination and his airline won't pick up the phone or give a crap. Unless it's us," added Morag.

She looked at Gertie's busy knitting hands.

"What IS that?" she asked, pointing at the misshapen black knit steadily growing under Gertie's flying fingers.

"Oh, it's a penguin," said Gertie. "Or it will be. I thought it might be . . . I thought it might be nice for Nalitha's other kid, when the baby comes."

"That is a brilliant idea," said Morag. She wanted to push Gertie again to take the job, but didn't quite know how. Regardless, Gertie had caught sight of her watch, and sat bolt upright.

"What?"

"Nine p.m.!" said Gertie.

Morag shrugged.

"Nine p.m.! Summer, *Love Island*; winter, *Married at First Sight*," said Gertie, shocked Morag didn't know. Gertie switched on Struan's big telly, which was tuned to a sports channel.

"Aren't those rubbish?" said Morag.

Gertie shook her head fiercely. "No," she said. "Because every single time, against all the odds, amidst all the nonsense—people really do, genuinely, when they least expect it, fall in love."

Morag watched the screen burst into life. "They do," she murmured, almost to herself.

Then she looked down and admired her cozy feet and waggled her toes.

"I may have to get Calum to incorporate these into the uniform."

Gertie suddenly saw herself standing side by side with Calum at a glamorous event.

"This is my personal designer," he was saying to someone. *"She designs my uniforms. As well, of course, as being the love of my life."*

Morag wiggled her warming toes and glanced out of the window. It was still terribly, unseasonably cold for spring; but it was bright blue out there, the sky fresh and washed clear. It was a Tuesday. The summer season, when the Highlands and islands were overrun with gleeful tourists, was a while off yet; they had a very light work day. Morag thought back to what Gregor had said. And how soon Nalitha was going to have to go off. She had an idea.

THE NEXT MORNING, as Gertie had found it hard to sleep without the familiar downstairs chatter and noise of women living in close proximity in the tiny cottage, she came down a little later. It was a lovely day. Morag was standing next to the kettle, still wearing her new socks.

"Uhm," she said gently. "Do you want to come for a spin?"

Gertie looked at her.

"I've got a spare seat on the plane. You can't bring your knitting. But you could . . . you know. Come along for the ride. Actually, do come," she said, more seriously. "Calum is down today and I want us to look busy and successful."

Gertie bit her lip. "Calum's around?"

Morag nodded. "Absolutely. Being a pain in my arse. Come on, isn't it your day off?"

GERTIE'S NERVES MOUNTED as they headed to the airfield that morning, until she ended up following Morag out to the plane as if she was being arrested. There had, in fact, been no sign of Calum Frost at the tin shed that masqueraded as an airport, which was disappointing as she had slightly imagined him saying, "*Morag showing you the plane? Why don't I come along too, get to know you better? For I am so tired of women who only want me for my money and status as an aeroplane person* (Gertie wasn't exactly sure about the exact nature of his job) *and really want someone who just loves me for myself. Also if she could knit, that would be a real bonus.*"

She thought of Elspeth too, and how proud she would be of Gertie, heading off out into the big wide world. Well, the archipelago. Which was more or less the same thing.

As they boarded—there had been no sign of Calum at the airport; she had absolutely definitely checked—Gertie couldn't believe how tiny the plane was; you couldn't stand upright on it, but had to crouch your way up and down. Morag indicated the front-row seat next to the window. She wanted Gertie to see everything. Next to her was a farmer who'd been down to a county show and was not just a nervous flyer but also feeling the effects of rather too much merriment at the Young Farmers' Ball the night before.

"Hey, lass," he said to Gertie. "Oh good, a friend of the pilot's. You'll have done this a million times, yes?"

Gertie bit her lip anxiously.

"So, is it time for putting seatbelts on or . . . ?"

Gertie hesitated. "Sure?"

Morag was close enough to hear—there was no door between the cockpit and the body of the plane and she didn't have her headphones on yet. She shook her head subtly, as Mackintosh was still fueling the plane.

"I mean, in a minute," said Gertie. And then, when it was time, she fumbled horribly with hers, not quite understanding how to make it click, and found herself nervously flushing again.

When the propellers started, she got a bit of a shock. Morag had taken second seat to keep an eye on Gertie, so Erno was captaining today.

"Rough night?" sympathized the Young Farmer.

"Something like that," murmured Gertie, staring at the tarmac disappearing under the tiny wheels of the plane, faster and faster . . . Suddenly there was a lurch in her stomach, and she shut her eyes, waiting and praying for it to be over.

IT WAS SUCH a beautiful day to fly and Erno had made a perfect take-off into the blue. Smiling, Morag turned to look at Gertie only to see her sitting, clinging tight to the armrests with her eyes closed. The Young Farmer was looking at her in concern, as if there was clearly something to worry about.

Once they hit cruising altitude she unbuckled and popped over. "Please open your eyes," said Morag, quite earnestly. It wasn't terribly helpful. Gertie clutched onto the tough metal and plastic hand rests and took a glance to her left, then gasped.

She had theoretically known what was going to happen, but it still seemed the most incredible thing; they had left a cool day, yet here they were above the clouds—on top of them. They looked like . . . well, to some people they look like waves, or cotton wool, or candyfloss. To Gertie, they looked like skeins of wool, or the fluff a sheep leaves behind if it has strayed too close to the barbed wire.

The sun felt warm on the window as Gertie peered out. They were flying south in order to turn round and follow the air corridor northward, keeping out of the way of the many Scandinavian airlines on the route and the great transatlantic liners, taking their shortcut across the top end of the globe.

A line of sparkle cut through everything, occasionally painting bright splodges here and there. It was, she was astonished to realize, the river Caras, which emptied into the whirling maelstroms of the sea. Here it looked like a glorious line of fairy lights unfurling ahead of her.

Down below she could make out, through breaks in the cloud, great long tracts of farmland, occasionally punctuated by tiny settlements, also sparkling in the sun. It was so strange; she knew she lived in a sparsely populated area. But compared to the vast empty land spread out far below here, humans . . . they were nothing. They were tiny.

"Gorgeous, eh?" called back Morag, over the din of the engines.

"There's so . . . it's huge!" said Gertie, suddenly astounded that her own world was so small. If she followed the land all the way over, it . . . it was curved. Gertie realized suddenly that she was looking at the actual curvature of the earth. The entire planet. And then she was even more gobsmacked than before. They turned northward and flew over the town and the place she had spent her entire life; where she had grown up and known life and all its joys and disappointments—and it was nothing. Just a little clump against patchworks of fields, and behind them, the mountains. Now they were real and solid, huge and looming. They looked gigantic. Everything natural and green looked real. Their little grid looked puny and silly from up here; the villages dotted around even more so; humans balanced precariously on the surface of a world that had a lot more space without them.

"Oh my," she said quietly. Morag smiled to herself. She so wanted everyone to love being in flight as much as she did; not to take it for granted, or complain about it, but to remain amazed that something so wondrous had become commonplace.

"What's that?" said Gertie suddenly. Far to port side was a plane going what looked to Gertie extremely fast.

The Young Farmer vowed never to fly again as the woman talking to the pilot was obviously a pure amateur. Plus he now wanted to throw up for about nine different reasons.

"Icelandair," said Morag, checking her watch. "En route to Glasgow. We see them every day along here."

"But they're going so fast!"

"So are we," Morag replied. "We're going 300 miles an hour. It's all relative when you're up here."

Gertie bit her lip.

"That's nothing actually," Morag added. "The Airbus goes . . . never mind, too much info. Don't worry. We see them every day. It's perfectly safe up here."

But Gertie wasn't really listening; they were approaching the mouth of the river, and beyond it the great sea, the islands looming up ahead of the sparkling waters. She put her hand to her mouth. She'd been on a school trip to Inchborn of course, everyone had, but they'd taken the little ferry, which had been an adventure in itself. There the water had been icy cold and there had been swells against the side of the boat.

The tan and forest colors coalesced around rolling tributaries below, and it was difficult to discriminate between roads or rivers. It was exactly like a relief map; Gertie felt she could put her finger out and follow them round with the tip; the conurbations—so few of them, and so insubstantial, it seemed—even if every day you read in the papers that the world was overpopulated. They looked like a few settlements of humans clinging to the very edges; to the edges of the sea and the river, with no thought for the endless spaces, shaped like Narnian maps, the rolling mountains and hanging cliffs. There were tiny rocks poking out of the water, miniature islands that couldn't even have names.

She had had no idea that Scotland could be so beautiful. That the *world* could be so beautiful. That the sea was so blue, the beaches so golden. She immediately wanted to knit in those colors; show off the glorious bracken, and the white tops of the mountains.

"We don't go very high up," said Morag reassuringly. "That's what makes it brilliant: you can see absolutely everything. I have flown everywhere, and I can tell you, few things beat the islands of Scotland. Ask anyone."

There was pride in her voice as she said it, as if she'd built them herself, Gertie thought. But maybe, when you were flying a plane, you felt like you had.

From here though the sea was a glinting paradise, bright turquoise near the shoreline, growing darker as they drew further from the land. She could make out the fishing boats, the towlines behind them in the wake, so they looked like white commas on a huge blue page; the fishermen couldn't possibly give a thought to their plane, high above. Gertie could see the shadow of the craft flicking across the top of the waves like a moth.

"Want me to buzz them?" said Morag, noting what she was looking at.

"Oh my goodness, no!" said Gertrude.

"Good," said Morag quickly. "Because I am absolutely not allowed to do that, and wouldn't have dreamed of it."

Gertie touched her finger to the heavy plastic of the porthole.

"It's not like what I thought," she said. "I didn't realize you could see so much."

"You can't always," admitted Morag. "It's a pretty good day for it."

Scotland looked, from the air, like a fantasy postcard version of itself. She saw a canal with boats up and down it; freshly tilled fields waiting for spring seeding; huge solar farms and, out to the far north, over the water they passed the huge wind farms that were powering half the country. It was like stepping into another world, being in an alien spaceship. The field of arms, in the middle of the sea, extended for miles and miles, gently spinning, out of sync then in sync with each other. Gertie had seen them pass on trucks a hundred times; she knew how massive they were. And there they were, planted like a field of beautiful sunflowers in the deep ocean. It was awe-inspiring. Even though she was in a plane, said to be utterly destroying the planet, she felt more optimistic about the future, suddenly, than she had for a very long time. There was something so benign about people doing something so difficult—planting great fields of windmills to harness the power of the earth—that you couldn't help loving it, and them.

"Wow," said Gertie again, gazing at the jaw-dropping scene in front of her.

They passed great sandbanks in the sea that Gertie could never have suspected were there; covered in birds doing goodness knows what. You could walk there, thought Gertie. Walk out, right in the middle of the sea. And nobody would ever do that, or know about you; your ship would suddenly run aground. A piece of earth—so much, it seemed to her suddenly, that nobody had ever stepped on. Not like the winding cobbles of Carso, which had been worn smooth, foot after foot, year after year, century after century. It was so strange that Scotland itself suddenly to her felt like an undiscovered land, full of places no human had ever walked; nooks and crannies of the mountain inaccessible to transport or anything except animals, birds, and to be viewed from the tiny window of a plane. She had not even suspected. Suddenly she wanted to bring her grandmother up, very much.

Gertie nodded, hypnotized. As they came in to land at their first stop, Larbh, she clutched the arms tightly again as the plane bounced and jerked through the clouds. That morning she had been very very frightened, but now, even as the view from her window grew grayer as they descended, Morag was so calm and matter-of-fact about her job, she couldn't be scared anymore.

"So," said Nalitha, arms folded over her vast stomach as they arrived back at the tin shed. "Are you taking the job, Gertie?"

Gertie, still giddy, her head literally in the clouds, stared around at the tiny airport, at the plane outside. Suddenly, she saw Calum Frost walk in with two men, high five Erno and Morag, and start chatting to them.

"Yes," she said. "Yes, I am."

CHAPTER 14

Struan was trying his best to be brave, but a summons from the head teacher was, even though he was a grown-up and also a teacher, still never an appealing prospect. Particularly when you were planning on announcing your resignation at the end of term and were slightly nervous someone might have got wind of it already. Also, he was worried about his primary 6s. Well. Most of them were fine, bellowing away as usual, but wee Oksana was still so quiet, and he wasn't sure what to do about it. He'd gone out to say hi to her mum, but her mother had looked very worried and asked immediately if Oksana was being a good girl, and he'd assured her that she was, at which the woman had raised her hands, as if to say, what the hell did he have to worry about then. This seemed reasonable, considering everything else they had going on.

As she left, Struan had noticed a skein of wool trailing from her bag, and thought briefly of his new tenant. It was so strange, he had no memory of her from school at all. Saskia would no more knit than fly in the air. As it turned out, flying in the air was very much on the agenda.

THE HEAD, MRS. McGinty, did not have her happy face on when Struan knocked and entered her small office. On the other hand, if she had a happy face, it was truly only visible when she was trying to suck up to parents, even—sometimes *especially*, Struan reflected ruefully—when their kids were absolute bampots, be-cause the parents who had the bampot kids were often the richest and most entitled parents in the area, and were often, quite frankly, bampots themselves, albeit bampots who brought Mrs. McGinty particularly nice presents at the end of the year.

He sighed.

"I see you were late again, Mr. McGhie," she said. Struan didn't want to admit that he hadn't been able to sleep the night before because he was in a new place and nervous about his upcoming audition, and had ended up in a corner of the tiny sitting room, sipping whisky and listening to Kris Drever on his headphones, which was rarely likely to cheer anyone up.

"Aye, I'm fine," he said, although he was conscious his shirt was unironed and his curly hair badly in need of a cut. Saskia usually told him when he needed to go to the barber, but she hadn't mentioned anything recently, which was, he realized now, a bad sign in itself; a sign that she didn't even care. Instinctively he touched the back; it was matted. Damn. As the supposedly cool young music teacher he got a fair amount of leeway about dress, but this was taking it a bit too far. The hole in his shirt probably wasn't working out brilliantly for him either.

"Well," she said. Mrs. McGinty liked to give the impression that as a peripatetic he was basically only just above pond scum and Struan felt it deeply: he often felt that way about himself anyway, and there were many many women in his life who had expressed it too.

He wasn't to know that in fact Mrs. McGinty had spent her distant youth madly in love with one guitarist after another—on distant stages or down at her local youth club, it didn't matter. And she hadn't been noticed by one of them. Not the lowliest member of the worst youth punk band had given her a second glance. One that she'd managed to glom on to, from a wedding band, had treated her absolutely horribly. Obviously, she told herself now, it was Struan's bad timekeeping and "eff it" (Mrs. McGinty didn't even think in swear words) attitude that she didn't like about him and not the fact that even though she was very nicely dressed in a new M&S Autograph collection trouser suit with matching gold necklace and earrings, and he was wearing a shirt that looked like he'd stolen it from a funeral, he still wouldn't ever have wanted to get off with her in a million years. She was only forty-five; that was nothing these days. Bloody divorce.

Fortunately she had a plan to punish him and was looking forward to bestowing it.

"Regardless, I was doing the Easter schedule, and it occurred to me, you haven't done the Outward Bound course for years . . ."

Struan straightened up. He hadn't done the Outward Bound for years, because it was on a weekend and he was normally working weekends. But he had been there once; they'd gone to Mure. There was an incredibly competent couple called Jan and Charlie who took the kids away and basically told the teachers to just leave and they'd get in touch if there was a problem. It was brilliant. There was the loveliest coffee shop in Mure Town, and a bar at the Harbor's Rest and a very pretty Icelandic girl who worked there . . . Struan remembered suddenly playing his guitar for the very pretty Icelandic girl—Inge something—and suddenly found himself blushing. Oh yeah.

"Well, okay," he said. He was finding this conversation difficult. Women normally liked him, at least until they got to know him, or—no, that wasn't fair. He had plenty of good women friends. At least until they tried to settle down with him and plan for the future. That's when it tended to go pretty wrong. But Saskia would be different. "Sure, that'll be great. On Mure, yeah? Love that place."

Mrs. McGinty was enjoying this. "Ah, unfortunately they're all booked up this year; they're taking on more kids in care. So we've found somewhere a bit closer to home—you're going to go with the mountaineering group in Archland."

"Mountaineering?" said Struan, unsure if he'd heard properly. He wished he'd had a shave: Mrs. McGinty was always so disapproving of stubble. He rubbed his chin. "The Primary 6s?"

He thought briefly of Hugh McSticks's generous padding and frowned.

"I mean, they're only wee. I don't know how they're going to get up a mountain."

"They'll be guided up," replied Mrs. McGinty. "It's more of a gentle stroll really—it's the north side that's famous. The south side has a path. Then camping for a night at halfway up, then getting nice and dirty and tired and going back to their parents. One solitary night without their phones. Everyone's happy. Of course you'll have to camp with them."

"Camp?" spluttered Struan, who hadn't camped since he was a child with his parents and had violently strummed Metallica songs on his guitar until the campground manager asked him to stop. After that, his parents hadn't taken him again. Even when his band played music festivals he'd turn down the cider and drive home late to get back to his own bed. "I have to camp?"

"It's character-building," Mrs. McGinty said crisply.

Struan sighed internally.

"I think I might be . . ." He was toying with weakly making up an excuse.

"Part of your contract states that you have to go on the rota for school trips," said the head teacher.

"Yes, I was thinking I might take them to see the Lost Spells Project . . ."

"I'm afraid that's already been taken. This is all that's left."

I bet it is, thought Struan.

"Who's the other teacher?" he asked.

"I'm still working on that," the head teacher replied.

STRUAN WAS HALFWAY to the flat, deep in thought, before he remembered he didn't live there anymore. He could maybe stop by quickly: he'd left one of his guitars in the hall cupboard anyway.

Morag wasn't in that day; just Gertie, rather shell-shocked after a nerve-racking interview where she'd asked for a possible sabbatical from the ScotNorth and instead of shouting "How dare you! Never darken these doors again!" as she'd imagined, Mr. Wainwright had actually been incredibly kind and said how much they'd miss her and that there'd always be a job here for her. He'd wished her luck. And then all the women had come forward and said how much they'd miss her mittens and vests and Gertie had promised faithfully to keep knitting for them and it had been an emotional day all round.

That was even before she'd gone to break the news to the KCs who were obviously delighted, but also immediately launched into the most terrifying plane-crash stories they knew; about the plane out of Malaysia that had gone missing and never been seen again. About planes crashing full-on into mountains because the pilot was having a crisis—although having discussed it fully they thought this probably wouldn't happen with Morag, even if she was over thirty and that young man didn't seem to be any closer to making an honest woman of her. She probably almost certainly wouldn't deliberately crash a plane because of that.

By the time they'd started on 9/11 Gertie had made her excuses. Elspeth though—Elspeth had been pleased, thought Gertie. She could always tell by the way her needles clacked as to her grandmother's mood.

"You'll take me up?" she'd said, the old eyes glaring at her.

Gertie was fishing rich browns and blues out of the oddments box. She had an idea she might write up something new for her knitting blog, even though she very rarely updated it; the fact that it was a blog, now, in 2024, and nobody ever read blogs, and the only people who read hers were the other KCs, who would write in the comments that everything was brilliant (Jean, Marian) or complain about the dull colors (the twins) or suggest she try something a little simpler (Majabeen, unable to help herself in case Gertie got too good, even though her own children were "too intellectual" to knit).

She was back at the flat, looking at her blog again, when the doorbell rang. This was a surprise, and Struan standing there was an even bigger surprise. She stared at him, feeling her mouth drop open slightly. This was ridiculous, she told herself. She was a grown-up, starting a new job, getting on with her life. She was not a schoolgirl. You can't be a schoolgirl forever.

Struan looked at this friend of Morag's. She had very long legs, which gave her an ungainly appearance, like a wobbly fawn, and she didn't look remotely happy to see him.

"Hi," he said, then grasped for her name and they both realized at the same moment he had forgotten it.

"Yeah, hi, I'm Gertie?" she said. "You remember. The person you take all that money off each month?"

"Och aye," said Struan. "Sorry. Long day. Have you knitted me a new guitar case yet?"

"I have not."

"Disappointing. Is Morag in?"

"I am now," said Morag, coming up the road behind. "Cor, what a day. They've built a new gin distillery on Larbh, and we were bringing back a consignment and one of the bottles broke."

"Thank goodness," replied Struan, standing back and holding

his nose. "I thought for a moment you were literally the drunkest pilot on God's green earth."

"All right, all right," said Morag, sniffing her sleeve. "Blimey, that's strong. What are they making it with, sheep dip?"

She pulled out her complimentary bottle. It was actually called "Sheep Dip."

"Huh," she said.

She glanced up at Struan.

"You know we live here now, right? You *don't* live here anymore. That's why we gave you all that money?"

"That's just what I said!" said Gertie.

"I just came to get one of my guitars," said Struan. "I'll get out of your . . ."

"Don't be daft, I was just teasing." Morag rolled her eyes. "Come and have tea."

". . . gin?"

THE HEAD'S DROPPED me in it," Struan was explaining. "She really doesn't like me."

"Is it because you keep staying out all night playing in bands and because you're leaving to play in an even bigger band?" asked Morag. Gertie had disappeared and reappeared with a large box of biscuits the ScotNorth had given her, only slightly broken, and everyone was delighted, as they went surprisingly well with the gin, which tasted as fresh as the watery place it came from.

"I'll be flying you up there, come to think of it," said Morag. "It might be fun."

"How is climbing up a mountain with a heap of ten-year-olds fun?" said Struan. "Do you want to do it?"

"Gregor never minds the kids," Morag went on. "They come over and pester him with questions about his goshawk."

"Yes, well, Gregor is of course perfect," said Struan. "Whereas, as Saskia keeps pointing out, I am very much not."

He chomped into a chocolate ginger, disconsolately.

"Have you got a boyfriend?" Morag asked Gertie, realizing this was the kind of question she should probably have asked before they moved in together, in case the answer turned out to be: yes, he's a professional bodybuilder out of his head on steroids all the time and every so often he comes round and breaks all the windows.

Gertie shook her head.

"Got your eye on anyone?"

Gertie thought of Calum Frost, coming in when she was in her uniform, saying would she like to go for a coffee after work sometime? I mean, it wasn't entirely appropriate with her working for him now, but it was only for a little while, wasn't it? Meanwhile he'd just have to hang on . . .

"I'm kind of off men," said Gertie. "They smell."

"They do," agreed Morag.

"Oi!" said Struan.

"Oh, you don't count," said Morag, reassuringly. "You're a teacher."

"And you don't smell," said Gertie, also trying to be reassuring.

"I think that's because Saskia cleaned the bathroom," said Struan, looking a bit glum. Then he perked up.

"Anyway, I'll soon be a sexy rock star again. I'm playing the town ceilidh on Saturday."

Morag rolled her eyes. Then looked at Gertie. "Hey, you should come! Loads of chaps there, all the young farmers!"

"What did I just say about not smelling?" said Gertie. "Plus my Knitting Circle always come and get stocious and embarrass me."

"Your mum is dead nice!" said Morag.

"She is," agreed Gertie. "She just kind of likes to sit and talk about me very loudly as if I'm not there."

Struan grimaced.

"Oh yeah, Saskia does that," he said absentmindedly, then looked surprised as both the girls stared at him. "But she is very hot," he added, as Morag made a mental note not to move too much furniture in.

"Right, I'd better head," said Struan, getting up.

"Get that mountaineering training started!" suggested Morag, and Gertie giggled.

Struan took the guitar and clattered down the stairs.

"Not a whit has he changed," said Morag, shaking her head.

Gertie wondered what Calum had been like at school. Adorable, probably.

CHAPTER 15

Nalitha had shown Gertie everything she could, and was now taking a much-needed day off to drive down south to the nearest John Lewis and start looking at blankies. She and Morag had reassured Gertie she was going to be absolutely fine, although neither of them were totally sure; she could be so shy.

Gertie did not sleep well, and left the flat early, before Morag was awake, although smoke was already skirling from the chimneys. The town was not quiet, because the tides were in, which meant the boats would have returned; not the little skiffs from her grandfather's time, but up-to-the-minute trawlers. They looked a little battered and bashed from the outside, but inside had the latest technology that told them where to find shoals, and also where the fish were low and needed to be left alone, to spawn and regroup.

At least it was a little airport, Gertie told herself, none of the scary lines to go through she'd seen on TV with queues that went on for miles and agitated, sad people sitting on their luggage, their children weeping, complaining about being stranded miles from home.

By contrast Carso airport, such as it was, was very much just a large tin shed at the end of the industrial estate. It had some cheeky flags and three flights a day: two by Calum Frost's large Norwegian line, which went to Aberdeen and Glasgow respectively, carrying oil people and tourists and local shoppers, plus MacIntyre Air, technically owned by Calum too, but fiercely clinging on to its own branding and show of independence.

Many of the people coming up via Glasgow were making the long trip north from around the world to visit their ancestral homes, or simply the beautiful chain of the archipelago: tiny Inchborn, with its preserved abbey and world war defensive zones and pillboxes; Cairn, the largest, its population, bird life and wonderful grazing; then Larbh, the remotest island, with a few tumbledown cottages, a very few remaining inhabitants; and uninhabited Archland, with its famously vertical mountain, the Mermaid's Spyglass, that drew climbers from round the world; the last island before the great expanse of sea before you hit Mure, Shetland, the Faroes, and on to the fjords.

It was a magical part of the world; so far north that in the summer it was rarely dark with an extraordinary quality of light in the bright yellow rays of high sun. Sunshine streaked across the blue-green water faster than the herons swooped from bay to bay, or the capercaillies circled the hilltops.

The airport itself had some pretty nifty branding along the lines of "Gateway to the North" and saltires and so forth, but inside simply tended toward the very drafty and so it was known by all as the tin shed.

The airport building, apart from the airlines, was run by a husband and wife team, Pete and Linda, who handled air traffic control for the three flights plus freight, helicopters and the teams that went out to maintain the wind farms and oil rigs, who had their only private transfers. Linda ran the office and the kiosk, with varying results.

The little kiosk sold absolutely terrible coffee from a horrible machine that really only qualified to be called "coffee" on a technicality, and was good at bringing together all nationalities, whatever their coffee heritage, from fastidious Swedes who expected a small biscuit, to Kiwis used to sensational patterns in their im-

maculate flat whites, to Americans who liked theirs tasting of
burnt electrical wire, to Italians who liked tiny defibrillator cups
you could only drink standing up in case your legs started twitch-
ing involuntarily, to Turks who liked to fill theirs with sugar until the spoon could stand up in it independently. There was not
a nationality that passed through that airport that didn't take a
sip from the million-degrees-Celsius super-thin plastic cup full
of watery brownish liquid who didn't immediately make a face
and agree amongst themselves that Scotland was brilliant at many
many things, but coffee was not one of them.

On the plus side, there was also a small supply of baking on sale
too; Linda made shortbread, fresh, and scones, warm if you were
up for the morning Inchborn flight or Edinburgh, and you could
sit by the big glass windows and look out at the little runway on a
sunny morning and frankly many locals came and did just that,
but they brought their own coffee in a flask.

There were two check-in desks: one for Nalitha, and one for
Calum's other business concerns, staffed by a rotating crew of unbelievably beautiful Scandinavians on Calum's flights, which had
real stewardesses on board, who also staffed check-in with formidable efficiency despite the fact that many of the male passengers
immediately went slack-jawed in the queue.

"That's what happens when you spend too much time with
sheep," Nalitha would point out, when even people trying to check
in to their airline kept craning round to look at the six-foot girls.

The other flight attendants were friendly enough but there were
just so many of them; it was such a huge company, plus they were
coming from incredibly well-insulated airports in Oslo and Ber-
gen and Aalborg, so it was understandable they would complain
about how cold it was in Carso, where the wind could rattle the
old aluminium sidings, for sure. Okay so the toilets *were* Baltic,

but that was good: Who wanted to encourage people to linger in toilets for heaven's sake? You could also tell the ones who'd been through Carso before by the inevitable coffee flasks.

THE FIRST THING Gertie had had to do was submit for clearance. Morag had tried to look completely unconcerned upon learning that she didn't have a passport and politely suggested she consider getting one of those. Then Pete made her up a laminated photo card that allowed her through the security gate, run by their son, Mackintosh. He was large and dozy, possibly as a result of having completely unrestricted access to shortbread and fresh scones every day, and Nalitha occasionally joked that she was going to walk through with a huge ticking ACME bomb, just to see what he would do. Gregor thought they should be searching people coming off the Inchborn flights, in case anyone had stolen rare or valuable eggs, but that hadn't gained much traction, particularly with the punitive consequences Gregor also proposed for anyone doing such a thing, which involved rather a lot of hot poker work, and some hanging.

GERTIE, HANGING AT the entrance of the tin shed, inhaled. When she'd arrived the first time she'd wondered what that smell was: kind of like if someone had heard of coffee and had tried to make it in a bin. She braced herself to be brave.

In the tin shed Gertie glanced, again, nervously, at the checklist and swallowed hard. Her first day without Nalitha there to help. It had been so many years since she had started a new job, and even then it was mostly just someone giving her a duster and telling her to unpack a box of shampoo.

"You'll be fine!" Jean had said, as convincingly as she could. "Just try not to daydream too much!"

Gertie had made an "of *course* not" face, as if she hadn't half-taken the job in the first place because of its terribly sexy owner.

She pulled anxiously on her uniform, with its tartan skirt—Gertie never wore skirts—and tartan piped shirt with the heather-colored waistcoat. Nalitha absolutely hated it, but Peigi made them by hand and refused to change anything about the ensemble. It was impractical—the shirt had short sleeves, which made it cold and uncomfortable, and was made of polycotton, which meant if you lifted too much and got hot, you would sweat in it—and the waistcoat was not remotely flattering to girls who had boobs, as Nalitha certainly did, nor girls who had flat chests, like Gertie, who looked—according to Jean—like a lad going to his first communion when she had modeled it for the KCs. Tara had told Jean to shush, she looked lovely, and also could she give her a lift down to Glasgow as she wanted to do some shopping and Gertie explained that it didn't work like that. In the same way that she couldn't give them free biscuits in the ScotNorth no matter how many times they suggested that there were already lots broken in the box, and Cara had said, "See!" to Tara very meanly and: "I told you that would be a stupid idea," and Tara had got a bit upset so Gertie had just got changed again and tried not to mention it.

But here she stood, finally, tapping carefully in her mid-heels, which were also new, and already giving her grief, and prepared to check in the 9:40 to Cairn, calling at Larbh.

There was a small queue of people already waiting at the desk, and she suddenly felt a bit panicked with having to log in and remember the correct sequence of events, but she breathed deeply and told herself not to worry about it. Nalitha had told her to call her anytime, but the thought of doing that was daunting, particularly as Nalitha had loudly made her pre-John-Lewis plans clear, vis-à-vis: lying down and watching YouTube videos of dogs falling over and eating jammy doughnuts, and Gertie thought she probably didn't want to be disturbed.

She could do this. She went up and keyed in the code that turned on the computer, which fired into life, then turned to the queue with a smile.

The first two customers were nice old ladies heading to Cairn, the largest of the islands, on a walking tour. They held on to their sticks and smiled widely, talking only about the weather forecast. This was going to be fine, thought Gertie. To her surprise, they hadn't even thought she was new or noticed anything amiss about how she served them, so she couldn't have stood out too dramatically.

Then it was a young family who traveled regularly, who greeted her cheerfully and recognized her from the supermarket, asking after Nalitha. Gertie swallowed. Maybe this was all going to be all right. A large group of hikers, no problem. Some Americans who wanted to ask her all about herself and told her they were Scottish and looking for old gravestones, in an extremely jolly tone of voice, as if traveling across the world to look for the gravestones of their ancestors was very jolly. She barely needed to check their IDs as they were all wearing matching sweatshirts that announced: IT'S HARD TO BE HUMBLE WHEN YOU'RE A WILSON, and sure enough there it was on the screen: Wilson x 8. She stopped feeling quite so panicky. That flight went fine. The number of passengers tallied with the manifest numbers; the luggage was the right weight. She'd been warned a million times that they had to be careful: the plane was so small that there was not a lot of margin of error with the weight limits. It was going to be fine. She was going to be okay.

She felt a lot more confident checking in the second flight, that afternoon—the return circle, picking people up. The little plane essentially flew in a circle. After two couples celebrating a birth-day, the next customer was quite different: a large, heavyset man, with an equally large, heavy-looking bag.

"Finally," he said, looking huffy.

"Hello!" said Gertie. "Welcome. Do you want to put your bag on the scale?"

The man looked irritated. "Not really, it's fine. Here."

And he brandished his phone, with the online ticket on it in tiny font, which Gertie couldn't see; and when she picked it up to try and scan it she must have pressed something wrong as it im-mediately started emitting a loud heavy metal song.

"Oh for Christ's . . ." The irritated man snatched it back from her. "It's there," he said, shoving it back in her face.

She checked the booking, wondering why on earth he was be-ing so aggressive. Was this how some people behaved in airports? Constantly ratty and glancing at their watches and sighing and tapping their feet and touching their luggage? In training Nalitha had said that people got anxious, and also airline staff had quite a lot of power to throw passengers off planes. If you missed one it would cost an absolute fortune to get the next one and if you were here in Carso, the next one wasn't until tomorrow anyway, so that was a problem. Hence people getting shirty with you.

Now she felt her face pinkening as the man stood there, look-ing cross as she checked him in, laboriously, desperate not to get anything wrong.

"I do need to weigh your bag . . . could you put it on the belt please?"

The bag came up as 27 kilograms. Gertie was not happy. Nal-itha had been absolutely adamant.

"I'm sorry," she said. "It's too heavy to go on."

The man snorted. "Fine. I'll pay *even* more."

"I'm sorry. You can't pay for extra baggage. It's . . ."

She hated having to do it.

". . . it's policy. We have to weigh our . . ."

She suddenly couldn't remember the name for the bit of the plane the luggage went into. She nearly said "boot."

"Uhm, hold."

"But I can take stuff out of my bag and walk on with it."

"Uh, yes."

The man shook his head.

"This is ridiculous, you realize that? Completely and utterly stupid!"

Gertie wanted the ground to swallow her. She didn't know what to do. If there was anyone really aggressive in the ScotNorth you just got Mr. Wainwright and he would come out and give them a hard stare until they put the cheese back on the shelf. John Paul was local and she'd known him all her life; she had no idea what this guy was capable of.

"You're bloody useless. Look at you! Computer says 'No!' Fuck's sake."

Everyone around was staring at their shoes suddenly, as if their shoes were very very fascinating things. Gertie swallowed hard and told herself she wasn't going to cry.

"Now you're going to make me open my fucking bag? Seriously, love, haven't you got anything better to do? Just let it go, fuck's sake."

Gertie breathed through her nostrils and tried to smile. "I'm sorry, sir. But I just can't . . ."

He mimicked her. "I'm sorry I can't . . . I'm sorry . . . I am a robot . . . controlled by computers."

Suddenly there was a stir in the queue.

"Excuse me?" came a booming voice. A man stepped forward.

He had blonde, slightly bouffant hair, Oakley sunglasses, and was wearing a ridiculously over-patched flying jacket, which, given the preponderance of weird slogans and odd bits of leather all over it, must have been extremely expensive. Gertie's heart leaped.

The man standing at the desk turned round, looking aggressive.

"Wait your turn, mate," he said.

"I'm not your mate," said the man, smiling nicely at him. "And I'm here to tell you, you can't board this aircraft."

"What?" said the man. "Piss off."

"I'm afraid so. I'm going to have to ask you to leave the airport."

"Get screwed," said the man. "Me and this girl were just checking in my bag, that's all. Weren't you, love?"

"I'm afraid she can't do that. As you are leaving," said a new voice.

"Who the fuck are you?" said the man.

"I'm the fuck who owns this airline," said Calum Frost stepping into view.

And just like that, the latest great crush of Gertrude Mooney's life jumped up a whole new gear.

CHAPTER 16

It happened. It actually happened. Calum and Morag's co-pilot Erno marched the man out of the terminal and dumped him on a taxi driver. Erno was on a diet for his heart, and his old intake of bacon rolls, sausage rolls, and occasionally sausage bacon and egg rolls had been cut off at the source by a family desperate to keep him alive, and a stringent air specialist doctor who was testing his cholesterol every five minutes and basically ruining his life, so anyone who looked like they needed a bit of roughing up was totally fine to Erno; he was in a bad mood anyway. This way he didn't have to think too much about the cashew salad he had packed for lunch. Also, he liked it when some of the passengers waiting in a queue they went past clapped.

The man, astonished, waved his fist at them and shouted a lot about suing, and how he knew his rights, but Calum had merely smiled and suggested he read the small print in his ticket, but good luck with everything and they had him on CCTV verbally abusing a member of his staff, which wasn't remotely true; unbeknownst to Gertie, the only CCTV was outside and looking after the planes, but Calum said it in a way that seemed it very much might have been.

Gertie was desperately trying to calm down by the time the men came back into the hangar. She had inadvertently told the next people in line, a nice young couple on their honeymoon, that it was her first day and therefore everyone had crowded round her, being incredibly nice and sympathetic and chatty. A bit too chatty in fact, as Gertie realized, to her annoyance, that

Majabeen's big son Krish was in the queue for the Glasgow flight and had seen everything, which meant that this terrible thing that had happened on her very first day would whizz round the KCs before she'd get a tea break.

"I'm completely fine," she said, trying to smile, even if her voice sounded a bit wobbly. She wasn't used to people yelling at her; Jean might—okay, definitely did—take on a chiding tone with her, but that was only when she was complaining about Gertie's hair. She'd never yell at her, and Gertie never did anything bad anyway. The teachers at school yelled at her to stop daydreaming, but not seriously, and she spent most of her schooling terrified that one would really get her into trouble. When in fact Jean would turn up to the parents' evening of her beloved only child to find the teacher had only the haziest idea of who Gertie actually was.

Calum came striding back across the floor.

"Well," he said. "Well done, you."

Gertie looked up at him, her knight in shining armor.

"Thanks," she said, going pink. "I didn't realize the owner was so aggressive!"

"I'm a pussycat," growled Calum, then smiled. "You're new, right?"

Gertie nodded mutely, going a deep pink.

"Do I know you?"

"I served you in the supermarket."

"You did!" he said. "You tried to poison me with . . . blue stuff."

"I . . ."

"I'm only kidding," he said, seeing her face. "Welcome to the team."

Meanwhile Morag, arriving to check the little twin otter, which was sitting outside pristine on its two little wheels like training wheels on a toddler's bicycle, gleaming in the cold sunshine, was surprised to see some people still not checked in yet, then remembered with some sadness that it was her first day without Nalitha. Her life returning to Scotland had been a lot to do with her best friend, and it was such a help having her there, running everything smoothly, whilst making incredibly rude and libelous statements about anyone and everyone to make Morag laugh. She wasn't sure about Gertie. She was so quiet, which was absolutely perfect in a flatmate; but in this job you needed people with a bit of grit.

Now, she came upon Gertie talking to Calum Frost, of all people, who as usual, irritatingly, hadn't told her he was coming down. It was a delicate relationship; he had replaced her aircraft when Dolly was out of commission, which was amazing. And MacIntyre Air was a wonderful advert for flying, the plane landing on the beach—the only beach-landing strip in Europe—and people came from far and wide to experience it. Calum had made his money, though, in not being remotely glamorous. He had turned flying into the opposite of exciting and glamorous, in fact, and he didn't give a stuff about it. It could be a tricky dynamic.

Calum was also a plane enthusiast who would probably have preferred being a pilot—Morag had met a few of them—but he had gone into the family business instead and was high profile and well known everywhere for his cavalier attitude toward customer comfort and the fact that he didn't give a stuff if people missed their flights or had to pay extra money for bags, or couldn't make their connections, or got dumped miles away from the town they actually wanted to be in, at one o'clock in the morning. His airline was cheap—that was all that mattered—and as such, he was right. It was incredibly successful and had made him very well off.

But Morag cared about her passengers, many of whom were repeat visitors, and cared a lot about the route they flew; a vital lifeline for the communities they represented; communities where ferries often couldn't manage through the rough weather or, frankly, were simply falling apart. She felt she owed something to the people she worked with. Calum very much didn't. He thought he owed something to connecting people for not too much money and that was all he thought about. They had a very uneasy truce, partly because she owed him so much and didn't like admitting it, partly because he was still after her route. Also, they received government subsidy because they acted as postman and occasional medical backup, and were providing a vital service. It wasn't much, but it kept them going in the windier months. Morag wasn't 100 percent sure Calum didn't also have a plan to do something with that subsidy and his tax requirements.

So she eyed him with some suspicion, which he blithely ignored, and chatted to her regardless as if she were his best mate, constantly offering her new staff or new uniforms or access to their global booking system whilst she smiled politely at him. She had a very hot boyfriend, *thanks*, with a big beard and holes in his jumper, and extremely tidy blondes didn't really do it for her.

And here he was, holding up her line and chatting up her newest staff member, which didn't matter to the people outgoing, as they weren't going to miss the flight until everyone was up there. But if they had a delay turning round, the people coming back from Larbh and Cairn would miss their connections to Glasgow and they would be furious and, unfortunately for them, the only B&B near enough the airport to take overnight passengers at short notice, and that the company would cover, was run by Malcolm McCue, by some length the grumpiest man in the whole of Carso. There was no explanation whatsoever as to why on earth this man had gone into the hospitality industry, given his utter contempt for all humans, heating his home, or making palatable food. Morag's spirits always sunk when he was called upon, and the returning passengers always looked cowed the next day.

"Hello?" she said. "Everything okay?"

Calum beamed and did that thing he did, which was to take her hand in both of his—he must have learned it from some bullshit management YouTube video—and squeezed it as if she were incredibly dear to him and he couldn't imagine anyone he'd rather be seeing.

"It's my favorite pilot!" he said, as he always did.

"I'm not your favorite pilot," said Morag. "I'm the only one you can remember because I had to crash-land a plane."

"Aha," said Calum. "But not one of MY planes!" He smiled broadly. "I like your new member of staff."

Morag looked at Gertie.

"Are you okay? What happened?"

Gertie, even pinker than ever, nodded vigorously. "Nothing—just a rude passenger . . . I'm fine . . . I should get back to work."

She looked up at Calum.

"Thank you," she said. "Again."

"You're doing a wonderful job for me," said Calum, doing the two-handed fist pump again, now with Gertie. "Just keep on doing it."

Fortunately, Gertie's next two clients in the queue were very frequent flyers indeed up to Larbh and basically talked her through it until she felt she was beginning to get the hang of things.

GERTIE WATCHED MORAG chat away—quite rudely, Gertie thought—to Calum, then take him out to do the pre-flight checks with Erno, as Calum liked to kick tires and check fuel lids and basically more or less pretend to be the captain and Morag let him. She managed to get through the entire line, carefully lining

up the baggage to go on the conveyor belt and carefully checking off every booked passenger—though three had not turned
up. Gertie stood, waiting to go out and help load the bags then
come back and let passengers through, staring outside through
the large dirty window at the handsomest man she had ever seen
in her life. The way he'd stepped forward out of the blue to rescue
her! The way he'd held her hand in both of his large strong ones,
looked into her eyes to thank her! Oh my God.

The KCs were all out in force that evening, almost putting their
needles down in their desire to hear all of Gertie's news. She'd
gone round there—she'd promised Jean—and they had baked her
a large cake, with only minimal fibers in it and absolutely no tack-
ing pins. Gertie found herself genuinely surprised by how very
happy she was to see them. She was really enjoying living with
Morag, and the new flat, and the new job—but it was a little over-
whelming, a lot to take on in a life that hadn't had much change in
it. Whereas the familiar grousing from the twins about the state
of the new baptismal font, what were the families going to think,
it was a disgrace, and complaining from Majabeen that it was getting so expensive to frame her children's certificates and Marian
wanting to try a new nail polish and Elspeth clacking away on the
sofa and the kettle boiling and too many people in one space . . .
It was home.

They all tutted when Gertie told them about the rundown state
of the terminal, and were very interested to hear about what happened to the rude customer, who, having missed the last flight
of the day, and the ferry that left in the morning, had to spend
a night at Malcolm McCue's. This left the man so inchoate with
fury (rather more deserved in Malcolm's case than Gertie's) that
he had dumped his entire bag of rocks and went to Fort William
to catch the sleeper all the way home rather than spend a night

more in this godforsaken hellhole, and went back to complain to all his horrible stockbroker hedge-fundy mates in Surrey that actually it probably wasn't worth establishing a huge cement works on the island of Larbh. Maybe they shouldn't bother using the rocks to make cheap cement and render to throw up screeds of cheap houses across Scotland's northern belt, sell them as second homes, price the locals out of the market and leave Argyllshire a scarred, pitted wasteland. So in fact in the end it all worked out rather well.

Jean wanted to know if she had met any hot shinty teams on tour yet, now she had a spare room; Majabeen was more interested in any oil millionaires and Gertrude had to say that she wasn't intending to use it as a pickup joint and the KCs sniffed, as if they would be the judge of that.

But as she moved through the week, her thoughts were completely filled with one man.

Back at the flat she had googled him straightaway. He was everywhere! There were profiles in magazines called things like *Fortune*, and the *Financial Times*. He was the wunderkind saving flying, according to some people, and an evil monster who stranded old ladies on purpose, according to some others.

Gertie wasn't about to go online and start correcting them—doing that, even anonymously, was not her thing at all—but she would have *liked* to very much, and she burned with righteous fury on his behalf at the people who had never even met him saying mean things about him.

He was divorced, it said, with homes in Oslo and Luxembourg, which made it a little strange that he spent so much time in Carso. In fact, Calum loved getting away from it all, as much as anyone who came there did. Away from the bright lights and the fast pace of running his businesses, he was very fond of taking long walks along the white islands, enjoying the white nights of his child-hood, away from how busy he was at home: he used his own jet to fly in and out, and as the weeks passed Gertie took to looking for its tail every morning.

Of course he wouldn't notice Gertie in a million years, she thought. Obviously. But she drifted off at night, finishing a scarf in the sweetest softest gray, with a red stripe running through it, like his flag, she thought dreamily; or perhaps he'd like a very smart striped one—that would be a lovely thing to do. Obviously it hadn't worked out last time, when she'd made the Valentine's gift for Struan at school, but they were stupid kids back then. And knitting was the very very best thing she did.

No, she'd knit it for him and present it to him *and his lovely white teeth would make a surprised grin and he'd say, "Why, Gertie . . ." No, nix that—she hated the sound of that. "Why, darling girl . . ." Yes, that would do better. "Why, darling girl, what a surprise . . . look at this."*

Then he would look for a shop tag and, not finding one . . . raise those light denim blue eyes to look into hers.

"You . . . you made this for me?"

And Gertie would nod shyly but sweetly but not too much in a way that made her chin go into her chest or anything. And he would shake his head in amazement and say, you know, people bought him presents all the time but never made him things, and still politely not asking her name again, would ask if she would like a cup of coffee later. Then he'd laugh and say, well, of course not the coffee here . . . perhaps you would like to join me in the jet?

And things got a little hazy here because Gertie didn't quite have an insight into what a private jet might look like inside, over and above what she'd seen on television programs. Also she didn't like thinking about the private jet crew she'd seen flounce through the airport from time to time, all of whom looked like supermodels, like they'd been hired to make a very glamorous and/or dirty film about pilots and air stewardesses.

Okay, forget that. Then he'd say, *"Let's go out and find something better,"* and then they'd go . . . *well, where exactly? The Silver Tassie on the High Street had the racing going very loudly at all hours, the Grapes was where the shinty team drank and was notoriously rowdy; there was a kind of wine bar that also did chips* . . . but use her imagination as she might, she just couldn't see millionaire Calum Frost kicking back there . . .

She sighed. If there was one thing she'd learned from reading novels and watching romantic movies, it was that rich men and princes really loved down-to-earth girls to distract them from all the shallowness of their rich world. And frankly, there weren't many people more down to earth than Gertrude Mooney.

CHAPTER 17

Once a month, there was a big ceilidh in the village hall. There always had been, for as long as anyone could remember, and no doubt before that, and Gertie did not always go, but the KCs absolutely did and, of course, *took their knitting*. Gertie firmly believed in being able to knit anywhere, a bit like how you could take dogs anywhere now, but at a social event seemed a bit much. Sharp needles and speeding, turning bodies were a bad combo. They sat round, drank whisky, gossiped furiously about everyone there, and watched the dancing. If you were a woman, you were wise not to dance too close to them, as it was entirely possible they would have views on what you were wearing and whether it was appropriate and whether or not you could do with covering up with a cardigan in case you caught your death and would you like a wee cardigan? Go on, it was easy for them.

It was also a bit old-school, and not many young folk went, when it was easier to light a bonfire on the shore and drink cider amongst the rocks in the great light months of the summertime, a hobby Morag had once enjoyed as much as everyone else but had rather grown out of, and Gertie had been far too shy and nervous to ever attend.

Morag hadn't been to the ceilidh since she'd been back. She had memories of being small and thinking it was the biggest fun in the world, when she and Jamie were up for the summertime, getting to stay up late, tearing about with the local kids in the summer evenings when it never grew dark, and the adults didn't care what they were up to (or were, she now realized, all quite drunk). They all played bulldog and various other games that are almost certainly illegal for children to play now. Later on, she'd shyly say hi to the handsome boys who were also visiting for the summer with their parents, who had also been dragged along. She had had her first kiss, with a lad called Colin, in the dunes behind the playing fields. It had been freezing, but he'd given her his cool denim jacket to wear and she'd felt very special and hadn't minded at all, until years later when Jamie had confided that he had also had his first kiss with Colin and it had given them both the ick for days. But Nalitha wanted to go now, and Struan was playing, and she was here now; she needed to get back into the swing of things.

"You coming to the dance?" she said to Gertie, as they sat companionably on the sofa watching old episodes of *Northern Exposure*, a show that was a bit of a guilty pleasure to Morag, being about a beautiful plucky lady pilot who worked in the far north, and completely new to Gertie, who liked it a lot. Gertie was knitting socks for Erno and also Morag's grandfather, both of whom had requested a pair once they'd tried Morag's as they worked miraculously well. The weather still wasn't heating up; it was proving a long, cold spring.

Gertie shrugged. "I have to. Otherwise I'll end up winding wool in a corner again."

Morag smiled and nodded. She'd always been surrounded by men in her life: her father, grandfather, brother, all flying obsessives, and was slightly fascinated by Gertie's entirely female existence.

"Doesn't it make it hard to get on with men?" she asked.

"A bit," said Gertie, squirming a little. "Basically the message is men are no good and not to be trusted."

"Some of them," said Morag, frowning. "But loads of them are nice."

"I don't think you end up in the KCs if you have a really nice man at home," said Gertie. Then she realized what she'd just said. "Wow," she said. "I never thought that before."

She frowned.

"They're just protective."

"So what are they like with your boyfriends . . . sorry, you like guys, yeah?"

Gertie nodded. "Well," she said. "I dated Murray Scott for a wee while."

Morag screwed up her face until she remembered him. "The butcher's boy?"

"Yes."

"And?"

Gertie told her about Murray, who worked for his dad the butcher even though he hated it and used to get upset even just seeing the lambs in the field, he found it so triggering. He was sensitive and that suited him and Gertie just fine, as they could both do quiet sensible things like try out new vegetarian recipes or go for beach walks whilst he talked about what happened to male chicks or the harsh realities of farming. It was a bit of a downer, but he was nice. The Knitting Circle on the other hand ripped into him mercilessly, often with a bacon sandwich on the go, and asking him about Big Murray. Big Murray was universally regarded as a bit tasty, which wasn't particularly nice for Wee Murray to have to listen to either and frankly the Knitting Circle scared the living daylights out of him, and he had eventually left Carso to go to Cambridge to study poetry and write long naturalistic verses about the beauty of the countryside and the skies of his home without ever actually coming back again.

Morag laughed. "Oh, poor Murray! I do remember. He was

always complaining about the vegetarian options in the dinner hall."

"Yup, that's him all right," said Gertie. "So yeah, I wouldn't say it's that easy."

"It's not that easy with all boys either," said Morag. "But I think you probably get a better feel for what boys are actually like. You know. The fartier side of life. You probably don't get the impression of them as amazing, mythic beings. I never fancied boy bands or stuff because I knew what lads are like."

"I fancied all the boy bands," said Gertie. "I fancied the ugliest one. Because I felt sorry for them. And because I thought that gave me more of a chance."

Morag smiled. "Well, that makes sense. What, even him out of One Direction?"

"His name is Niall and he is actually doing very well for himself," said Gertie primly, before she could stop herself.

"Well, maybe he'll fly with us sometime," Morag said with a laugh. "But in the meantime, we should round up some more people for the ceilidh."

ERNO, MORAG'S CO-PILOT, had frowned when she'd asked him the next day.

"Is it compulsory?"

Morag rolled her eyes. "No! But it might be fun. It's good exercise."

Erno sighed. "But I do not want exercise. I want to watch television and to be left alone."

"I bet your wife would like to come," said Morag, accurately. Katrin had done a lot of worrying and nursing of Erno over the last nine months or so. She had possibly not considered, when marrying the handsome young fighter pilot in Helsinki, that she was going to end up in a tiny village in the north of Scotland, with a grumpy overweight middle-aged man. Or maybe she had, but it was probably still worth asking.

Erno sighed. "I will ask her," he said, and was then somewhat taken aback by her enthusiastic yes, and her hurling herself at him in glee, and he made a mental note that actually he should probably take her out a little more often, so it all worked out for the best.

"WHAT ARE WE all talking about?" came the loud, confident voice as they headed back into the tin can the following day, still discussing the ceilidh. Gertie looked up. It was Calum, who had just appeared in the terminal. Gertie couldn't stop herself grinning and was glad she'd put some lipstick on that morning. Jean had kept insisting at the KC meetings that it was what cabin crew did, and she'd finally given in.

"Why are you here?" said Morag, with an edge to her voice.

Calum nodded toward two men standing in deep conversation at the far end of the corrugated hut.

"The lads took me up," he said, proudly.

The two men turned round and saw Morag, grinned and walked over.

"Hey," said Morag, smiling now. It was Jim Crown and Gavin McVeigh, the helicopter pilots. They were for hire if you wanted a particularly expensive and noisy and cold way of looking at the lochs and the islands from a height, or you could learn to pilot a helicopter with them so you too could take people up somewhere very cold and noisy to look at things from far away.

They also ran the search and rescue office; fortunately they'd had a very quiet winter. There had been plenty of snow, but plenty of sunshine too, for which everyone had been extremely grateful. Although the spring was cold as all out, the snow wasn't shifting at all at higher altitudes.

Jim and Gavin liked talking engines with Morag and arguing over what was better—planes or helicopters—and Morag liked it too; she wasn't averse to some shop talk, particularly about something as clearly inferior as a helicopter.

"Hiyah, youse," she said cheerfully. "Buzzed any daisies recently?"

"Landed on any beaches and sunk your vessel?" said Jim happily. They'd rescued Erno the year before, when he'd had a heart attack and they'd had to make a crash landing on Inchborn. Despite not remembering much of it, Erno was always slightly embarrassed by this fact—they'd had to cut off his trousers—so he'd slunk off to call his wife.

"Did you get that update . . ." began Morag, and Calum frowned. He liked hanging out with flying people, but they always seemed to have a subtle way of reminding him he wasn't one.

Gertie noticed and found herself leaning forward.

"Did you have a good day?" she found herself asking Calum, pink as she was.

Short of anyone else to talk to, Calum turned round and saw the new staff member. She looked skittish as a rabbit.

"Oh hey," he said. "Yeah, it was a beautiful day to be up there."

Gertie nodded.

"How are you getting on?"

"I went up!" she found herself saying quickly.

"Uh-huh," said Calum.

"That's why I took the job. It was my first time up in a plane. I loved it."

"Hang on, we hired a non-flyer for my airline?"

"It's my airline," said Morag without interrupting her flow of conversation.

Calum stared at Gertie, ignoring Morag.

"You're kidding me."

"No!"

"Well!" said Calum. "That's amazing! Great stuff!"

Gertie grinned then. She had, as Jean never ceased remarking, a beautiful smile; her teeth were white and even, and her mouth was warm and generous.

"Thank you!"

"You should celebrate!"

"I think we're going . . . I think . . ." Gertie almost stuttered. There was feeling bold and there was doing something completely out of character. But then again, she remembered what Elspeth had said: *Live every day. Grab it.* And it was working out well so far, wasn't it?

"We're all going to the village ceilidh on Saturday," she said. Then, before she could think about it: "Why don't you come?"

CHAPTER 18

Gertie worked solidly all week, barely noticing the hum of KC gossip when she popped in to see them and only just answering all the questions they had about who was going were—"I can't tell you! Data Protection!" she'd say loudly when they asked if Phil O'Meara really was visiting that farmer friend of theirs in Larbh again and if so was it long term or short term. When she'd indignantly protest that she couldn't tell them that, they'd take it as absolute confirmation that the whole thing was back on, and quite right too, lovely lads the pair of them. It was only right they got to have some fun and come on it wasn't doing anyone any harm, and did he take flowers with him or anything checked in that might have looked like an engagement ring?

But Gertie was busy working very carefully on the loveliest thing she could think of; it was just a scarf, in the softest of wools with different colors of stripes, all carefully chosen to blend in the same palette of ocean greens and pale blues and grays. It was utterly beautiful. Or, in Jean's opinion, "awfy drab." It could be from Paul Smith or some expensive Bond Street shop—but it wasn't. Because when she had asked Calum Frost if he wanted to join them for the ceilidh on Saturday night, he had said, "Sure, why not." And it was a date.

She had a whole drawer of knitting, but had decided on carrying on the fine stripe in the gray. The KCs couldn't really help making fun of her—well meaning she knew but still, saying who could possibly be interested in such dull colors and such thin knits in the weather; it just wasn't practical.

People wanted Fair Isle and bobbles and big chunky buttons; everything she did was too delicate and flimsy and devoid of color; although Gertie didn't think they were devoid of color. She took the colors from what she saw around her: the greens and grays of the sky, the orange and ochre and ombre of the stones on the beach and the pretty shells—in their country colors—weren't primary and shocking and in your face. Majabeen came back from visiting relatives in Kolkata every year with loads of bright new wool, full of stories of luminous pink and hot scarlets and gold everywhere, the beautiful colors of her other home (although it was worth pointing out that whilst she was in India she had talked quite a lot about the beautiful cool breezes and fresh wind of her actual home).

Gertie felt so washed out, so plain. But she didn't like bright colors when she was knitting; she felt in stones and gray and rust and heather and a sense—it sounded so silly she would never have told anyone—that she knitted in a way that connected her to the land she came from; that soothed her eyes just as the motion of making the tiny delicate stitches, over and over again, soothed her. Her knitting had love in it, in every stitch, love learned and handed down through the generations. Would he feel that? And would he like her scarf?

Calum was a rich man, after all, with taste—she could see he was stylish. Maybe. Maybe she just had to be bold. For once. Struan had been different. He had been a ridiculous schoolboy. But Calum was a man.

Monday she wrapped it in some tissue paper with a tartan ribbon, put it behind the desk, and waited.

After a few hours, Calum finally did show up. He had a new idea about ferrying tourists to the mountain, properly called Beann Tur, on Archland, which stood straight up like a fantastical sculpture; its odd-shaped protrusions instantly recognizable as the Mermaid Spyglass all over the world. It was a sensational tourist route, known everywhere, and would link perfectly to his Glasgow and Edinburgh services. Plus, Calum was very used to everyone saying yes to him. Morag's determination not to give in pleased him, but the Mermaid's Spyglass had two routes—a reasonably straightforward walking path with just one or two bits of actual climbing, which local schools often used for trips, and a terrifying north face for professional and highly skilled climbers only. They didn't need it overrun with people who didn't know which was which; the tourists would be in a right pickle.

"Well, I will save them in my helicopter," said Calum, and Morag made a face. Gavin had pointed out he was absolutely unsuited to flying a helicopter, as helicopters required deep concentration on the matter at hand linked with good hand/eye coordination and the ability to listen to instructions, and he, Calum, had none of those things and really had to stop trying to take his telephone out whilst they were up in the air. Calum had failed to listen, however, and was now on his ninth lesson, all of which was the same lesson repeated, the number one beginner's lesson, but Calum hadn't noticed. It did mean, however, he was spending a lot of time in Carso.

"Hello!" said Gertie, who was wearing lipstick again in case he walked in, which he had. He was wearing a jumper that turned up at the collar and twisted round the neck in dark fuchsia, a color so unpleasant Gertie figured the jumper must have been very very expensive, which it was.

"Hey . . . you," Calum said, regretting once again not taking that course on remembering employee names.

"Hey," said Gertie, going pink as ever.

Calum smiled. He had five minutes to kill.

"How's life treating you?" he said. "Anyone being rude to you again? If they are, let me know and I'll get on it."

"Ach!" said Gertie, beaming. "It's good. I like it a lot. Also I . . ." She reached under the counter.

"I got you something. To say thank you."

Calum frowned. He'd forgotten all about it. "For that mean guy? Oh yeah! Think nothing of it."

"Well, I did think something of it," muttered Gertie. She handed him the parcel, feeling very red. Oh my God, what if he thought this was really cringe and stupid?

Calum raised his eyebrows and pulled off the ribbon. He had been expecting—well, something terrible frankly, and was genuinely surprised. "What's this?" he said. "Is it for me?"

He pulled the scarf out. Truly it was a thing of beauty, Gertie thought. The softest of blues and greens absolutely matched his eyes; if he wore it, his face would change like the weather. She smiled excitedly.

Calum stared at it. "You knitted me a scarf?" he said.

Gertie nodded.

"Uh. Thank you," said Calum, nonplussed. There was a moment when Gertie thought he was going to put it on. But he didn't.

"See you Saturday," she said quietly.

"Uh-huh," said Calum. "Great! Thanks!" and he waved heartily, and went off to join Jim and Gavin.

Gertie watched him go. Wow. He had been so completely overcome, he had barely known what to say.

CHAPTER 19

Struan didn't have so much time to worry about the upcoming school trip, as he was driving in every day behind the big RVs that moved in to colonize their small roads earlier and earlier each year. The very polite ones pulled off into lay-bys to let the cars pass; the rest seemed to enjoy leading parades. Anyway, he was still teaching every day as well as playing the village hall ceilidh that Saturday, and Saskia wasn't at all happy about it. She wanted them to go duvet cover shopping for reasons he found utterly mysterious, as well as getting him to practice for this big audition she'd found for him. There was an opening she'd come across for a guitarist in a big touring legacy band, their hits decades behind them, which meant their fans had deep pockets and were happy to shell out for hospitality packages to come and relive their youth for a couple of hours. Big UK tour, possible European extension. Terrific money.

He'd quickly learned the parts—there wasn't a huge amount to them—and sent off a self-tape to his "agent," in reality a retired bartender in Glasgow called Nimoo, to please Saskia, and then was surprised and a little perturbed to be summoned for an audition. Saskia was delighted and convinced this was the start of something. She wanted him to hand in his notice to the school, and focus on his music career, and by the way, that wasn't how you loaded the dishwasher. After the Outward Bound trip, he kept saying to her. Soon.

So he had a lot on his mind. The night of the ceilidh was a fair evening; it wasn't raining and that was the big thing, everybody said. Okay, it had been freezing; very very cold for early March which was, after all, practically Easter and whilst it wasn't entirely unusual to still be scraping frost off your car window then, nonetheless winter had been going for a long time and was showing absolutely no signs of stopping anytime soon, even if the daffodils were out.

But it was no longer getting dark at three o'clock in the afternoon, so that was something, and the northern light was clear as glass, bright sunshine on blue water. As long as you were wrapped up or behind double glazing, it absolutely was not so bad.

All the hairdressers—well, all two of the hairdressers, A Cut Above and Talk of the Town on the high street—were booked out with people getting elaborate dos that would only last until the first eightsome reel and would then, no doubt, come tumbling down quicker than mascara running down the face, but that didn't matter.

The hall was being decorated by the cubs and brownies who had made spring bunting with varying degrees of enthusiasm (some of the rabbits may have originally being toting machine guns, until Akela had told them all off), and a rough bar was set up in the corner, selling bottles of BrewDog, or drams, or some absolutely terrible prosecco that tasted like carbonated candyfloss and coated the teeth in more or less the same way, which was exactly how the locals liked it.

Struan and his band went along pretty late to set up; he was on guitar, Jake, who was nineteen and an absolute wunderkind who could play anything, on fiddle, complaining that his neck rest was giving him acne, but nonetheless reasonably cheerful about his chances of pulling the prettiest girl at the dance with his rarely failing method of serenading them with a love song with their eye color in it. "Brown Eyed Girl" or "Baby's Got Blue Eyes" or "Bette

Davis Eyes" if he wasn't exactly sure or was seeing double by then. Harris was the grunting accordion player-cum-caller, stout and heavily bearded.

And that was the three of them, Struan setting the rhythm and responding to Harris "One, two, three." A "Gay Gordons" and a "dashing White Sergeant" to get everyone warmed up, then they'd go as difficult as the audience was in the mood for. Oddly, the tourists swelling the ceilidh ranks since the emergence of Tik-Tok hadn't been that helpful, as they didn't know how to do it and tended to bump into each other.

Back at the Shore Close cottage, the KCs were getting ready, with the help of some of the same candyfloss prosecco awaiting them at the church hall. Or rather more accurately, they were getting Gertie ready, who had popped in to pick up a dress she'd forgotten when she had moved out. Gertie wasn't even taking her knitting! She wasn't even going to be sitting with them! She was going to be with Morag the pilot and her new friends from her exciting new job! The KCs smelled gossip afoot. This was the most exciting thing that had happened to them since Marian's lobe piercing got infected. Jean was utterly delighted, and a wee bit sad at the same time.

Gertie, as she put her makeup on, and tried to stop Jean from suggesting she wear more colorful eye shadow and add the blue mascara, couldn't deny feeling excited too.

She was wearing the prettiest, boldest thing she had: a daisy-print dress, which she had originally thought was too childish but now as she tried it on in the evening sunlight, swung about in its full skirt, saw that the wide neckline was flattering to her small chest and her long legs stuck out the bottom. And she had made herself just the thing: a tiny cardigan, little more than a shrug, knitted in pale blue silk, the exact same color as the underprint of the dress. It was chic and, in this weather, entirely necessary and she was incredibly pleased with it. She looked at herself in the mirror. She could fly. She'd been up in a plane. There was no reason—okay, there were a million reasons—why she couldn't pull a multimillionaire, and it was a ridiculous idea.

But she thought of Calum's generous, keen smile; the way he spoke to her straightforwardly, never seemed to take the piss out of her, like everyone else did. He had a clearness about him.

And he was single; she'd checked. And he was coming, because she'd asked him. And the airline and helicopter pilots were coming so he'd want to hang out with them anyway. Her heart quickened with excitement as she added some more mascara and combed her curly black hair out with the most expensive unguent she could find in Lloyd's pharmacy, and added some extra lipstick, which was very unlike her. She even borrowed some of Jean's blusher and was amazed by what a difference it made to her face.

Gertie stood up in the tiny bedroom upstairs in the cottage, and moved into the freezing bathroom, which had the only full-length mirror. Downstairs the chatting was getting pretty loud already so the pre-party was in full swing. Heavy laughter reached her ears. Outside, people moving up the high street were all dressed up, the men in kilts or trews, their tartan trousers, depending on how much dancing or sitting they were planning on doing. Kilts favored dancing. Trews were often cut rather snugly and offered a variety of hazards to the more enthusiastic of the dancers.

The women were dressed up too, hair all done, fancy outfits on, often in prints or just plain black, but it was undeniably the men who were the stars of the evening, the tartans bright and glowing in the light; sharp and colorful, like the Lindsays, full of purple, or deep and mysterious, like the hunting Cameron. Men walked taller when they wore the kilt, Gertie always thought. And she wondered, suddenly, what Calum would wear. Of course he was welcome to wear the kilt as an incomer—plenty would wear a Stewart tartan and all were welcome. But perhaps he would wear something from his own country? Formal wear in Norway? She had a vision, suddenly, of him wearing white tie and tails with ceremonial medals. No. This was ridiculous, obviously. She shook it from her mind, feeling pink. Nevertheless, he would take her hand, with her new pink and white manicure, and sweep her onto the dance floor and . . .

"Gertie! Get your arse in gear!"

It was Jean downstairs. They had finished the prosecco surprisingly quickly, and were gathering up their wool. Gertie frowned at them. They were looking rather motley. Tara appeared to be wearing a ballgown that didn't quite fit her, in a slightly startling fuchsia, whilst Cara, presumably to differentiate herself, was wearing a patchwork jumper that made her look like she was protesting a nuclear power plant in 1986. Jean was in sparkly black mohair, as per usual, which looked rather good with her dramatic black eyeliner and freshly dyed hair, but was going to get unbelievably hot in about fifteen minutes flat. Underneath she only had a camisole on. Gertie fervently hoped it wouldn't come to that. She may have to keep an eye on the prosecco. Marian looked good actually, a simple black long-sleeved top on, then a small black kicky skirt that emphasized her fantastic legs, and a nice bun at the back, which may not have entirely been her own hair, but was none the worse for that. Majabeen was in hot pink. Elspeth was staying behind—she was, thank goodness, strong enough to stay at home on her own now; seemed so much better. But she had been promised every scrap of gossip.

There was a general chorus of approval as Gertie descended the stairs. Jean, looking at her, felt a sudden stab. She had just got so used, over the years, to seeing Gertie in her supermarket tabard, or her comfies, and had always been so pleased to see her that she hadn't thought enough about whether Gertie should have been out more, having more fun, getting dolled up. Even now, it was only the village ceilidh, and only the old KCs.

Elspeth beamed. She always thought Gertie looked beautiful.

"Have a wonderful time," she whispered into her granddaughter's ear. Elspeth didn't think the ceilidh was a small night out—not at all.

Jean brightened, however, as they opened the front door and there was Morag heading toward the village hall with Jim and Gavin the helicopter pilots, and a lumbering Nalitha beside them.

"On you go," said Jean, kissing her daughter's hair, and shoving her out the door before Gertie got a chance to get too nervous about it. It was primary school all over again. "You go on with them—we'll see you in there."

But in complete contrast to school, Morag turned round, smiling, and beckoned Gertie to join them, and Gertie's heart opened up, so happy and relieved. Even more so when even Nalitha, huge but somehow resplendent in a tight purple top and her maternity jeans, admired the silvery blue cardigan and was astonished that she'd made it herself.

"Would you like me to do something for the baby?" Gertie asked, and Nalitha had smiled and said, normally when people knitted for the baby they sent some awful itchy Fair Isle that would more or less kill a baby with overheating, but if she could do something as delicate as that, well . . . she'd absolutely love it—she loved the penguin—and that made Gertie happier than ever. She met Morag's boyfriend, Gregor, for the first time and was impressed by his quiet, careful manner. His kilt matched his eyes, which were gray. She'd rather assumed Morag's boyfriend would be like Gavin or Jim—a loud confident type talking loudly over everyone—but Gregor was gentle, and she saw it right away. And how she longed, in fact, for someone who did what he did— wherever Morag was nearby, Gertie noticed, Gregor always knew; their eyes met. Constantly.

You could hear the noise from the hall as you approached, half the town drawing closer and closer, along with excited-looking tourists wearing hired kilts that came down past their knees, or up, rather awkwardly, to their groins, or, on one memorable occasion, worn completely back to front with the flat bit at the back, which you had to admit did give them a certain practical use vis-à-vis sitting down.

They smiled and waved at the people they knew, and Gertie felt prouder again when they passed a group from the ScotNorth, promising to come over and say hello whilst feeling that she was with a bunch of cooler people. And even though it was just a ceilidh in a small town at the very top of the country in a cold March; it felt to Gertie like she was stepping into a New Year's ball at the Ritz.

CHAPTER 20

The cubs and brownies had, to be honest, done a wonderful job making the old Scout Hall feel hospitable and party-like. The bunting was jolly, the colors mismatched but it didn't really matter; in fact, quite the opposite; it added to the general sense of celebration. The band was warming up in the corner but there was already a stampede toward the bar. Jean meanwhile marched straight up to the corner nearest the door. Had it been in a posh restaurant it would have been called a power table, because you could see everything that was going on without being too near the band. There were some tourists sitting there, looking nervous in their fleeces because they hadn't packed formal wear and were now worrying about it (which they really didn't have to do, because the farmers would be along soon enough once they'd tucked the cows in for the night, and they'd be lucky if they changed their trousers).

Regardless, Jean immediately decided they were fair game, and marched up to them staring and, when that didn't work, said, "I'm sorry, this table is reserved," and they jumped up like somebody had given them an electric shock, even though everyone knew you couldn't reserve tables. Regardless, the KCs swept in and took all the best places, beaming smugly, and opened their knitting bags, dispatching Marian to get more prosecco, and an orange juice for Majabeen, who didn't drink because it might affect her ability to communicate with her grandchildren on the level they required, being geniuses.

Safely ensconced, they looked around the room, beaming at

their friends and giving stink eye to their enemies, of whom there were more than realized they actually were enemies, including Sadie McInnes from the other hair salon who had said something mean about Marian's eye makeup in the bar at the Silver Tassie, which got back to them, meaning they had all boycotted the place right away, whilst also buying Marian some new, slightly less spidery eyelashes as a birthday present. Also Pamela McGinty who had, back in the dim and distant past, given Majabeen's grandson Beni a B on an essay for which eternal enmity was called for and if some of the KCs thought, well, perhaps it wasn't the worst thing for Beni to get a B on something (he was rather a bumptious child, fond of pontificating on what he was going to study at university, but not the University of the Highlands and Islands; he was going to go to Oxford or maybe Cambridge, despite the fact that he was only nine and a half) but the Law of the KCs meant that they had to hate Mrs. McGinty anyway—they didn't make the rules.

It felt odd without Gertie, Jean noticed. Like they didn't have someone to tease. Normally they'd be trying to push her out to dance or have fun. She looked for her daughter. There she was, standing with Morag and the lads from the helicopter, Nalitha sitting down looking absolutely ready to pop and pretty cheesed off, as if she had been determined to show she was totally cool and ready to come to this, but then realized when she got here that she wasn't and all she wanted to do was be at home, which was a pretty shrewd observation on Jean's part.

For everyone else, though, there was something different in the air. You could feel it. Gertie could, at any rate. The first sense of spring; the promise—sometimes fulfilled, sometimes not—of warmth in the sun, of the feeling of light on your back as the evenings got longer and longer. In midsummer, it wouldn't really get dark at all; just a tentative twilight.

But tonight, thought Gertie. Tonight held the promise. She always felt it, like magic in her veins: that special night in the spring, particularly after a long winter; and the Highlands had had a very, very long winter, which had been wonderful for the ski fields of the Lecht and Glenshee, who had had a startlingly wonderful season, which was lovely for the people with the wherewithal to ski there, but quite chilly for everybody else.

But tonight she could feel it on the breath of the air. Spring was a promise; a fragility brought on the blossom, that could be sent off with the first breath of a late season's wind.

This was the night of the ceilidh; the early promise had been fulfilled and the air was full of the scent of gorse, as the doors of the uninspiring community hall were thrown open and the dancers could burst out onto the lawn (although woe betide them if they strayed onto the bowling green which, thankfully for everyone, not least the local Facebook page, they did not). The sweet sounds of the band wandered down the street, causing toes to tap that didn't even mean to.

One family, tootling along the North Coast 500 on a tour that had not gone well as their harassed, anxious city kids had barely looked up from their iPads, came through the sweet little town, with its toy-sized airport on the outskirts, parked in the harbor for free, paid their £5 each at the door (£2 to locals, only fair), and the children danced and cartwheeled happy as Larry all night long. They looked at the room filled with happy people and beautiful music, and decided straightaway to take their kids out of their overstuffed loud competitive schools, sell their boxy house for a fortune, and move. They never regretted their decision, not in all the March days to come that were gray as granite as the children tore around and grew strong and bonny and developed musical local accents and ate chips and drank Irn-Bru on the harbor walls and the little one got over her fear of seals, and they never once missed a ceilidh in the town.

"So you look lush," said Morag, which was the truth, and Gertie beamed. "You SO have your eye on someone."

This was going to be awkward, Gertie realized, when Calum walked in—after all he was her boss—but she'd deal with that as and when. And anyway, Calum was so charming—he'd just manage to skim over it lightly. For sure he would. Not a problem. They'd probably be quite casual at first.

"Oh no one in particular," she said, pretending that she was the kind of person who might just dress up for any occasion. And for a moment, she felt like she was. It was a nice feeling.

"So what's single life like?" said Nalitha, avidly. She adored Mo, but nonetheless, it was still interesting, and now Morag was all settled she'd lost the fun that comes out of hearing that it is absolutely terrible out there, pure hell on earth.

"Oh God, don't remind me," said Morag, sipping her drink and looking a touch smug and squeezing Gregor's hand.

Gertie shrugged. "I don't know," she said. "I don't . . ." She flushed. "Well, I do like someone . . ."

"Spill! Spill!" yelled the girls. Gregor politely moved away to insert himself into Jim and Gavin's helicopter conversation even though, as a mechanical dunce, he had less to contribute than he would have done to the Gertie's love-life discussion.

Gertie was suddenly desperate to talk about nothing else; to talk about his lovely smile and his great teeth and his casual dress and his enthusiasm and his aura, and how funny he was and . . . but she knew she couldn't. Even though they were nice, these people, they were still her bosses. And he was *their* boss. So it was a bit of a palaver. But soon . . . her eyes strayed toward the door again, and Morag and Nalitha exchanged raised eyebrows and excited looks.

STRUAN WAS PLAYING well, but only on half attention, he realized, still thinking about the audition. He glanced out into the crowd. He knew everyone pretty much; they had some very loyal attendees. He'd nodded gracefully to the KCs because firstly Jean cut his mum's hair, so he wasn't messing with that, and she had always been very generous with the lollipops.

They were speeding up on an eightsome reel, trying to get the balance right between the speed the locals would like—murderous—and what would be best at not tripping up the visitors.

The room was growing very warm, even with the doors flung open and people forming fairy rings in the garden and dancing out there, the sunlight glinting off highlighted hair, and pints of foaming beer. Okay, so he had a lot on at school, and things might be a bit tricky in his new place, but he couldn't help loving the groove, that moment of bottled lightning where everyone was playing in total harmony, the fiddle weaving in and out of his solid rhythmic lines, the accordion a counterpoint, the feet banging on the scuffed wooden floor making their own percussion, along with the off-beat double claps and whooping of the onlookers.

It was a fine thing, right enough, watching the lassies with their skirts flying: some of the prettiest girls clumsy as drunk giraffes; some of the most heavyset, serious-looking women with lines on their faces and rock-solid Presbyterian hair suddenly turning into fleet-footed beautiful dancers as they took their turn on the floor. The years turned back with every spin they made; their gray-haired partners long used to having their hands exactly where they needed to be, even if those hands were spotted now, their grips less sure; seeing though, in the women dancing opposite them the young girls they had been, long ago, in homemade clothes, full of giggles and hope, on a night very much like this one, even as the young people there were eyeing each other up, and couldn't believe the oldies were getting in their way. What were they even doing there anyway?

As Struan was letting the music force through him, him only the conduit, on this sweet evening, the giggles of the children rolling down the tiny hill of the lawn cutting into the top lines of the melodies, Gertie was looking around. Any moment, Calum was going to walk in and she couldn't have wished for a better evening. Okay, so he'd missed the "dashing White Sergeant"—Gertie's absolute favorite, with its flirtatious bobbing and dancing, between two men—but there were plenty more tunes to come, and she was angling her face to look its best for when he entered. She nipped to the bathroom, redoubled the red lipstick, and added the daring mascara that had lengthened her normally colorless lashes. The dress was lovely. She didn't look like herself at all, as had been rather unflatteringly pointed out by absolutely everyone, particularly the ScotNorth table.

The band took a break as the music stopped. Gertie walked back carefully around the dance floor, just in case he'd arrived whilst she'd been in the bathroom. A sunbeam came through the door and hit her hair as she turned, her face prepared into a nice, but not too enthusiastic, pleased smile she had practiced in the mirror. "Oh, Calum, how lovely to see you!" was her plan.

Instead, just as she prepared her big smile, she caught, accidentally, Struan's eye.

And, suddenly, Struan had the oddest thought.

"I know you," appeared, fully formed, in his head, as if someone had chalked it up on a blackboard.

"I know you. I have always known you."

He blinked. She was his tenant, obviously, and apparently she'd been at school with him . . .

But it felt like more than that. It was an intensely strong feeling; a very strange thing, as she stood there, her dark hair outlined in the sun, her face happy and excited. That she knew him and he knew her.

Gertie was still staring at the door, ignoring the rest of the party, who were getting animated—the helicopter boys reckoned they could design Nalitha a better stroller and were getting excited drawing diagrams on napkins—in the intermission, whilst background music played and the band went to get a well-earned pint. Struan couldn't help himself. He was just so surprised.

"Hiyah," he said, softly. "How's it going?"

Gertie turned to look at him: handsome, unshaven, old jeans on long legs. It was so strange to her after all this time—that he wasn't who she was looking for.

"Hiyah."

"How's the flat going?"

"Since yesterday?" She grinned. "Oh, we have some post for you. I think the pizza delivery company misses you."

He smiled and shook his head.

"Thanks for that. You know . . . I can't believe I don't remember you from school."

"Maybe you were just too busy playing your guitar all the time."

"Probably," said Struan softly.

"And you're off to the big world soon anyway . . ." said Gertie, looking around the Scout Hall.

"Aye," said Struan.

Gertie looked at the bright light pouring through the open door, listened to the laughter of the children rolling around the hall; the sound of friends and neighbors meeting each other with great cheer, or in the case of the KCs, occasional sniffing.

"It's not so bad here," said Gertie, and at the precise moment, the sun still illuminating her hair, Struan would have found it very difficult to disagree with her.

Gertie looked at him. For a moment, with him standing right in front of her, she felt dangerously wobbly, her old self; like she would fall back into those silly old ways.

No. She wouldn't. She was the new Gertie now. In fact, she decided, she was going to tell him. So they could laugh about how silly it had been. Get over it properly. Yes.

"You know," she said. "I used to have such a . . ."

Struan was straining very hard to hear when: "Mr. McGhie! Mr. McGhie!!!"

It was Shugs, his gravel-voiced Primary 6. Struan glanced up and sure enough, Big Shugs, his dad, was standing by the bar sinking pints with all his mates from the farm. The only difference between Wee and Big Shugs, both dressed in shorts and T-shirts and trainers, was that Wee Shugs had a thatch of thick red hair and Big Shugs had no hair at all. Apart from that, they were completely identical.

"Hello, Shugs," he said.

Shugs frowned. "I thought you were a teacher. Why are you here?"

"Teachers can do other things," Struan said. "I don't live at the school."

"I didnae think that," said Wee Shugs, who had.

"This your girlfriend, sir?"

"No," said Struan, incredibly quickly.

Gertie noticed. She couldn't not.

"God no," she said after that, too quickly, hurt.

Struan looked up at that, surprised at her vehemence. He had just been trying to redirect the child's interest in his personal life. Also, why should she care?

Gertie looked at the child in horror—she knew Wee Shugs well, and was used to gently batting his chubby fingers away from the lollipop jar when she was cashing up for his mum—and was about to move away when another voice came in.

"That seems a weird question."

And walking into the room was Saskia, looking extremely good—she wasn't dressed up, she was just wearing very tight black jeans and a black vest but it looked sensational on her, and her wide pouty mouth was pouting even more than usual.

Saskia came up to the small group.

"Hi," she said, in her husky voice. "I'm Saskia. Struan's girl-friend?"

"Hi, sweetie," said Struan, turning pink. As was Gertie.

"Nice to meet you," Gertie said, rather stiffly, furious inside that this woman thought—definitely thought, by the way she had her arm round Struan now, quite possessively—that *she* had been trying to chat him up, rather than him coming over specifically to tell her she looked nice. "Struan's my landlord."

"*You're* the new girl?" said Saskia. "Huh. I thought you said she was . . ."

Gertie stiffened. What was Saskia about to say?

Struan wouldn't have put it past Saskia, at that point, to repeat that he'd called her a mouse.

Happily for both her and Struan, Wee Shugs piped up.

"Because you know she works in the ScotNorth? She can get

you like free ice cream sandwiches and everything! She doesn't though," added Shugs, sadly.

"I don't work there at the moment," said Gertie.

"Did they catch you stealing ice cream?" said Shugs, in conspiratorial tones.

"No!" said Gertie, deciding she had had quite enough of this conversation.

"Well, I'm glad you and your landlord are getting on so well," said Saskia, for whom the appearance of Gertie—who she could only see as a very pretty, leggy young woman whispering in the ear of her live-in boyfriend—confirmed 100 percent the reason she wanted Struan closer to her where she could see him.

Gertie got none of this, naturally, and just wondered why Struan's incredibly beautiful girlfriend—it was absolutely no surprise why he'd followed her—was being so hostile. Maybe she knew she had once had feelings for Struan! But then, how could she, when Struan himself didn't remember who she was? This was absurd. She was changing these days. She was a different person.

She stuttered a goodbye, then turned and walked against the flow of people heading back in again for more dancing or drinks, happy and flushed and eagerly enjoying their night and saying hi to their friends. Smoke drifted across the open air, presumably from the naughty vaping teenagers on the other side of the hall. Some children had started a game of football, and were veering further and further away from the hall, presumably in case a parent caught their eye and realized it was getting late to take them home. Two little girls were solemnly coupled up, waiting for "Strip the Willow" to start, and trying to inveigle others to join them. Tragically the boys were having none of it.

The sky was softening into a range of purples and pinks; a chill was blowing in from the sea and she pulled her cardigan closer and looked up and down the street. And as she did so, she realized something. It was empty. Everyone from town was either already inside or had settled down in front of the telly for the night.

And suddenly she knew, with an ice-cold certainty, that Calum had just been polite. He wasn't coming.

He wasn't coming and she was unbelievably stupid with her little fantasies. He was a millionaire international businessman, and she was literally nobody. She was such a fool, an idiot, to think that Calum Frost—Calum Frost who had been in *the papers*—would ever turn up to a little village dance. How stupid was she?! Even stupid bloody Struan McGhie had told his girlfriend—his super-hot girlfriend—that she was, well, she hadn't heard exactly what, but it was clearly nothing good.

Oh God. She felt that familiar ice splash of reality she hated so much. At least—her one massive point of relief—she hadn't told anyone who she thought was coming. They had just thought she'd got dressed up to look nice. Or they suspected something, but they wouldn't know.

Gertie stared down the road, her daydreams dribbling away. Oh God. She was practically thirty, not fourteen. How could it still feel like this? How could she be waiting for her life to begin? It had felt so much that way with the new job, but underneath she was still just plain old stupid Moony Mooney.

Inside she heard the band start up, but they sounded a bit odd.

"Ladies, gentlemen, and anyone who wants to be here . . . we're just waiting for the last member of our band . . ."

STRUAN WAS STANDING, staring at Saskia.

"I have to . . . I need to be onstage," he said weakly.

"Oh for fuck sake, Struan, it's hardly the London Palladium."

"I know, but it's my job."

"He's got another job," said Wee Shugs helpfully. "He's my teacher."

Struan turned to him. "Wanna run along, wee man?"

Big Shugs stirred himself at the bar and gave Struan a strong look. "You telling my lad to run along?" he inquired, holding on to his pint.

Struan screwed up his face. "Not at all," he said, only just managing not to add "sir" to the end of the sentence.

Saskia, who was facing away from Big Shugs, gave him a look. "This is why you're giving up your job, remember?" she said.

"Look, I just have to . . ."

Kenny was looking at them both with mildly disguised impatience.

"Okay, everyone, we're just going to line up for 'Strip the Willow'—groups of eight please. Lassies to the right, laddies to the left, but of course go wherever you feel free."

Kenny was very proud on how up to date he was on his audience chat. Everyone immediately started to form lines that would be chopped up into neat rows of eight to form the dance. Two dancers at the top of the set would hold arms, and couples would then swing round, join hands, and race under the marriage bower. People were starting to form around Struan and Saskia, assuming they were going to take part.

She was still looking at him, her lovely face distraught. She had tried so hard.

"I don't . . . I mean. I thought you wanted. To move away. With me."

"Look," said Struan. "We've moved in, aye. But that doesn't mean I dump everything: my job, the kids, my band, this town, my work here."

Kenny was now going through the dance, for the benefit of the new families and any other strays, rather than the locals who'd been dancing it since they were in nappies, and indeed, the very small children just out of nappies who were standing all ready themselves.

"But you don't . . . you don't seem like you want to leave any of it."

Struan didn't know what to say to that. "I want you?" he said, finally.

"Hurry up!" said Annalise, one of the outside-girls-only set.

"That's why you're sixty miles away, chatting to other women."

They looked at each other for a long moment.

"Do you want to dance?" said Struan, finally.

"No," said Saskia. "I want to go home. To our home. To spend time with you."

The music sounded awful without Struan; they couldn't keep time.

"But I have to . . ."

She nodded.

"You do know."

"I do," she said, turning round, looking defeated. "I do, Struan. I really do."

CHAPTER 21

Jean was fizzing with excitement that Gertie had gone missing—missing! Gertie never went anywhere! Where could she have gone? It wasn't like Carso was full of options. She was disappointed that she hadn't been introduced to whoever the mystery man was—that there was one, Jean was in no doubt. Gertie had been mooning about for weeks, Jean recognized the signs—but maybe the new couple had just taken a nice walk.

After the final waltz, the "Auld Lang Syne," naturally, which saw everyone form a huge circle and dance in and out, there was the usual half an hour of slightly drunk parents trying to round up their now-feral children who had their party outfits covered in mud and had decided they wanted to build nests and sleep in the trees. There was much agitated grousing as people made their way home across the fields, and some concern from the number of teenagers who had gone missing in couples, so it was all pretty much normal.

Jean got back to find Gertie upstairs; she'd gone home, to sit with Elspeth. When she'd arrived Gertie had gone into the bathroom and taken off all her makeup almost savagely. Stupid, stupid idiot.

Then she sat with Elspeth, comforted by the quiet breathing, letting their tea grow cold, and letting big fat tears drop down her cheeks. She'd run away with herself—that was what it was. Thought she was fancier than she could ever be. What an idiot. What a stupid idiot. Elspeth, half-asleep, grasped for her hand.

"You are my best girl," she said, half-asleep, and Gertie felt comforted. A little. Not enough.

JEAN IMMEDIATELY PUT two and two together and got five.

"What happened?" she said. "Did someone do something to you?!"

Gertie shook her head. "Oh no, nothing like that."

"Was someone mean to you? Did you go out and meet a lad?"

"I didn't meet anyone, Mum."

Jean was confused. "Well . . . well is that Morag MacIntyre being mean to you? She's just your boss for a bit, you know; she's not allowed to bully you."

Gertie shook her head again. "I'm fine," she said. "I'm completely fine. I just felt tired. And I was worried about Gran."

This was a terrible lie, and Gertie felt incredibly immoral, using the old lady for her own purposes. But she couldn't face explaining to her mum what had actually happened. What if she laughed? And she certainly would tell everyone in the KCs. Gertie couldn't bear their pity either. Also she knew they would say oh, she could absolutely have that stupid Calum Frost, he didn't know what he was missing, and she couldn't bear *that* either, now she knew it wasn't true, and that she had been so stupid for ever thinking it might be. How could it be?

She went and looked at his Instagram after telling herself a hundred times that she wouldn't. On his own account, nothing since a post about a month ago with him taking delivery of a new plane. She checked him in tagged. Sure enough, there he was, just his elbow, behind some . . . she sighed. Some very pretty blonde girl and her friend pouting into a camera. In London. You couldn't see Calum, but he'd been tagged anyway so obviously they wanted people to know they'd been out with him. Gertie frowned. The girls were from a different planet. They were showing huge glossy lips to the camera and wearing tiny bikini-strap dresses. Maybe he didn't take any pictures because he didn't really want to be there, thought Gertie, desperately trying to hang on to her last, most faint hope that it was all an accident. She looked at one of the girls. It couldn't be. Was one of them . . . was that *her scarf*?!

It was! He had taken the beautiful scarf she'd put so much time and effort into . . . and given it to another girl. There was devotion in every stich of it and he'd just hurled it away.

She pulled up her laptop, looking at her stupid blog, considered deleting it, then looked at the Instagram picture, much larger, and bit her lip. God, her stupid blog, all about the joys and peace of crafting and knitting and creation and it was all pointless. Pointless and stupid and nobody gave a crap.

Furiously, she went downstairs, and decided she couldn't care less, she was going to have some whisky. Then she had a little more. She wasn't a big drinker, Gertie; she normally let the rest of the KCs get jolly. But this, coupled with the prosecco earlier, plus the fact that she'd barely eaten all day from excitement, found her vision blurring. She went back upstairs and picked up the laptop again.

"Are you all right, love?" Jean was asking, knocking at the door.

Crossly, Gertie decided she wasn't going to stay and face them. She stomped down the little road home.

She went to bed, the room spinning, and fumed, until she finally fell asleep, awaking in the morning with a parched mouth and a shocking headache, still wearing the stupid dress, which she tore off. Thank God Morag was off first thing to Inchborn. She took an incredibly long shower, necked some paracetamol, and went straight back to bed to sleep half the day away. There weren't any messages on her phone—there often weren't. It never even occurred to her to check her old laptop.

CHAPTER 22

There was one thing Jean Mooney knew. Gertie had been perfectly happy, until she'd spent the night with the staff of MacIntyre Air and come home furious and drunk. And now it was the next morning and Gertie wasn't answering her phone. Before she knew what she was doing, Jean got dressed and marched off to Ranald's to give him a piece of her mind for whatever was upsetting her darling daughter, who'd been absolutely fine until she'd started at this wretched airline of his. Those girls were bullying Gertie—she knew it. And if the helicopter pilots had been giving her grief, she'd move on to them next.

Ranald MacIntyre was working less these days, but he still enjoyed it immensely. Morag taking over had been the most wonderful thing, more than he'd ever dared hope for, even if she'd moved out.

Jean Mooney, likewise, wasn't scared of much. She had been through, more or less, everything life could throw at her: a husband who hadn't worked out, raising a child alone, enduring poverty and cold, and always working. She was tough, deeply loyal, and up with much she did not put.

She had tried to raise Gertie the same, but her vulnerabilities sometimes seemed so on display, her face so scared-looking all the time. She was her dad's absolute double.

Jean, on rare occasions, suspected that she smothered Gertie a little. But there had been times, Elspeth notwithstanding, that they felt they only had each other to love, to cling on to, a tiny island in the great sea of the world. That was why the KCs were so important. Both of her sisters lived far away—one in London, one in Korea of all places, somewhere Jean had trouble even imagining—and rarely got home.

She had never expected her family to be so small; never hoped for it, the day she was wandering over Ben Eiris, and the sun was low and golden in the sky, lighting the amber fields with the heavy colors of a tired summer, and she had seen him, tumbling down from his parents' croft, in his old patched cords and his untidy hair and a shy smile he could not hide in the glorious evening of the beautiful day. He asked her if he might walk her into the village if she was going that way and she said she was, and he pretended he hadn't been waiting for her to walk that way with a basket full of gorse and she pretended not to know exactly what he was doing as they walked over the old stone arched bridge at the foot of the town, past the field of Highland coos with their elaborate hairdos, keeping the flies off them in the sweet air of harvest season.

They went to the Young Farmers' dance, which was so loud and sweaty that they could barely speak to one another, which suited Robert absolutely fine, but, had Jean only realized, should have been a warning sign that sitting and having long conversations and joining in might not be the kind of thing the lad did best. But when you are caught up in a mass of wild dark hair, and the sweet blue eyes Gertie peered out of now, well, whether you were suited to the long winter evenings together was not the first thing on your mind. And now he was in the city, hair long gone, with a younger, hard-faced woman who made Jean shudder.

So Jean had always done the lot, she thought now, as she headed over to Ranald's old drafty house. Gertie had gone to work for MacIntyre Air, and now she was sad and that was simply unacceptable to Jean.

Jean put on her warpaint: she had perfected her makeup routine in 1974 and had absolutely no intention of changing it now. Blue frosted eyeshadow, glutinously thick black mascara, frosted lipstick, and a lot of hairspray, along with her very best gold threaded blouson cardigan with the shoulder pads and chenille flowers, which meant she sometimes had to go sideways through doors, but gave her confidence nonetheless.

Gertie would have been horrified of course, just as she would have been horrified if she had known that Jean had also once had words with her supervisor at ScotNorth, who had never bothered Gertie again about her choice in work shoes and in fact stayed out of her way entirely until they conveniently found another job in Wick, and moved, with some relief. Equally if she'd heard some of the words Jean had used on Pamela McGinty, in those days Gertie's Primary 4 teacher, with a tendency to mock children who, like Gertie, did not enjoy speaking out loud.

Furthermore Gertie also didn't know that when she was seventeen, she had been targeted by Connal Bjornesson, local tearaway and all-round bad egg, who used to come in when she was working on the service desk and make her bend down to unlock the cabinet to get out his rolling papers, which had made her turn very pink indeed, although she still, notably, always managed to serve him. Jean had also had words with him vis-à-vis her little girl, not for a moment taking into consideration any idea that Gertie actually might quite like a bit of a very bad boy, would love a shot on his motorbike, and wouldn't mind a bit that Connal was nobody's idea of a good, marriageable prospect.

Unfortunately, Connal's mum Senga was even harder than Jean and had absolutely no truck with this, leading to something of a stand-up fight in the high street outside the Silver Tassie that Jean had to lie to Gertie about and say it was about the run on the discount silver four-ply that Senga knew fine well Jean had her eye on but had taken anyway without a care.

JEAN MARCHED UP the high street in the early morning sunshine. Very few people were awake, after the celebrations of the night before; there was a side street shinty match being played by some small boys but even they looked a bit peaky; presumably they'd been up till all hours. She passed the open bakery, which smelled fantastic. She'd get some doughnuts on the way back; even Gertie's mood would surely be lifted by hot doughnuts. They could fix everything.

Ranald's housekeeper Peigi answered the door. The women knew each other of old, and exchanged strained nods.

Peigi's horrible dog Skellington, a bad-natured spaniel with a dribbling mouth that hung open over sagging jowls, pus-filled eyes, and mucky ears, wuffed at her balefully. Jean gave him a stare.

"Aye all right there, dog," she said, calmly. Skellington tried out an explanatory growl.

"Skelly! Good boy!" said Peigi, who like all dog owners considered their perfect animal beyond reproach.

Skellington made a noise somewhere between a cough and a bark, left a spurt of wee on the carpet, farted noisily, and turned and headed back in.

"He's such a character," said Peigi, with which Jean could only agree. "What do you want?"

Peigi had her arms folded and was wearing a flowered housecoat. Jean shook her shoulder pads.

"Sorry, is this *your* house?"

Peigi shrugged. "I live here. What are you after?"

"I need to speak to Ranald."

"He's sleeping."

At this Jean raised her eyebrows and Peigi got rather pink.

"Don't be ridiculous, Jean Mooney—he always rests in on a Sunday when there's no planes. And I've got kirk to go to."

"I don't want to talk to you," said Jean. "I want to talk to Ranald."

"And I'm saying he needs his rest."

"He's not sick!"

Above their heads, a window slid open.

"I'm not deaf either!" came a voice. There was Ranald, dressed in a blue dress shirt, looking down on them.

"Hey!" said Jean. "I want a word."

"Come in then."

Peigi looked absolutely furious. Standing on the doorsteps with her arms folded telling people they couldn't do things was absolutely her favorite way to pass the time.

"So what is it you couldn't text me about?" said Ranald, after the kettle had boiled and they'd sat down with tea.

Jean looked at Peigi.

"I thought you were going to kirk."

"The minister will wait for me," said Peigi.

"Will she though?" said Jean. There was absolutely no way the Very Reverend Jill would wait for Jesus himself if he was tardy, so Jean wasn't buying this for a second. And even if she did, the twins would probably get things going all by themselves.

Peigi sniffed loudly and went looking for her hat, an unpleasant waterproof purple cloche with burgundy cherries on the brim. She kept up a stream of reminders to Ranald about what time she'd be back, what they were having for lunch, whether Morag was going to be there (Peigi hated Morag but for Jean's ears spoke about her as practically her own beloved daughter) and how he should go looking for the fresh daffodils in the front garden and bring a few in for the table.

Ranald and Jean both watched her go.

"Your girlfriend's nice," said Jean eventually, after the old wooden door had swung shut.

"She's not my . . ." Ranald didn't finish this sentence as he had more or less given up from letting people speculate about what Peigi was to him, given it wasn't her looks or cooking ability or delightful personality.

"Well, Mrs. Mooney, what can I do for you?" he said, sipping his tea. Peigi had made it and it was bitter and slightly stewed. Jean winced at hers. Being able to make tea seemed a fairly essential quality for a housekeeper but there you go.

"Your company," she said.

"Uh-huh. I haven't seen you on a plane for a while," he pointed out.

"Well, why would I? I've got everything I need right here."

"You never fancy a wee trip to Inchborn, walk the sand?"

"Too busy," said Jean.

Outside there was a wind along the promenade, but the sun was out too; the rushes on the shore were bending slightly but not lying flat.

"Nice day for it," said Ranald.

"You sound like you're missing it," said Jean. "On your one day off."

Ranald smiled. "I know. Funny isn't it? Do you still like cutting hair?"

Jean shrugged. "Actually I thought you could do with a trim."

"I could."

"Well then." Jean took another sip of her tea and made a face.

"Oh sorry," said Ranald, looking confused. "I think I've just got used to it."

The sun danced and glittered off the sea.

"Want to take a walk down to the harbor and pick up something at The Point?"

The Point was a new coffee roasting place, run by bright and enterprising young people in the town, with long beards and a tendency to corner you if you weren't paying attention and talk to you an awful lot about coffee. Jean hadn't sussed it out yet the way she normally did to catering operations—marching all of the KCs in there with their knitting bags, taking over most of the tables, talking loudly and seeing how well the staff tolerated it—and had been meaning to check it out. Ranald was already pulling on his old cracked leather bomber jacket that hung by the door, the one he'd inherited from his own father, who'd flown in the war, and, unusually for her, Jean found herself without much of a choice.

It was sharp in the wind, but the sun made everything better.

"I love this time of year," said Ranald. "Evenings getting longer, everything stretching out ahead of you, a summer full of parties and weddings and folks needing to get places. I like taking the young brides; they cannot stop yelling on the flight."

Jean smiled.

"We were thinking of running a midnight sun flight this year. It's some tourism thing, but they're all over it. Take-off at 11:30, land on the beach in Inchborn at midnight, when it's not quite dark. Light a bonfire or some such. I don't know if that will come off."

Jean looked at him. She'd never known Ranald well; he was older than her and had been a fixture in the town for so long. Now she looked into his enthusiastic smile and rather liked the lines around his blue eyes, formed by decades of squinting in the sun above the clouds.

Morag had spent a lot of time trying to convince him to use his undoubted talents as a pilot to fly long haul, travel the world, do any of the fascinating routes that were available to him, but he had always loved doing what he did now: performing perfect, accurate maneuvers in a plane without nine onboard computers doing all the hard work; without being locked into sky trails like bus routes, completely at the whims of air traffic control, stocked in a circle in the sky like flying in a car park round Heathrow or Frankfurt or Abu Dhabi or Singapore.

He liked knowing his passengers in the small communities; few were better than him at sniffing out, and coping with, difficult weather. He liked being on hand for the babies being born, for the necessary deliveries. He loved his community and liked being wanted.

Jean didn't know any of this; she just thought he was the rich pilot, although now having been inside his house she didn't think he seemed rich at all, which was a correct analysis, as he very much was not.

"So," she started. "My kid is working for you."

"Gertie!" he said. "Of course! I didn't realize she was yours."

Jean nodded. "Lovely girl," he said. "Quiet one, though, right?"

Gertie had barely managed to stutter out a word to Ranald on his part-time shifts.

"Well, yes," said Jean. "She is shy. And sensitive."

"And she's chosen a job on the front line of an airline?" said Ranald. "Ballsy move. I respect that."

"Well, no," said Jean, who felt this was getting rather out of hand. Normally by this time she'd be announcing that she'd said her piece and swanning off on a cutting line. "The thing is, I think she's unhappy."

Ranald frowned. "Is this one of those millennial things where you have to give them an award every day or they don't turn up?"

"No!" said Jean, about to lose her temper. They had reached The Point, which was indeed on the corner of the harbor, in an old white building, next to the ice cream parlor, which did a roaring trade during the summer. Also in fact a roaring trade during the winter, when people were cold and it was a bit dark, so what better to cheer you up than an ice cream, and it did well in the autumn when people took long walks kicking leaves with their dogs if there was the promise of an ice cream sandwich at the end and in fact it was doing well today in the spring, as people saw the sun and, even though it really wasn't warm enough, wanted to remind themselves that ice cream days were coming.

"It's about how . . ." She tried to think. "Well, they just need to include her. Just because she's shy doesn't mean she isn't a very good person."

"You want me to tell Morag not to be . . . shy-ist? Is that it?" Ranald smiled. "Och you know, I think I would like that. Morag's always calling me every 'ist' under the sun and being very correct about everything and calling me an old dinosaur. Aye, I think I would quite enjoy telling her that."

"I mean, I just don't want them to not include her . . ."

"Did they not go to the dance together last night?"

"They did," said Jean, uncomfortably.

"Well then. Tell her not to get involved with one of those helicopter lads."

"Why, are they bad? Maybe it's them who's upset her."

"Probably them," said Ranald. "Helicopters. Terrible things."

He seemed unwilling to expand on this opinion, and stopped just before the coffee shop, bang in front of the ice cream parlor.

"Ooh," said Ranald. "Is it a sin to have an ice cream on a Sunday morning do you think?"

They both glanced at the kirk, looming up in the highest point of town, made of sandstone. It had a small, careful graveyard with a special, tiny section given over for sailors, lost and washed up without a name down the centuries. The sound of a small congregation doing its best with "The church's one founda*shun* / is Jesus Christ *oor Lord*" made them both feel a bit guilty.

"We're already going to hell by not being there," pointed out Jean.

"Exactly," said Ranald. "Better stock up on cold items."

And they found themselves grinning at each other, and then found they both liked pistachio and didn't think anyone else liked it and Jean thought, you know, that probably was it—Gertie was probably mooning over one of the helicopter laddies and she'd gone out, at least. And Ranald asked her how old Gertie was and she told him she was thirty and he raised his eyebrows and she did, indeed, think it was probably a bit late to be worrying about her daughter's love life. And they finished their ice creams and then got tea to take away from The Point, even though the nice young man with a beard couldn't believe they didn't want to try his new Guatemalan blend, which had been pre-digested by cats, and they felt bad about disappointing him.

By the time they got out, kirk was out, and the congregation was bearing down on them—many of the congregation thinking that ice cream was a sin on a Sunday if you hadn't been to kirk, but if you had got up early and dressed nicely and been to kirk then it would probably be all right to have an ice cream as long as the

Very Reverend didn't see them. It was all right for the Very Reverend to tell them not to sin or be worldly on a Sunday when the Very Reverend spent all her Sundays visiting the elderly whether they wanted to be visited or not, and reminding them about eternal hellfire, and eating all their custard creams.

Jean spied Peigi again out of the corner of her eye, chasing after them. It was hard to miss the purple hat. Plus Skellington had been tied up outside and had started a very unattractive howling noise when he saw his mistress. Peigi's lips thinned when she saw Jean and Ranald together, and all her thoughts of hanging back at the kirk to complain to the Very Reverend about slackness in the church cleaning rota were forgotten as she bustled her way down.

"You're *buying* tea from a *shop*?" she hissed, in absolute puzzlement. Jean and Ranald exchanged guilty looks. There was a pause.

"Well, anyway. I'd better get on with Sunday lunch. No rest for the wicked."

This was clearly meant to be a joke. Jean felt bad. Peigi was kind of a joke in town, being so in love with Ranald that she'd moved in, but she didn't like making fun of the older woman, and she was suddenly reminded uncomfortably of Gertie, sad in her own kitchen, presumably over some silly helicopter boy or other. She didn't want Gertie to end up like Peigi; that was for sure. Because if there was one thing Jean knew about getting older, it was how little, really, anyone changed on the inside, no matter how gnarled their hands became, or set in their ways they were.

Jean turned to Ranald. She couldn't remember really what she'd come to complain about. Someone was making her little Gertie sad and she was going to kill them for that but she couldn't deny . . . she'd had a nice morning. There. She'd admitted it to herself, with some surprise. It wasn't what she'd been expecting at all.

"Thank you," she said.

"Not at all," said Ranald, his wrinkled eyes twinkling at her.

Ranald watched her go. He rather liked her forthrightness and had a lot of time for a woman who showed quite as much enthusiasm as he did for pistachio ice cream. Also fortunately for Jean he was not a man who knew anything about women's clothing and hadn't even noticed the shoulder pads.

CHAPTER 23

Gertie, who still hadn't returned her mum's call, as if it were all her fault, tried to hold her head high for work the next morning. She had her makeup toned down and pulled her hair back in a ponytail; after the glorious weekend, the weather had turned dreich again. Worse than that: it was freezing. She felt that that moment of glamour; of triumph even—she remembered the heads turning as she walked in, the dress swishing, the golden evening—it had been an illusion.

Well, she was going to forget all about it. She was going to get on with the job.

The tin shed was in chaos that morning. Morag out ignoring everyone, doing some touch-ups on Dolly 2, flying with Erno, who as usual wasn't showing till the last minute, but already in the departures area were a sheep, a sheepdog, and a chicken, queuing patiently.

"You are kidding," said Gertie. Pete, who ran the shed, shrugged his hands at her.

"Uhm, hello, everyone," she said, checking the departure time was on the chalkboard—they still did it by hand—along with any delays and the weather conditions, which normally some wag would rub off and replace with "MONSOON" or, occasionally, "MORDOR" on particularly dark mornings.

"Okay, uh, who's first?" said Gertie. The woman with the chicken moved forward, whereupon the dog set up a ferocious barking.

"Hush bye," said the man to the dog, who completely ignored him.

"Well I have to check in, but you can't let that dog on," said the woman.

"Aye on yoursel', Senga Albright. I'm bringing Roddy so you can just shut your mouth," said the man. "It's only a stupid chicken."

"Would you listen to that?" said the woman, putting the chicken on the desk, where it fluttered and hopped in its cage, and folding her large arms. "I think he shouldn't be allowed to board for abusive language."

"She started it by being rude about my dog!" said the man.

"How was I rude about your dog?"

"You called him 'that dog.'"

Senga rolled her eyes at Gertie.

"See what I mean?" she said. "And he called my chicken stupid."

"All chickens are stupid!"

Senga ignored him. "He can catch the next flight."

"Well, as it happens I cannot," said the man. "As I actually have a real job and a real farm, and a dog to get bred with a bitch that is in heat and that canny wait as you know fine well."

"What could I *possibly* know about your disgusting dog practices?"

"Mating a dog to make another excellent sheepdog is not a disgusting practice!"

"Well it is if you think that's an excellent sheepdog. Excellent at barking his bloody mouth off if you ask me."

Gertie screwed up her face. "Uhm . . ."

"And I was here first," said the woman, banging the chicken cage down on the table again. The chicken borked uncomfortably. The dog made some warning yips. The sheep looked very very nervous.

"Don't you be letting that hound near my prize ram," said the next farmer, a very tall man with a red-veined face that had spent its life facing the wind. "He's got a busy schedule too."

Senga frowned. "Whit?" she said. "You're telling me this entire plane is sex-trafficking?"

"Ooh," said a couple of ornithologists who had just rolled up with large suitcases full of very expensive binoculars, cameras and a lot of wet-weather gear. "Sex what now?"

Gertie regarded everyone. This kind of thing never happened in the ScotNorth.

"Okay."

She looked at her diagram of the tiny plane. This was like one of those "farmer crossing the river in a boat" puzzles. She frowned.

"You're going to Inchborn?" she said to Senga, who nodded.

"My nephew is there," she said. "This chicken's sick."

Gertie wasn't quite sure what to make of this.

"Oh, let us have a look," said one of the ornithologists. "What's up with her?"

"Well," said Senga, tilting the cage. The chicken borked crossly again as the ornithologist made to undo the latch, whereupon the dog wuffed even louder.

"Do not set that chicken free please!" said Gertie loudly, a sentence she hadn't expected to utter in her new job, or indeed any job.

Morag had arrived back and hovered by the door, unwilling to intervene, but ready. A full-on dog/chicken/sheep loose in the cabin scenario wasn't worth thinking about. Obviously the ram would go in the hold, but even so. She sent Erno off to supervise fueling.

The line was now full, or as full as it got—sixteen people—but only Gertie there to check them all in. She glanced around.

"Okay. You with the chicken. You're in the back row, in the corner, okay?"

She rang up the ticket.

"Actually I'd rather be . . ."

"That's where you're going. Man with dog, you're waiting till the very end and going up in the front."

"Hahahah!" said the man. Senga harrumphed.

"None of that," said Gertie. "And if I notice any more behavior from that dog, I'm going to deny boarding. Which I can totally do. I think."

The dog whined.

"I'm not saying you're bad," she said to the dog. "I'm just saying, you have to behave for this trip, okay?"

The sheepdog bent his head and came up and nuzzled Gertie's hand, much to the chicken's alarm.

"You are very nice," said Gertie. "Just don't upset anyone on the plane."

"What about me?" said the man with the ram.

"He's going in the hold."

"I'm not going in the hold."

"Your animal," said Gertie. "He can't be in the cabin."

"Why? Did I have to order it? Is it like getting a special meal?"

"No. He can't be in the cabin because he's an untrained sheep."

"What, and the chicken is trained?"

"STOP DISSING MY CHICKEN."

"Do you want to get on this plane or not?"

"With this boy's sperm I could buy this plane," muttered the farmer.

"I'd love another plane," said Morag from where she was watching.

Grumbling, everyone checked in their respective animals then removed themselves to three different corners of the hangar to sit and wait for boarding, slagging off the others mightily.

"Well done," said Morag, coming forward. She didn't want to

sound condescending, but Gertie had handled it all with aplomb. "That was a tough crowd."

"I don't think I managed to persuade the ornithologists there isn't going to be a big sex party," said Gertie, frowning. "And it's you who has to fly them all."

The woman with the chicken stomped up to them.

"Morag!" she said.

"Hi, Senga."

"You know this chicken is for Gregor!"

"Gregor is fine for chickens."

"Yes, I know but it's injured. He can fix it."

"I expect he can," said Morag, whose voice always went rather soft when her boyfriend came up in conversation.

"So I think I should sit up the front of the plane, don't you?"

"I'm so sorry," said Morag. "But my cabin crew's decision is final."

And Gertie felt a little better. And there was no sign of Calum anywhere, which was also useful.

CHAPTER 24

N ow come on, my seconds, come on!" Struan was saying, raising his hand and sure enough, just at exactly the right time
and pretty much exactly in tune, except for Wee Shugs, they all
came in, gloriously splitting the melody on the downbeat of "The
Water Is Wide."

"Oh, that was very good," said Struan. "Very good!"

He looked at them mischievously.

"I don't suppose . . . no."

"What is it, sir?" said nervous wee Oksana who had joined from
Ukraine a year ago and was miles ahead of everyone academically,
to some deep embarrassment, but very slow to speak up in class.
But she was gradually improving. She still carried a teddy bear
everywhere, called Bodhan, which was a little unusual in a P6,
but Bodhan had become a bit of a class mascot, so that was fine.
Struan wished she would sing out a little more, and felt concerned
she didn't appear to have many friends, but wasn't sure at all what
was best to do.

"Och no . . . it would probably be too much for you . . . the
Drumnadrochit kids, maybe."

Now they were properly stoked.

"No, no, tell us what it is."

"Okay," he said, reluctantly. "You know how you're coming in
on two different notes and it can be a wee bit difficult to hold in
your head? But you're doing it absolutely fine now, right?"

They nodded smugly; he'd drilled them so much that many
of their parents were surprised to hear them constantly singing

around the house, to the hens or during the morning milking, whilst brushing their teeth or playing on their Nintendos.

"Well," he said. "You know we could split it again. Go three ways."

He played three notes on the piano to form the triad chord. The kids stared. This had not occurred to them.

"I mean, it's high-level stuff," said Struan.

"What will it sound like?" asked Wee Shugs.

"Well, if it's you it'll sound like a coo fart," said Jimmy Gaskell, which was met by laughing and a sharp intake of breath from Oksana who loved music class and didn't want their teacher to change his mind, even if she found it impossible to join in.

"Okay, if you don't want to," said Struan, pretending to pack his notes away.

"No, sir! No, we do!"

"Okay," he said, heading back to the piano. "Right, listen to this."

And he played the top two notes they already came in singing, then added a lower D, two tones down, which gave a beautiful sonorous closure to the chord.

"So, you go again."

They did, and this time he sang the D in so they could hear it. Then he looked around for volunteers. He needed someone musical but not so musical he'd be removing a vital tentpole and collapse the others.

"I can do it, sir," said Shugs, reading his mind.

He absolutely couldn't do it, so Struan said thank you, and asked Jimmy Gaskell, who stuck his tongue out rudely at Shugs, who instantly looked like he wanted to kick his head in.

"And what about you, Oksana?" he said. The girl was so eager, but so timid, she tended to clam up when they actually started singing; she couldn't quite find her voice. "Do you think you could do it?"

Oksana turned very pink and she shook her head mutely, clutching her bear. Anna-Lise, next to her, who volunteered for anything and everything, stuck up a chubby pink hand.

"Okay, then—Anna-Lise and Oksana, you try, with Jimmy."

He played the note again. Then the notes for everyone else to come in on. Once he heard them all humming it, he played the intro.

The effect should have been instantaneous. Unfortunately, Shugs had decided to completely ignore the instructions, and join the low part of the song. Misjudging it completely, he sounded like a ship maneuvering through thick fog. The rest of the class groaned. To most children this would have been a moment of supreme embarrassment. Shugs, however, was profoundly unconcerned.

"What?" he said. "I nailed it!"

"You did," said Jimmy Gaskell. "You nailed it into a coffin then buried it in the ground."

Everyone laughed at that but Shugs still couldn't care less. He loved to sing and that was that.

Struan glanced at his watch. It was time to wind up the lesson anyway.

"We'll work on it again on Friday," he said. "Oksana, Jimmy, and Anna-Lise, look the song up on Spotify and see if you can get the low note when it comes in?"

"Yeah I don't even have to practice," said Shugs proudly.

"And Hugh . . ." Struan thought quickly. "Perhaps we might introduce some percussion."

There was a groan from elsewhere in the room.

"What," said Jimmy Gaskell, "because he sucks at singing he gets to play the drums? How's that fair?"

Thankfully the bell rang before Struan had to figure out that rather tricky question.

"Oh, and don't forget," he said, as they reluctantly began packing up—music was their favorite lesson, and after the glorious weekend there was hail going sideways in the playground. "You've got to bring back your camping parental forms and give your parents and guardians the kit list."

"What teachers are going?" asked Jimmy Gaskell.

"Why, will that change whether you go?" said Struan, genuinely interested. There was a groan.

"Naw you have tae go," said someone. "Unless you've got a medical condition."

"Well, we've all got ADHD but they don't accept that," said someone else, sadly.

"We're going on the wee plane and climbing a mountain," said Shugs, clearly baffled. "It's going to be braw!"

"All of the teachers would be good," said Anna-Lise, class suck-up, and everyone else groaned again.

"Well," said Struan. "It's Mrs. McGinty."

There was silence at this. Nobody was immune to the frosty headmistress, except Anna-Lise who brought her fresh cheese from the farm and talked about how the head had promised to have her to tea one of these days.

". . . and, uh . . . me," said Struan, and was unusually gratified by their pleased faces. Home may be tricky. Work was . . . work was all right. He really wasn't looking forward to giving it up one bit.

CHAPTER 25

"Why am I flying this zoo express?" Erno had remarked in horror, and the ornithologists had been talked down once again from attempting to treat the chicken themselves. It was obviously too much like an exciting version of a medical drama for them, a scene in which a beautiful stewardess asked, "Do we have a doctor (for chickens) on board?" but Gertie managed to get them all onto the plane on time. It all went all right, apart from Senga muttering about Roddy getting his stupid seat up the front, and everyone coming up to pet the dog and talk about what a beautiful dog it was, which only seemed to rub salt in her wound.

Morag dropped the others off first on Cairn and Larbh, where they unloaded the ram, which made the dog sit up and start making a noise, but it wasn't for long, and finally she got them turned round, traveling south, into the sun, heading back for one last stop at Inchborn.

She got off first at Inchborn. In her career, she had seen the sunrise in Singapore, glancing off the hundreds of huge ships lining up to take port; swept round the towers of Hong Kong; crossed pink deserts and seen the cooking fires of the wandering people below. She had flown over Table Mountain; banked so Paris looked up on its side, the Eiffel Tower a prong in the air. She had flown into Chicago when its evening sun was setting, lighting up the skyscrapers.

Nothing, but nothing made her happier than the swooping landing at the beach, coming down low—if the water was calm, you could see the little Cessna's reflection on the water; if it wasn't, which it normally wasn't, you could see the ripples and shimmies and ever-changing directions of the water. Either way, she loved it—checking the headwinds carefully and lining up the plane. Where you would expect a runway was only a long flat beach, heading directly into the dunes.

Morag had had to make an emergency landing here the previous summer, but her training had kicked in; nobody had died, and all sorts of things had happened so she didn't feel the least bit nervous about it. This was her plane, this was her turn; this was, as far as she was concerned, the happiest place in the world to her, because Gregor lived there.

He came down the dunes toward them, his face beaming.

Morag got up herself, to open the door that had the steps inside it. She secured them to the ground, then helped Senga out with the chicken.

Gregor dashed up to her.

"Is it very unprofessional to kiss a pilot while she's wearing her hat?" he said. "I can never remember."

Gregor cared about her career but was often hazy on detail.

"You can," said Morag. "But not in front of your Auntie Senga."

"Oh yes."

"She put me at the back of the plane," said Senga crossly.

"Not me!" said Morag.

"There's only ten rows," said Gregor.

"They put a dog in business class and they put me at the back."

"We don't have a business class, Senga."

Gregor wasn't listening to either of them, he was picking up the cage and gently opening the latch, making a low noise, which Morag thought might be clucking.

"Come on then, girl, what's up with you?"

"Well, the bloody sex plane certainly messed with her nerves," said Senga, incomprehensibly, but Gregor had turned and was heading back to the house already.

On the scrubbed wooden table was set a plate of fresh scones that smelled heavenly, and the kettle was whistling on the old stove.

"Och you're a good lad," said Senga, eyes lighting up.

A ray of watery sunlight came through the huge old single-paned kitchen window and Morag suddenly felt a real yearning to stay awhile. Except she couldn't—she had mail to take down to the post office before it shut; she had two passengers sitting there to be dropped off. Fortunately they were tourists who thought making stopovers on the beach was so cool and they were busy taking self-ies. Rather tourists than the wind farm executives who thought they were terribly busy and important and thought Morag's plane was basically their private corporate jet because they all knew Calum, and treated it accordingly.

Gregor was now examining the chicken on a dishcloth on the table, very carefully, his long fingers keeping the creature calm (and only someone who has ever tried to calm a chicken will know just what an exceptional skill this is). Morag was almost faint with longing watching him. Behind her, Barbara the goat wandered through the open kitchen door and nudged Morag from behind. They watched him work together, a truce of sorts.

"Ah," said Gregor. "Here it is."

Carefully, he grabbed what Morag belatedly realized were her expensive eyebrow tweezers, and carefully pulled a fat blood-filled tick from the chicken's abdomen.

"This can't have been making you feel very good," he said, stroking the chook carefully. "Morag, can you hold her?"

"No," said Morag.

"I'll take her," said Senga, as Gregor carefully disposed of the wriggling tick, counting its legs carefully to make sure he had it all, outside far from the other birds, and then went and washed his hands.

"You're not going to squish it?" said Morag.

Gregor shrugged. "It's a living thing. It's not its fault."

"What if it jumps onto something else? What if it crawls up your butt while you're sleeping?"

Gregor shrugged. "That's why I put it so far away. Outside butt-crawling distance."

"Maybe that's what everyone thinks, before they find a tick *up their butt.*"

Gregor smiled as he dried his hands.

"And sterilize my tweezers, thank you."

He grinned again. "Oh hey," he said suddenly. "I have to tell you something."

"What?" said Morag. "Is it about something else gross my tweezers have been doing because if it is I'm not sure I want to know."

"Oh no, it's something Calum said."

"Calum Frost?" said Morag, surprised.

She glanced at Senga, who immediately stood up and said, "Ooh I wouldn't want to interfere in work news," and took the chicken out into the garden to try and make it more of a holiday.

"When were you talking to Calum Frost?"

"He popped by."

"You do not *pop by* to Inchborn."

"Oh well, you know. You do if you're taking helicopter lessons."

Morag rolled her eyes. "He doesn't land it himself though, right?"

"Not everyone has to be a pilot to be a good person," said Gregor mildly, pushing his glasses up his nose.

"Huh," said Morag, who had been raised in a flying family and therefore although she theoretically realized that, it didn't quite get in her bones.

"How often does he come here?"

"Well, he likes my cooking."

"I get that."

"And just hanging out."

Morag sighed. "They are all the things *I* like. You're not having sex with him?"

"We play a lot of chess," said Gregor.

Morag pouted. "What?"

"Well, chess can get sexy."

"Not necessarily."

"It did that time we played it."

Both of them thought back to those winter nights, the stove crackling, the darkness covering the island like a blanket. Gregor glanced at his watch but it was impossible. She'd be back on Friday, he told himself sternly. And his aunt was outside.

"Well anyway," said Gregor quickly, clearing his throat. "I'm not sure how to tell you this but . . . apparently he's been . . . he got a . . . message. From your staff."

"What kind of message?" said Morag, frowning. "And who?"

"Uhm," said Gregor. "There was an email. And a scarf, I think. He's a bit weirded out by it all."

"What are you talking about?"

"Your new . . ."

Gregor had only met Gertie very briefly and couldn't remember her name.

"Gertie? No," said Morag. And then, immediately: "Hang on, how come you live on an island by yourself in the middle of the North Sea and you know more gossip than I do?!"

She frowned.

"Hang on, she's been bothering Calum?"

"Apparently. She knitted him something."

"Is that all? She's a good knitter."

Said like that, it sounded rather sweet.

Suddenly she had a terrible thought.

"Hang on . . . it can't be. I wonder if that was who she was . . . oh Lord."

"What?"

"She was waiting for someone at the ceilidh. Then she stormed off home. And she's been kind of a bit cross ever since. Oh. Surely not."

"Well anyway," said Gregor. "I'm just passing on . . ."

"Thanks," said Morag, kissing him, and shaking her head. "God, I slightly miss the days when all I had to do at work was fly the plane. Do you think he's going to want me to sack her?"

Gregor shrugged. "I don't know. But he'll probably want her to stop. Mind you he did say he was used to it."

"Oh for God's sake," said Morag. "He's so cocky and annoying."

". . . but not from people who've accessed his private email address on the airline's system."

"Argh," said Morag. "This is my 'flatmate.' Mind you, kudos to her for setting her cap at the millionaire. Okay."

Senga appeared at the door, chicken-free, looking expectant.

"She's going to be all right," she said. "Now, Gregor, you're going to make me dinner, aren't you? And we can have a good long chat."

She shot Morag a look as if Morag would not be coming off well at all in that chat.

"I'd better get back. I'll see you on Friday."

It was so hard, kissing him, smelling him, and having to leave.

The evening light was soft with mist coming in from the sea, but they were going to beat it, she knew, as she clambered into the cockpit and suggested Erno take first chair, which he grumbled about, so she could concentrate on what Gregor had told her. It was so strange, she had only been impressed just that morning by how well Gertie seemed to be doing. Please let it not be all for nothing.

CHAPTER 26

It was to Morag's mild irritation that Calum was as nice as he could be about it. She saw him at the airport at the start of their day.

"She's just a kid," he said.

"You think it's totally obvious that everyone would have a mad crush on you," she said primly.

Calum shrugged. "I have all my own teeth and an airline," he said. "I have to tell you it happens quite a lot."

"What is your current setup anyway?" said Morag, suspiciously. "Aren't you in, like, a throuple?"

Calum laughed. "Let's just say I'm flexible."

"But not flexible enough for Gertie."

"Sorry," said Calum. "I'm rich—I can't help it. I only date really really good-looking people, most of whom are also rich. Is this news?"

"Gertie's pretty," said Morag stoutly.

"Yeah, lots of people are 'pretty.' *You're* pretty," said Calum. "But you still wouldn't make the cover of *Czechya Grazie*."

"That sounds alarmingly specific," muttered Morag.

"I mean, of course, you might make a nice calendar of, uh, Scottish lady pilots," Calum mused.

"Shut up now," said Morag.

Presently, Gertie arrived. She immediately flushed bright pink when she saw Calum there, and Morag saw it, clear as day. Then Gertie looked at the two of them and instantly twigged what they'd been talking about. Morag realized when she was flying with a big airline she had really resented HR departments with their endless training and nitpicking and checking, but now, she would have very much liked one around. Calum had one of course, but they were still technically a separate company.

The tin shed was an absolutely useless place to have a quiet meeting. People were already milling around waiting on the Glasgow flight, or preparing to take helicopter classes. There was a back office that Pete used to go up to the air traffic control tower, and keep their files in. It was freezing and a mess and made of glass so everyone could see who was in there, but it was the best they could do.

"Uh, Gertie, could you . . . pop over here?" said Morag. Goodness, she'd only been here a couple of weeks. This was incredibly awkward.

Gertie knew immediately what was up. It had dawned on her very slowly after the ceilidh when she had that unsettling feeling she had done something terribly terribly wrong, and it had taken her a while to scroll back on her laptop to realize what it was. A long, rambling, clearly very drunk email complaining to Calum about breaking their date and how he hadn't noticed her and . . . oh God. Gertie had deleted it right away and hoped he'd done the same, but obviously it was too late. She covered her face with her hands. Morag couldn't help but feel sorry for her.

"Uhm, Gertie?"

"I'm sorry," choked out Gertie. "I'm really sorry."

"It's fine," said Calum. "I understand."

And his voice sounded so sweet and gentle Morag got quite annoyed with him, because it didn't seem a good way to get someone off having a crush on you: by being very very nice to them.

"I think you got caught up because of my stupid aeroplanes," he said. "I know it's daft. It was all my dad, really. I know it looks impressive, but it's just the family business . . . I'm sorry. I know I'm spoiled. It's terrible."

Gertie shook her head. "No," she said, in her quiet throaty little voice. "It wasn't. It was you."

Oddly for a moment Calum looked a bit taken aback by that, like he wasn't expecting it, or as if it wasn't something he heard very often.

"Well, anyway . . ." He coughed. "And obviously, let me say, nice as it might be . . . we have a strict no-fraternizing staff policy."

Morag frowned slightly as this was news to her and also they didn't work for the same company, but every little bit helps.

"So I'm afraid I can't accept . . ."

He pulled out the scarf.

Morag gasped. She couldn't help herself. "What are . . . you sent him this?"

Gertie flushed harder. She had poured her heart and soul into it. To have it flung back in her face was very hard.

"It's lovely," said Calum. "But I just can't . . . my, uh, friend, she loved . . . anyway."

Morag picked it up. "You *made* it?" she said again.

Gertie shrugged awkwardly.

"I thought you stopped at penguins. Oh my God, I love it," said Morag.

Calum looked at it as if he was rather regretting having to give it up.

"Well perhaps I've been a little . . ."

"Were you going to give him anything else?"

Gertie shrugged then and, feeling she had nothing left to lose, opened the box in her drawer. Inside was a beanie, in more resistant wool, done in descending shades of gray with a yellow rim. She had thought he might like that next.

"I would wear this, like, right now," said Morag. "You are really really talented," she said, shaking her head. "This stuff is amazing. God, I'd go out with you. Sorry, I mean . . . We can't really have this kind of thing at work, Gertie, I'm sorry."

"I'm sorry too," said Gertie.

Calum looked rather yearningly at the hat, then back to Gertie.

"It was very kind of you to knit for me."

"I thought with all the helicopters you get on and off, you must get cold early in the morning."

Calum cleared his throat. "Uhm. Well. You're right. I do."

There was a silence.

"Am I . . . am I getting fired?" said Gertie, finally.

"Oh my God, no, we would never do that," said Calum quickly. "You're . . . you're wonderful at your job."

He fingered his scarf-free neck unconsciously.

"Okay well, if we're all sorted out . . ." said Morag. She had a flight to get going, including a gaggle of very excited pensioners on a day trip, the types that had to be told they couldn't go from side to side to look out different windows, without the plane unbalancing quite dramatically, so she'd better get on it.

"Gertie, could you finish check-in?"

"Of course," said Gertie, jumping up.

She stopped at the door.

"I'm sorry again. For sending you that message. I never should have done. It was very wrong."

"Don't mention it," said Calum, looking rather regretful.

CHAPTER 27

Walking home with Morag later was a bit awkward. Gertie was quiet, and Morag kept trying to think of something to say that wouldn't make things worse.

"You know," she said finally, "once at flying school . . . I pretended not to understand ATPL theory to get this really hot guy to help me out. Then I passed the exam and he failed and he called me a Super-nerd Cow and never spoke to me again."

Gertie appreciated the sentiment. "How old were you though?" she said.

Morag frowned. "Nineteen."

"I'm nearly thirty."

"Does it normally work, knitting for boys you like?" said Morag. Something tugged at the back of her mind, but she couldn't put her finger on it.

"Not really," said Gertie.

Morag patted her on the shoulder.

"I just feel so dumb," said Gertie.

"I share the man I love with a goat," said Morag.

"Well, as long as the KCs don't hear about it," said Gertie, a completely vain hope, as the vicar had been arriving in from an ecumenical conference in Dundee and overheard the airport discussion, and in an error she would regret for a long time, had gone back to the manse and asked the twins why Gertie was looking so upset, which had immediately sent them into a frenzy until they had discovered the truth.

"We could have a fish supper?" said Morag, cheeringly.

"I'm going to go sit with Elspeth. Now she's better, she's just bored."

"Good," said Morag, fervently. "Bored is what we're after."

THE NEWS EVEN made its way back to Ranald. As a flying man he'd been on the receiving end of a few crushes in his time and, in fact, he had Peigi living in his house right now, so he understood a little bit about it.

He didn't deliberately go and hang out near the wool shop; he just happened to be heading by to pick up some fish and chips. His son Iain, Morag's dad, was in town, and point-blank refusing to eat Peigi's food. Ranald had worried slightly that even after all this time he might feel that Peigi was trying to fill his mother's shoes. Apparently he had dealt with that a long time ago; it was simply that Peigi was a terrible cook, in a way that Ranald had learned not to mind.

Anyhow, it was a chilly evening, despite the sun, and the queue for the chip shop was in the shade, which wasn't ideal, and Jean was standing outside the wool shop, looking cross.

"Hello yourself," he said, pleased.

Jean looked up surprised. "Hiyah!" she said, noting that he was looking well. His arms were tan in short sleeves, and surprisingly muscular given his age.

"Just waiting for chips. You choosing wool?"

"Not from here," sniffed Jean. She'd been at war with Janet in the wool shop for years; Janet got annoyed that Jean got all her wool except for odds and sods from mysterious circumstances, and Jean was annoyed that Janet wouldn't sell their work in the shop, instead preferring her own, rival group, who specialized in baby matinee jackets with copious frills and matching knitted dollies. Jean thought they were common and had said as much within Janet's hearing, so that meant that visits to the shop were often fraught, yet necessary, it being the only knitting shop between here and Oban. Sometimes you just needed a set of number 6s and that was that.

"Okay," said Ranald, who had only the very faintest idea of what knitting actually was and how much wool you would need to do it if you did it.

"Uhm, I hope Gertie's okay after today?"

"What do you mean?" said Jean, her senses prickling. "She's fine!"

In fact, Gertie in truth was not at all fine. She had sobbed her heart out, on her lonely bed, then gone back to her old house so she could sit next to Elspeth and cry quietly, whilst her gran got her up to date with *River City.*

"Oh good. I'm so glad that's settled then."

Ranald got to the front of the line.

"Chips?" he said suddenly, out of common courtesy, and Jean rather surprised herself by saying, why yes, and shortly—Ranald would come back for the fish suppers—they found themselves down on the front, sitting in the sunshine with a bottle of Irn-Bru between them, and plenty of salt and vinegar on the hot crispy utterly delicious irresistible chips, staring out to sea as the seagulls circled with their normal air of impatient menace. They warmed their hands on the chips and their faces in the sunshine, and Jean, to her surprise, found herself very content.

"I haven't done this in ages," she said. "Do you remember when you were a kid, you'd get chips and sit out, like, all night."

Ranald smiled. "We'd do tricks on our bikes to impress the girls."

"Did it work?"

"It *did* work," he said. "And I still have the stitches in my arm to prove it."

Jean laughed. "You're older than me. It was skateboards by my time."

"Okay, well then, that sounds a lot cooler."

"It was, thank you."

"So it worked on you?"

"Come on," said Jean. "It's Carso. What else were we going to do?"

And they both laughed, and irresistibly found their gazes drawn to the old red telephone box on the shore, still working, but no longer the center of group activity it had once been. The boys would call the girls, or they'd all dare each other to call someone in particular, or make prank calls to the head teacher whilst killing themselves laughing. Those had been good days too.

Jean smiled. Then she looked out to sea, watched the windmills turn, and glanced at the cargo boats just visible on the horizon and she thought of her daughter.

"What happened to Gertie?" she asked, quietly.

Ranald was just thinking very briefly, and no doubt stupidly considering his age (and what these chips would do to his cholesterol levels he didn't want to mull on), that he felt young again. It was nice to sit out on a sunny evening, by the sea, with a girl and some chips and some Irn-Bru, feeling there was nothing ahead but possibility: no responsibilities, nothing to do later, just a girl, some hot crisp greasy chips, the salt stinging his tongue, the vinegar making him blink, the Irn-Bru blessedly sweet. Everything perfect.

Well, anyway. He felt himself pulled back, and chided himself for being ridiculous. And then he told her.

Jean went very still. She looked at the crumpled empty shining paper in her hand, bundled it up and stuck it in the nearest bin.

"Sorry," said Ranald. "Maybe I shouldn't have told you. It's just a bit of silliness."

"No, I'm glad you did," Jean replied. "They never stop being your kids, do they?"

Ranald thought of his son Iain, back at the house, refusing to talk to Peigi.

"Not really," he said. "You think they will but they don't."

"I mean, it was easier for us, wasn't it? Don't you think? None of this internet, or traveling about, or choosing from everyone. You just found someone you liked . . ."

"Ate some chips . . ."

Jean smiled. "Aye. But for the young folks now . . . it seems so complicated. And those boys on the apps . . . I don't trust a one of them."

"Not a single one?" said Ranald, smiling and throwing one of his chips for the seagulls even though he knew it was a mistake that would start a massive noisy barney and he was correct in that.

"Those bloody things would eat a babby," said Jean. "Don't do that, they're velociraptors."

"I know. It's just been a while."

They stared out for a moment.

"Aye, I think it is harder," said Ranald, finally. "It took Morag forever to find the right man. And look who she ends up with! Some birdwatcher who lives like a hermit on a remote island!"

Jean laughed. "Oh yes, so she did. Mind you, she seems happy."

"She does, aye," said Ranald, beaming.

"You're so happy she's back up here, ey?"

He nodded.

"Sometimes I think Gertie should go further away. Spread her wings," said Jean. "But I'm not sure I could bear it. She's all I have. That makes me sound so selfish."

Ranald nodded. He understood.

"If she'd traveled a bit more . . . seen a bit more of the world. She wouldn't have been so caught up in . . . I mean, Calum Frost. Seriously."

"Ach, it's easily done."

Jean nodded. "I know, I know."

"I wouldn't be young again for the world," said Ranald. "Well. You know. Apart from the knees."

JEAN WAS ABSOLUTELY ready to be full of sympathy for Gertie when she got back, glad she'd run into Ranald wearing a full face of makeup. She'd worn it mostly to annoy Janet, who veered toward the mumsier end of the scale, so it worked out pretty well in the end.

The twins looked up. Majabeen was in England with the genius babies; Marian had gone to visit her dad, who was traditional, so that was always tricky. Elspeth was sitting by the fire and the twins were passive-aggressively racing to knit up two sleeves of the same jumper. They had also been full of vicarish sympathy for Gertie, and told her not to worry about being single; it was fine—although of course it helped if you had an identical twin sister. So Gertie had ended up feeling awful all over again, and gone upstairs to her old bedroom.

"Come on, Gertie," shouted Jean up the stairs. "I've got a brew on and I'll get out the good biscuits."

Gertie though had lost herself in a daydream in which *"Oh here I am in hospital,"* said Calum, *"with a terrible chest cold . . . pneumonia maybe. If only I'd had your scarf, Ger . . . Miss Mooney, everything would have been so different. And yet you are still happy to nurse me back to health when all the shallow models I knew have abandoned me completely. I don't deserve someone like you, I really don't. Will you ever forgive me? Oh, my expensive pajamas appear to have become unbuttoned . . ."*

"GERTRUDE!"

Jean calling her Gertrude really was a five-alarm situation.

Gertie, bursting out of her daydream, screwed up her face. She couldn't stay up here forever. Or could she? Plus she was absolutely starving.

Her door nudged open, but nobody came in. Instead, a long tube of Jaffa cakes was pushed through. Goodness, Jaffa cakes were for very, very special occasions. How bad did they think she was? How bad *was* she?

Tentatively, she moved a little closer to the Jaffas. This was absurd; it was one of the ridiculous novelty one-meter boxes they normally did at Christmas. Jean had obviously got it in the January sales and was saving it for a special occasion, which would be a very Jean thing to do.

On the other hand, Gertie really was very hungry. She bent down and stretched out . . . whoosh! The Jaffa cakes jerked back.

"Mu-um!" said Gertie. She crawled toward them, but they got yanked back again. Gertie couldn't help it—she smiled.

"Mum, I am not going to crawl downstairs for Jaffa cakes!"

Jean's face, eyes rimmed with the familiar spidery mascara, appeared behind the door.

"Then would you crawl downstairs for me?" she said, opening up her arms.

"THE THING IS," said Tara, unnecessarily, as Gertie was fussed over and petted and poured extra tea and given more Jaffa cakes than even she wanted, which she wouldn't have thought possible.

Obviously Tara had been formulating a speech whilst Gertie had been upstairs.

"The thing is, those books and TV shows you like, Gertie . . ."

Elspeth and Gertie exchanged worried glances. Gertie was frogging wool from another beautiful scarf she'd started for Calum; it hurt far too much to continue on with it.

". . . they're not real. You know, rich and famous rock star meets a backstage girl and despite the fact that they're really rich and famous and get to meet lots of glamorous people all the time, what they really want is someone to ground them and tell them the truth," went on Tara inexorably. "You know those are just stories, right?"

Cara nodded, as if she was an expert in matters of the heart also. "I mean, look at rich and well-known men. They marry supermodels and actresses."

"Miserably," pointed out Elspeth from the sofa, peering over the tops of her spectacles and trying to count stitches. She kept losing her place. She hadn't told anyone about it. She knew the pattern for a sweater off by heart; she'd knitted enough of them down the years. The last thing Elspeth wanted was to worry Jean by telling her she didn't understand the patterns anymore. She'd only fuss unnecessarily. Elspeth was just tired; that was all. It was nothing.

"Yeah, they always get divorced," agreed Cara.

"Yes," said Tara. "And then the handsome famous guy marries someone even more beautiful and famous and *even* younger than the last one. So what's your point?"

Gertie sighed.

"I mean there's nothing *wrong* with you," Tara went on, as if she was being extremely kind at this point.

"Well, thanks very much, Tara O'Farrell," butted in Jean, sharply.

"No, but you know what I mean," said Tara. "The rich million-aire looking for a poor nice girl . . . it's . . . I mean, you are *very* nice," she added at the end.

Gertie stared at the floor. "Thanks for that, Tara."

"It's a bit like me and Rod Stewart," said Jean, thoughtfully. "I mean, I think Rod Stewart would have loved to have been married to me probably instead of all those leggy supermodels."

"Calum is nothing like Rod Stewart, Mum!" said Gertie with some force.

"Oh, I don't know," said Jean. "They're both blonde. But you know, I think . . . well, Rod would love coming round for some cock-a-leekie soup."

"Don't be ridiculous, Mum!"

"He would though," insisted Jean. "He's Scottish."

"He isn't! He's from Essex!"

"All the more reason why he'd like a pure Scottish person then, isn't it?" said Jean, putting her knitting down and folding her arms. There was really no shifting Jean once she got onto Rod Stewart, and Gertie was daft to even try.

"So anyway," Jean continued. "That's what I'm saying. It's nice to think about Rod Stewart."

Tara, Cara, and Marian all nodded emphatically. Gertie stayed schtum.

"But it doesn't mean that if he came to Carso he would imme-diately fall in love with me."

There was a disappointing lack of dissenting voices.

"I mean, it's not out of the question," said Jean, raising her voice slightly, and rather undermining her entire argument.

"Are you saying it's not out of the question that a world-famous rock star with a gorgeous leggy blonde supermodel wife would run off to live with a size-sixteen middle-aged lady in a small town in Argyllshire?" said Cara. "I'm just trying to clarify."

"Well we wouldn't live *in town*," said Jean crossly. And they were still arguing about what, exactly, they would do with Rod Stewart when Gertie headed home, feeling undeniably better, if sworn off all men, famous or otherwise, forever.

PART TWO

CHAPTER 28

Struan woke with a heavy head. Saskia had already left for work, which was just as well. They had not been getting on. And the makeup sex had been good. Very good. But Struan was coming to the uncomfortable conclusion that this wasn't quite enough. That he had been trying to find a settled relationship and do things in his life he was supposed to do—but it wasn't making him happy, and he felt awful that he wasn't making Saskia happy either. She wasn't a bad person. She just desperately wanted him to be the kind of person who cared about lampshades and house insurance deals and bringing in lots of money and going out to fancy places and, well . . . He thought he might be like that too. But what if he just wasn't? But he'd moved, and he didn't have a home, and he had the audition and how would he tell her? It felt horribly complicated. It was weird, the most relaxed times he'd had in the last month were when he'd popped around to his old gaffe.

Meanwhile, the job he still had was full on. It was almost end of term, the last few days of school before the Easter holidays, which meant absolutely everyone had been completely unmanageable, not least the teachers. There was a lot of chocolate cake brought into the staff room, which meant that wee Mrs. Fichen was all sugar hyped by the end of first break and was letting her P1s run with scissors. Mr. Stryde, who had been teaching P6s for as long as anyone could remember and knew where to put a semicolon, had somehow been convinced that *Guardians of the Galaxy 3* was a totally appropriate end-of-term film. That sounded about right until it got to the vivisection and blind bunny rabbit scenes and half the class erupted into devastated sobs and couldn't be calmed down.

Struan was trying to keep his class straight for the trip, when they were nearly peeing their pants with excitement and staring out of the window, or peppering him with ridiculous questions he couldn't answer, apart from the obvious (No, Anna-Lise, there won't be a McDonald's there). It wasn't really the best music lesson to stay calm and prepped for their big trip, particularly when they bugged him to let them put some TikTok songs on and show off their dance moves and he reluctantly agreed. He was going to have to repair the damage out of his own pocket, Mrs. McGinty had sternly informed him. Struan had, yet again, managed to defer telling the head he was leaving which made him, Saskia did not hesitate to point out, completely pointless in every way.

The night before he'd had a gig with the band. They'd been playing for a wedding—first of the season. The wedding party were all heading for a blessing on Inchborn the next day. Judging by the amount they had consumed at the wedding reception there was going to be a fair number of sore heads joining the blessing. It had been a very rowdy affair, even by Scottish wedding standards; two west coast families, one protestant, one Catholic. They had wanted a ceilidh band though their first dance hadn't been a traditional waltz; it had been a heavily choreographed *Strictly*-style number to "When I Fall in Love."

Except, unfortunately, the rather over-refreshed husband had forgotten what were presumably carefully rehearsed moves, and his new wife, also quite well refreshed, had gotten very annoyed and vocal with him. This had confused him even more, and she ended up pushing him quite sharply on the shoulder, then marching off the dance floor in tears even though the song still had an endless six minutes to run. Struan and his bandmates had jumped in and timed a waltz as they turned down the recorded music, and he had encouraged all the other guests to come on and dance, which they did, until finally, rather shamefacedly, the bride and bridegroom did too, although notably not talking to one another.

They'd stuck with the fast songs, as people got steadily quite stocious, and Struan had drunk a couple of pints to deal with the heat rising in the village hall. A bridesmaid had grabbed him at the disco and made it very clear that he was going to have a dance and ideally more with her, and he'd had to politely extricate himself. It also looked like she might turn nastily physical, but Struan had always had very strict rules about drunk women, even—especially—very keen drunk women, so he sent her back to the bar. It was staffed by local students, now looking fundamentally terrified, but the distraction gave Struan a chance to make a run for it out of the fire exit with his guitar and amp, without even saying goodbye to the other lads. It wasn't his finest hour.

The couple of pints had still made him restless though, as well as having to get back to Saskia's flat, which he still didn't like, plus worrying about the upcoming school trip. He had slept very badly, particularly as he remembered his sleeping bag was in the loft at his old flat.

Instead he dragged himself up early. Saskia was up too, in the gray dawn. She looked at him and he looked at her, neither quite ready to admit the obvious.

"Well, bye then," said Struan, and she offered up a chilly cheek to kiss and he felt sorry for her, and sorry for himself.

He left the quiet estate, and texted Morag that he was coming over early. She didn't get the message because she was already at the airport, busy with something else, something rather concerning.

CHAPTER 29

Morag was busy, because the weather had gone into reverse. It had just got colder and colder. That morning, the morning of the school trip, the radio had buzzed in the tin shed very early.

Morag had headed up to the control tower to answer it, sure it would be Gregor. There was no mobile signal on the island and the radio was their only mode of communication. It would be a lot more romantic and sexier if it wasn't an open channel that anyone could listen in to if they had the inclination which, there not being loads to do in Carso, and loads of old retired skippers living there, plenty did. Morag wasn't entirely sure the KCs didn't have an illegal scanner rigged up, the speed they got all the gossip. So it was rather tentatively that she picked up the receiver in Pete's control tower. You could see for 360 degrees; it was a bright clear day, cold for the time of year. It had been a ridiculously cold spring; people had been scraping their cars down in the mornings for what seemed like a hundred years, but a good day for flying, she thought.

"First Officer MacIntyre," Morag said, just in case it wasn't Gregor for whatever reason and she said "hello, honeybuns" or some such, even though that wasn't the kind of thing she was likely to say. On the other hand, even very sensible people say very stupid things when they're in love.

"Morning, First Officer," came Gregor's typically amused voice, and Morag felt herself smiling. Pete rolled his eyes as he arrived at the office, but she didn't notice, and he was doing it from a very affectionate place.

"How can I help you? Over."

"First Officer, have you looked at your weather forecast?"

"Obviously," said Morag, unimpressed. "An area of low pressure coming in from the north, with bands of rain, windspeed mild to moderate."

"Yeah," said Gregor. "I don't believe it."

"You don't believe in the weather forecast?"

"I do believe in weather forecasting as a concept as long as it's very short range and based on observable patterns and cloud formations . . ."

"Uh-huh. How is the sick chicken doing by the way?"

"Janet? She's grand yes."

"Oh well, worth my best tweezers then."

"I would say so. I'll make you the best Spanish omelette when you next come."

"Deal."

"Bring peppers. And tomatoes. And onions."

"Uh and potatoes?"

"Potatoes I have."

"Will do."

"Listen," said Gregor. "Just be careful. They're predicting rain but I was out looking at the radishes, and they're still shaking off frost."

"Your radishes are telling me to disbelieve the weather forecast?"

"That's exactly what I'm telling you."

"*The radishes are shaking off the frost* sounds like you're trying to pass me spy stuff in code," grumbled Morag.

"Well, I'm not," said Gregor. "I mean it. Have a look."

"Also it would be a terrible code," added Ranald, listening in.

"Gramps, this is meant to be your day off."

"Doesn't mean I don't have a passing interest in what you're doing to my plane."

"Hello, sir," said Gregor.

Morag couldn't help it, she liked how respectful Gregor was to her grandfather. They came from totally different worlds, but they each respected the other for their commitment to what they did. Both workaholics too. Morag wondered briefly if a therapist would have a field day with it—how she'd fallen for someone just like Ranald—then batted the thought away. If Gregor was as good a man as her grandfather, and she had every reason to suspect he was, then everything was going to be all right.

"What are you thinking, Gregor."

"Actually, Gramps, this is a call to me?" said Morag. "And I think I'll be making the judgment?"

She heard a noise from the terminal building beyond the door and winced slightly. There was a wedding party who were getting their marriage blessed in the abbey on Inchborn and they looked rowdy, even first thing in the morning.

"I'm just saying," said Gregor. "They're predicting heavy rain. And I think it's not going to be rain."

It was the end of April. Frankly, anything could happen. You could turn up and marvel at the soft gentle air and the bluebells that stretched for miles and miles; perfumed the air with their scent; rendered the world gentle and beautiful and lifted the heart.

Or you could watch lambs in the fields being born to harsh cruel winters and scouring winds; jump out of your car and run to the door before you got blown over; walk, wrapped up in a big duvet coat, down to the sea front to see the waves ten, twelve feet over the esplanade front, might in their power, the windmills whirring, the fishermen grave, setting out on their travels deep into the night.

CHAPTER 30

The bell woke Gertie from a not unpleasant morning half-dream in which Calum had started a new route to France and needed someone to walk down ancient cobbled streets trying croissants with and . . . BUZZ!

Maybe it was him! She thought suddenly, sitting bolt upright, running her hands through her knotted hair. Maybe he'd had a night lying awake thinking about her, and he couldn't wait a second longer. Maybe the helicopter was right outside.

She pulled off her old *Friends* pajamas and replaced them with a black dress she grabbed from her hanger, dashed into the bathroom.

BUZZ!

To rinse her mouth out with toothpaste then downstairs, slapping her cheeks a little to put some color in them, all the while trying to tell herself to stop being ridiculous, it was probably a delivery driver for Morag.

Struan was standing on the street, holding two cups of coffee from The Point, which opened early for the fishermen.

"Ah," he said. "Hiyah."

"But don't you have a key?" she said.

Struan shrugged.

"Aye, well, it's your house, aye?"

"I suppose . . ."

She stood back to let him in.

"Is your . . . was your girlfriend all right?"

He winced. "Not really. Sorry if she was rude to you."

Gertie shrugged, only relieved she hadn't managed to follow on her instincts and tell Struan about what she'd once felt for him. God, what was she thinking?

Struan explained his mission, and Gertie sent him up to the loft, where he managed to dig up a waterproof jacket, which was fine. The tents would be provided, but his sleeping bag . . . he pulled it down from the tiny loft. It did not smell good. He hadn't used it since last summer, when they'd been playing little folk festivals and camping. Good times. Sadly not good enough for him to remember to wash his sleeping bag. He sighed. Maybe they'd put him in a tent by himself. Surely he wouldn't have to share with the headmistress . . . A chill went through him. No. Definitely not. Oh God, why couldn't they have booked with their normal people on Mure? The idea of having to undress in front of . . . no. That wouldn't happen. Not in a million years. So he could stop panicking.

Struan grabbed his bag containing his deodorant and all his socks and looked around at what had used to be his apartment. Gertie was in the shower, which felt odd, although of course she had to get to work too. She had looked terribly fetching in her black dress and bed head, he found himself thinking, then shook that thought right out of his head.

He sighed once more and grabbed another one of his guitars down from the attic, just out of habit, tuning it absentmindedly. Then he remembered they were going hiking and put it down again. Then he thought, well, it wasn't heavy. And they were going to be moving at the pace of ten-year-old children, so it wasn't going to be a speedy thing to be doing. And the kids might like it round the campfire . . . It might make things more bearable anyway. So he strung the case around his rucksack. By this time Gertie was out of the shower and dressed in her uniform and she kindly filled his flask with very strong hot coffee.

"Actually this might be good," he said, taking the coffee with thanks. "A bit of fresh air, a bit of exercise, get the kids singing as they move." Even now, years on from the pandemic there were still a few, even up here, in the great free wild air of the very far north who had never quite escaped the trap of their bedrooms and their phones. Whereas on this trip all phones were confiscated and left at base, to save the children from trying to order pizza or call in a helicopter or simply to send messages to their parents of the heart-rending deprivation and terror involved in being outside for more than fifteen minutes.

Gertie looked at him. "I thought you were off to be a big rock star," she said. "This is a slightly different kind of rock."

He smiled. "Aye. But it'll be all right. No phones. Nobody bothering me. Few songs around the campfire. Maybe a scary story."

"About a man who gave up his lovely flat in Carso?" said Gertie, and Struan smiled again, then looked rather wistful and stared out the window.

The sun was pinkening over the sea, the waves white-capped. Tiny lines in a mackerel sky were crossing above that, as the light hit the rolling hills, the sheep already up and grazing.

"It'll be a beautiful day to fly," said Gertie.

"Aye," said Struan, watching gusts shear the water's edge. It was chilly, out there, but so beautiful. In the distance rose Inchborn, like a drawing of Narnia; beyond it Larbh and Archland.

"I suppose when you're touring it's cozy and you get to go to new places," said Gertie. "And no children!"

"It's all hotel rooms and buses," said Struan. "Everything looks exactly the same. And don't tell the wee buggers, they'll get even more unmanageable but . . . I quite like the children."

THEY WERE HEADING in the same direction—there was a coach picking up the kids from school, and Gertie would walk on further that way, so they left together into the freezing cold, sunny morning, Struan clanking under the weight of his rucksack.

"I don't think I've been camping since last year's festival circuit," he said, to break the silence.

"I wondered what the smell was." Gertie allowed herself a small smile.

Struan wrinkled his nose. "Oh Christ, it's my sleeping bag isn't it? I knew it was awful. Then I got used to it and kind of forgot. Oh no. The kids are going to rag me something stupid."

"That's if you don't render them unconscious with the dope smell first."

"Oh God, really?!"

He twisted his head round comically to sniff his sleeping bag and Gertie really couldn't stifle a full grin then.

"It's that bad?"

She nodded. "Maybe just keep yourself very far away from their tents."

"Oh they make the teachers do that anyway, don't worry."

Gertie shivered. The morning was clear, but colder than it looked, or than it should have been for the time of year.

"It's going to be right cold up there, isn't it?"

"This is Scotland," said Struan. "I think that's a given."

"But you have your trusty stinky sleeping bag."

Struan sighed. "Maybe they'll have a spare at the Outward Bound center."

Gertie laughed. "You would actually get inside a stranger's discarded sleeping bag rather than your own? What went on in there?"

Struan looked sheepish. "Oh, I don't . . ."

"I mean I think they have some old sheep blankets probably?"

She was teasing him and he found himself smiling back. They came to the bottom of the hill, next to the road with the school. A large coach was already there, belching fumes, along with a gaggle of children, their parents, bags, and general uproar. They didn't technically need a coach as the airfield was only a kilometer away, but it helped make sure they could count them in and out.

Gertie sensed an immediate slowing down from Struan and it took her a second or two to realize what he was doing. He was hanging back so that nobody there would think they were together, it being so early in the morning and everything. He was completely terrified of the idea that anyone might think they were a couple, or knew each other. He didn't want a repeat of the Wee Shugs incident.

She flushed quickly. What had she told herself after Calum? *Stop it.* Struan had probably heard about it—that was even worse. Probably thought she was completely desperate.

"I'm just turning down here," she said quickly, going off across the road.

Struan, who had not heard about it, had barely realized what he was doing; it was only just dawning on him that he was about to turn up in front of the whole school with a young woman who was not his girlfriend. He was just planning out a tactful way of explaining to Gertie how much unimaginable ragging he would get if they showed up together, and even worse when they saw her at check-in later, when he turned his head to see she was marching off, again. Oh. Well. She must have had the same thought first, how awful to be seen with him early in the morning in front of people from the town. Huh.

He walked on, rather crossly, toward the clutch of very excited children, and parents who clearly hadn't got quite as much sleep as they would have liked the previous night.

CHAPTER 31

Ranald was inclined to listen to Gregor's warning; Morag too, obviously, but although there was freshness in the air, there wasn't any news coming over of anything worse. The clouds didn't look ominous—she'd been caught in a horrible storm before and the air didn't feel like that at all. Just cold. She prepped the plane just in case there was ice around. Erno looked at her very oddly. Being Finnish, he reckoned he knew all there was to know about ice. But he respected Morag, so he let her at it.

The wedding party was now at either end of the hall, glaring at each other. There appeared to be shopping bags full of what looked suspiciously like whisky bottles, and Morag wasn't crazy about that. Gertie had arrived as Morag descended the stairs, and was efficiently arranging everything on her desk.

So they were doing two runs, one specially for the schoolchildren. They did it every year—a special cost-price addition to the schedule just for the P6s. For many of them, the plane ride was the most exciting part of the trip, even though there were fewer these days who hadn't at least been to Spain on their holidays.

The children rolled out of the coach like little padded Michelin men, all of them in their big hoodies. They were bursting with excitement, carrying their rucksacks, which were more or less the same size as they were, and fussing madly about who was going to sit next to who on the plane.

Morag looked at them all.

"Mrs. McGinty?" she said. "Can I have a word?"

"Yes?" said Mrs. McGinty.

"It's just . . . the weather forecast . . ."

"Yes?"

"The weather forecast says it's going to rain . . ."

"Yes, I can see that," said Mrs. McGinty. "I have a smartphone you know. We're not total amateurs."

"No, I realize that."

"Nothing wrong with a bit of rain! Will be good for them! Get them off their iPads all day!"

"I don't think there's anything wrong with a bit of rain either," said Morag, a tad desperately. "I'm just saying, that it's very cold, and there's a small possibility . . . well some people think . . . it might turn into snow."

"It's almost May!" said Mrs. McGinty. "Don't be ridiculous. Who are these people?"

"Well, Gregor . . ."

"Your boyfriend thinks it might snow? Anyone else?"

"Uh, not really."

"A *little* bit of spring snow is hardly going to hurt them."

"No, I guess not . . ."

"Are you still happy to fly us? Through a small amount of cold weather?"

"Of course," bristled Morag, who had also had bad experiences of Primary 4 with Mrs. McGinty.

"Good," said Mrs. McGinty, dismissing her.

Mrs. McGinty was wearing brand-new very expensive climbing gear that had obviously all been bought as a matching set as well as a shiny new sleeping bag. She sniffed at Struan, which he would normally have considered an incredibly rude thing to do to someone, but he had to concede with his sleeping bag that she probably was well within her rights, and he was very relieved that they wouldn't—as it turned out—be sharing a tent. He'd be sharing with the guy who ran the course, and she'd be sharing with the woman. The campsite wasn't far up the mountain; they'd set up camp one day, sleep over, then make the summit the following day. It was a fairly straightforward walk, with one small sheer cliff in the middle they had to do some exciting stuff with ropes to get over.

Gertie was behind the desk of course, and gave absolutely no sign of acknowledging Struan at all beyond a professional nod, which he returned.

"Your hair is sticking up, sir," said Anna-Lise instantly.

"Thank you, Anna-Lise," replied Struan.

"Maybe he likes it like that," said her best friend Bronte, who was as in love with him as a ten-year-old can be in love with anyone: that is, she couldn't quite distinguish between how much she loved Mr. McGhie, how much she loved pizza, and how much she loved her cat, but all of those things were Very Much.

"Oh sorry, sir," said Anna-Lise.

"Okay, you two," said Struan. "On we go."

When Gertie had first heard about the school flight, she had liked the notion of it very much, and made a special point of printing out all the boarding passes, inputting Special School Flight on to them as the code, and bought little plane stickers to show they'd checked in their baggage. Morag thought this might be overkill. Ranald thought it was brilliant. They were rostered together that day; Ranald wouldn't miss the school flight for anything. He stood by the desk, gravely saluting them all as they came in.

He also answered their questions—yes, they would fly very high; no, not to space; no they couldn't "just go to America"; no, there wouldn't be a film on the flight nor any coloring books; no, Moss could not "have a go at flying a plane," and Ranald did not believe him when he said he had in fact flown "loads" of times before. Mrs. McGinty quietened down the vigorous infighting in terms of who got the window seats going out.

Finally all twelve children and two teachers were belted in, some kicking their legs with excitement. Most had flown before, but flying in the tiny twin otter was always exciting, and they could feel every bump and piece of stone on the runway surface; the super short take-off of the small engine, and the immediate, precipitate rising, straight into the blue. There was an audible *oooh* of excitement from the cabin and Morag and Ranald swapped glances, smiling at each other.

Struan looked apprehensively at the weather app on his phone before they took off. It was still saying rain. Very heavy rain. Or, "it's only a bit of rain" as he kept hearing parents and other people say in his presence. The trip never got canceled for rain—if you start canceling things in Scotland for rain, you are not going to get many things done. Apparently the tents were "heavy duty" and there was a cave, and the kids would have a "great time whizzing around in the mud" which sounded to Struan like an ideal situation to get some arms broken, but he didn't mention it. More than one person had asked if he was taking a hip flask.

But as they circled the town, all his dreary thoughts and his tired brain lifted. He couldn't help it. The children's faces were in awe. All their phones were gone, locked away in one big bag; instead, they were staring out of the window, pointing at the houses, jostling to see their own; staring at the mummies all frantically waving in the gardens, often with baby brothers and sisters being held up too to wave at the little plane. They did circles in the sky, round the playground where every other class was watching, the Primary 7s with superior smiles from having already done it; all the others in an agony of anticipation for the incredibly far off time when the Great Day of the Camping Trip would be bestowed upon them.

Then, amidst encouraging shouts to "dive bomb" into Inch-born Abbey, where Morag had already discharged the fractious wedding party, or loop the loop—a perennial favorite (Ranald's dad had once done it with him in it as a young lad and he would tell the story at a moment's notice, vomit and all)—Ranald pointed the plane up to the sky and broke through the cloud cover into the bright white sunshine beyond. After a long hard winter even just feeling the sun on their faces through the windows was a joy and relief.

The flight didn't take long at all before they were coming in to the strip at Archland, the towering height of the Mermaid's Spyglass looking thin and small from on high then, as they pushed on over the sea and pounding waves, taking on a more sinister aspect. The children looked at it with interest.

Waiting in the tin shed at the end, waving frantically as they touched down perfectly were the Outward Bound mentors: Skellan and Denise. They were beaming widely.

Morag watched the children descend, a little quieter, more tentative and nervous now they could see the mountain up close and their parents were far away. "It's awfy big," seemed to be the genuine consensus, and their eyes were wide. A lot of the earlier confidence had gone, although not all. Moss, the one who had thought he could easily fly the plane, also loudly opined that he could run up to the top and back before tea. Wee Shugs talked about looking forward to killing some rabbits which may not, considering Big Shugs, have been bravado. Morag grinned, and looked at the teachers. Mrs. McGinty was already talking to the Outward Bound staff in that way of hers, as if everyone was five years old, and a particularly dumb five at that. Even from up in the cockpit, Morag could see their smiles becoming increasingly fixed.

Meanwhile Struan was looking around as if he wasn't quite

sure what he was doing there. His guitar was surgically attached to him as usual. Morag smiled at that too. Same old Struan. She knocked on the window and gave him a wave, and he waved back, easily.

Everyone got their bags right there outside the tiny hut, and Ranald prepared to make the big circle round to take off back the way they'd come. Morag checked the cabin. It did feel cold through the open door, Gregor had been right. Very cold for this time of year. But who knew what the weather did these days? Morag was very sensitive to weather, having been caught in a fair storm or two up these parts. But you wouldn't meet anyone who flew, sailed, or walked around the northern isles of Scotland who didn't have some very hairy stories to tell; that was for sure. Nonetheless, it was chilly out there and she let Ranald take the controls whilst she went and heaved the door up, helped on the other side by Skellan from Outward Bound, who knew what he was doing, thankfully.

The kids on the sidelines waved furiously at the twin otter as it pootled along, taking off quickly straight up into the sky. Ranald was unable to resist twisting right round the top of the Mermaid's Spyglass and buzzing down over the hut, in the hopes of the shock making the head teacher jump, which she did.

CHAPTER 32

"They look so cute," said Morag, watching the kids disappear behind, the island itself getting smaller and smaller as they moved away.

"It's fun to do things like this with the we'ans," said Ranald.

Morag nodded.

"I'm so glad you came back," he added.

Morag sensed something was coming and waited for him to speak.

"It's so wonderful you came home again. I love having you near . . . It's just lovely when everyone is getting on . . . nobody's falling out . . ."

Morag gave him a look.

"Are you talking about Peigi? I didn't fall out with her! She's just horrible to me all the time!"

"That's just her way."

"Being horrible is her way?"

"Ach, her marriage wasn't easy, you know."

Morag didn't say anything to that, because that was sad. In fact it all seemed a little sad.

"I'm fine you've moved out. I just . . . I just miss you coming over, that's all."

"Doesn't she have any other family she could go to?"

"She's got a sister down in Peebles. They don't really speak."

Morag frowned. "So what you're saying is, she's been so horrible to absolutely everyone her entire life so now you just have to put up with being poisoned on the daily?"

"She's not poisoning me."

"She is," said Morag. "Just really *really* slowly."

Ranald tapped the altimeter; not that there was anything wrong with this one, it was an immaculately managed aircraft. It was not his original twin otter, but a replacement, whilst the old otter was being kept in the hangar partly for tinkering rights; possibly, someone had mooted, also as a museum piece.

"Isn't there anyone else?" said Morag, quietly. "I mean, of everyone in the whole world, I know nobody can be Gran . . . but does it really have to be her?"

And at that, strangely, Ranald went quiet.

Later, Morag went home and found herself very much looking forward to learning how to cast on and sharing a slightly bashed box of Maltesers that the staff at the ScotNorth kept slipping Gertie, only to learn that Gertie had got a sudden call to go and sleep over with Elspeth. Jean had been asked out somewhere at short notice and very much wanted to go.

GERTIE DIDN'T KNOW what woke her. Her tiny bedroom in her old house was freezing, absolutely perishing cold, but that wasn't unusual. She stared straight up at the roof, then turned her head.

Instantly she realized what was wrong. She crept to the window. It was snowing. Not a little flurry but a proper white-out, huge flakes of snow. It was late in the season but not at all unheard of; you could still ski down in the Cairngorms. It had been a harsh winter, and the weather was getting less predictable all the time.

Gertie shivered and thought immediately of the children.

They wouldn't be out in this, of course. They'd be down in the bothies near the airstrip, totally warm and cozy and safe. Of course they would. Nothing to worry about.

She glanced at her phone: 4 a.m. Should she call Morag? And

what would they do anyway, in this? White-outs might be all right for jumbo jets, but could small planes fly in it? Gertie had absolutely no idea.

No, she was sure everything was fine. Gertie was just new to this type of work; that was all. She was more used to being comfortable in the supermarket. This kind of stuff was in the hands of people who knew exactly what to do about it.

She realized belatedly she had absolutely no chance of getting back to sleep.

"Gertie?" came a querulous voice. "Is that you?"

She went into Elspeth's room. The only KC that never annoyed her, not even a tiny bit.

"You're not asleep?"

Elspeth tutted. "I never sleep, lassie. Sleeping is for young busy folk. Have you seen that weather though?"

Gertie nodded. "Can I get you some hot milk?"

Elspeth nodded.

"That'd be nice," she said. "Will you come and chat to me whilst I drink it?"

Jean had drunk rather more than her fair share of Lambrusco the night before and could be heard snoring cheerfully in the big room, so she wasn't much to worry about.

"Of course," said Gertie. But when she went downstairs and saw out of the sitting room window, that faced toward the north, she forgot her promise. Because there, in the distant airport tin hut—invisible through the swirling snow except for one tiny point—there was a light on.

GERTIE RESCUED THE milk just in time.

"I can't chat," she said, regretfully. "I think something's up. Although . . ."

Suddenly she could hear Jean's voice in her head: *"Why would they need the check-in girl?"*

Elspeth sipped her milk carefully. "Well," she said. "If something bad is happening they'll need all the hands they can get. And of course they'll need you. You'll be wonderful. Look how good you are at looking after me."

Gertie blinked.

"I'm not sure I say that enough," said Elspeth.

Gertie kissed her soft cheek, then wiped off some of the milk.

"I'll let you know," she said. "I'm sure it's nothing. I'm sure they have people on this."

Elspeth looked out of the window at the swirling flakes.

"I'm not sure about that," she said. "In 1968, wee Willie Piper on Larbh just froze to death right there in his hut."

"Yes, but it was a shepherd's hut," argued Gertie, who had heard this story before. "In January. They didn't have, like, super arctic sleeping bags and stuff back then."

"Left behind three fatherless mites . . ."

"Okay, okay I have to go," said Gertie. "I think. At least, just to see."

She glanced around and, on impulse, stuffed a load of socks and whatever came to hand in a rucksack. Just in case. She pulled on her own socks and waterproof trousers and a huge puffa jacket which meant that regardless of how everyone else was doing, she would be more or less impermeable to the weather. Then she set off out into the snow.

SHE HAD BEEN right: Morag and Pete were indeed sitting up, looking at the radar forecast. Gertie slipped into the tin shed—Morag hadn't locked the door behind her—and up into the glass lookout tower.

"Where the hell?" Morag was saying. The radio was open; Gregor was sitting on the end of it. He, of course, had an entire bad-tempered wedding party who were supposed to have been picked up by the ferry at 11 p.m. They had, it transpired, not been, and were now all crowded into his house. Gregor wasn't terribly keen on company at the best of times, and now he had to deal with a bunch of drunk wedding guests including a hysterical woman who had always wanted to be a May bride and instead was being treated for possible pre-hypothermia.

Pete was frowning. "It wasn't on any of the official forecasts. Well, it is now."

Morag sighed. "Yeah. Can we raise them at Archland?"

They clicked the radio again, trying to get through to Skellan and Denise.

"They'll be asleep," said Morag. "Anyway. Everything will be completely fine. It's just a blizzard. That's what being in a tent is for. Cozy and fun in a snowstorm."

Gertie thought of Struan's thin sleeping bag, meant for summer festivals, and some of the children's, which had unicorns on them, and wondered about that.

Morag looked outside. Pete looked at her.

"You would go out in that?"

Morag frowned. "You could land her on Everest, Pete."

"Yes, but would you? Let the helo guys take this one."

"We don't know there's anything wrong," said Morag. "We haven't heard a peep from the coast guard."

"There's an AAS," said Pete, meaning an Attention All Shipping warning from the Met Office. "The ferry won't be out tomorrow at this rate."

"How long is it going to last?"

"It's a huge front. And it doesn't seem to be shifting."

Morag frowned. "Okay. Keep me up to date."

She suddenly realized Gertie was there, and startled.

"God!" she said. "I thought you were a ghost in the window!" Then she looked at her watch. "Why are you here?"

"I saw the light," said Gertie. "I wondered if anything was up."

"And you came down? Through this?"

Gertie shrugged. "I have a good jacket. And I brought . . ."

Gertie pulled out a flask from the rucksack.

"Oh my God is that coffee?" said Morag. "I can't drink the filthy shack stuff anymore."

"Oy," said Pete.

"Oh come on, you know what I mean."

"You mean we have disgusting coffee."

"Yes! Because you do! Everyone knows that!"

Morag cradled her hands around a mug of Gertie's coffee. The tin shed was not warm at the best of times, never mind 4:30 a.m. in a snowstorm.

"Are they going to be okay?" said Gertie, as they peered out into the wild, flurrying white, so far away from the gentle spring weather of the ceilidh, which seemed such a long time ago now.

"I am . . . I am totally sure they are," said Morag sardonically. "That's why I'm down here at four o'clock in the morning. We'll probably have to pick up the wedding people, if they can hang on till daylight. I mean, we could go in on instruments, but I'd rather not if nobody's in danger. You can't tell which way is up in these storms."

"Really?" said Gertie. "You could fly upside down and not know?"

"Not a clue," said Morag briskly. "Till it was too late."

"I wish I didn't know that," murmured Gertie but Morag had already picked up the radio.

"Can you handle them until the morning, Gregs?"

The radio crackled.

"I can technically," he said, drily. "But I might have to kill them all myself. Is that okay?"

From behind him they could hear the sounds of people shouting.

"It's only been snowing for forty minutes," said Morag. "Have they resorted to cannibalism already?"

"I remember someone who didn't like being stranded here by bad weather," said Gregor, alluding to the forced landing that had brought them together the previous year.

"Well, I didn't make a big fuss about it." Morag smiled to herself.

"You made a *huge* fuss!" Gregor laughed.

"Well, I grew to like it."

"I don't think I have time to make them that much toast."

"I didn't learn to like it through toast . . . alone," said Morag.

"Uhm, if you two want to stop flirting, we can probably patch through the radio to Archland," said Pete, rolling his eyes.

Morag bit her lip and returned to the matter at hand. Gertie inched closer.

The connection was very crackly, and you could hear the high sounds of the wind swirling in the background, and what sounded like a tent flapping.

"Hello? Hello?"

"Hello, Archland, this is Carso Control. Over."

"Yes, hi, Carso Control. This is Archland."

"Hi, Skellan. Everything okay? Over."

"So, yes, it's pretty wild out there . . ."

There was sudden silence in the control room. The connection was lost.

CHAPTER 33

The odd thing was, Struan felt, the day had started well. They had waved off the plane, then it had been assumed, correctly, by Skellan and Denise that everyone had already gobbled their packed lunches, so they revealed they had prepared some cheese sandwiches—white bread, no salad cream in case there were any nervous nelly eaters in there. Which there were, obviously, so that all worked out very well.

Then there'd been the safety briefing. Skellan had played the tough guy warning them if they didn't do everything he said they'd be in terrible danger, and Denise had been very nice and mumsy and assured them that everything would be absolutely fine. They sometimes did it this way and sometimes did it the other way around depending on the group. Sometimes if Denise was too nice the children called her mum by mistake and got a little tearful, but this lot seemed fairly resilient; they'd lived in the shadow of Archland all their lives. It was hardly news for them. It was the nervous city kids they had to watch out for, who'd never seen a rabbit in the wild, never mind a puffin or a kestrel.

The tents were already up there, stored in a waterproof box in the cave, so there was a quick round of toilet stops then a second round of toilet stops, because the staff were experienced, and finally it was time to go. Although it was cold, they set off in fine fettle, tackling the gravel scree and large clambering rocks with ease. It was a clear day and they were excited with how high they climbed and, as they did so, how the other islands—Larbh, Cairn, Inchborn—and the mainland gradually came into view. Most of the kids wanted to stop every five seconds to look at some bright flowers, or try and smuggle some rocks to throw at each other later (the guides had a pretty good eye for this kind of thing) or drink the amount of water they had all been terrorized into believing they had to drink these days. Skellan and Denise gently chivvied them along. It was chilly but sunny—a nice day to be on the mountain. Struan found he was almost enjoying himself, although he started regretting carrying the guitar very quickly.

"I'll leave it at base camp," he said every time someone asked him about it banging against the backs of his legs; he was tempted to leave it in a cave they passed, where the children dared each other to run in and out, and screamed with glee when they did so.

"Something will pee in it," predicted Skellan gloomily. "If it's a fox, seriously, you don't want to know."

"No, keep the guitar!" said Wee Shugs. "We can do our song for Skellan and Denise!"

"Maybe we could do it without Shugs," said Jimmy.

"Shut it," said Shugs, aiming a kick up the scree but missing completely.

"That would be lovely," said Denise with quite a lot of enthusiasm for someone who'd listened to so many middle-management and Christian groups take out a guitar around the campfire, when she'd rather be listening to a podcast instead.

But he didn't mind it, Struan found, as they headed on, the children growing quieter as the exercise and fresh air took effect, and he couldn't quite believe, looking round, that he hadn't been up here for so long.

When he took in the extraordinary beauty of the Northwest Isles spread beneath his feet, he was struck once again by how lucky he was to live where he did. The air was fresh and sharp but so clear; the clouds scudding across the sky, reflecting onto the choppy waves beneath. Mure, the Faroes and Iceland were in one direction; America in the other, and due south to the landmass of Scotland, with its mountains and beautiful glens. He couldn't think of a better place to be. The higher he got, the further below him all his problems seemed. No wonder people climbed so much. It was a joy.

Struan beamed, even as the guitar hit him on the behind once more as he navigated a slightly tricky rock fall. Ach, well. He'd leave it at the camp and come back and get it the following day. The idea of making the summit was suddenly quite exciting, even if they weren't doing anything terribly complicated with ropes (there was one rope section, the fabled cliff, but it was carefully managed for the children and very straightforward, with a tiny bit of abseiling too).

The top of the Mermaid's Spyglass looked far overhead, which gave them the impression that they really were climbing; it was much more adventurous than he'd expected. If he got this touring job . . . he glanced round at the kids laughing and joking and arguing and saying the first thing that came into their heads. You knew where you were with kids. He thought about Saskia again and felt bad. He had, he was thinking, taken a wrong fork. Somewhere. Gone the wrong way. It wasn't like this mountain, where the path was difficult—but you could see where you were meant to be going.

He shepherded the children when they took a break.

"Do I have any volunteers to carry my guitar?" he said, swinging round to the scattered class, who were munching on chocolate bars.

"Nooooo!" they said in unison, except Anna-Lise, who shot up her hand and said, "I'll do it, sir," and everyone else groaned and rolled their eyes and Anna-Lise looked defiant.

"Thank you, Anna-Lise, you are a diamond amongst coal," said Struan, eyeing the tiny girl carefully. The guitar was about the same size as she was. "But actually I should stumble on my weary way. Thankfully as a musician I am always in tip-top physical condition."

"Why aren't you a proper musician, sir?" said Khalid, he of the annoying little sister.

"I am too!" said Struan, slightly offended.

"No, I mean, why aren't you like Harry Styles and that? Why do you spend time with us?"

"Because I prefer being with you?" said Struan.

They groaned again.

"No way," said Jimmy Gaskell. "You'd much rather be Harry Styles."

"I wish you were Harry Styles," said Oksana, very quietly.

"So do I," said Mrs. McGinty suddenly, and then put her hand over her mouth as if she'd surprised herself. The children were so shocked they didn't know if they were allowed to laugh or not.

"Harry Styles would be a terrible teacher!" said Struan. "He'd have to fly in on his private jet every day and he'd be exhausted! And all the girls would scream all the time and you wouldn't *learn* anything."

"I think we would still like our music teacher to be Harry Styles," said Bronte eventually.

"Yeah, yeah, okay. For that I am not sharing my chocolate," replied Struan.

"You haven't got any chocolate!"

"I forgot to bring any chocolate. Can anyone share their chocolate?"

Anna-Lise's hand was already in the air and he accepted one solitary, slightly manhandled chocolate button with good grace.

He then eyed up a rather large KitKat Mrs. McGinty was un-wrapping.

"Absolutely not," she said. "Besides, you'd have to share it with everyone."

Struan gave the children a look that made them laugh, teachers playing up outside of school.

They had reached the bottom of the "cliff" which was 15 meters of flat rock, clips already hammered in. This was the most thrilling part of the climb, which was otherwise mostly an amble.

Skellan patiently explained to them how to use the ropes and how he would clip them in and out, and how they couldn't fall off even if they wanted to, but also not to jump off just to be funny because it wasn't funny. It was possible to bang yourself on the cliffside if you weren't careful, and then he had to pull you up and his arms got tired so who knew what might happen? The children looked slightly frightened again until Denise bustled in with a bag for their chocolate wrappers, reassuring them they'd be all right. Skellan clambered up first, like a monkey, which impressed absolutely everybody, whilst Denise stayed at the bottom to encourage the nervous climbers.

Jimmy pushed his way to the front as soon as volunteers were required, grabbing the helmet from Denise. Struan would rather one of the other kids went first—it didn't do any good to bullies when they got their own way, even when they were only showing off. They needed to be quashed immediately, for their own good as well as everyone else's. But Struan's fears were tempered when, halfway up, Jimmy skidded and lost his footing and did indeed end up dangling, feet bouncing off the bare cliff face, as Skellan hauled him up and everyone managed to smile about it. Jimmy could not take it in good part, and looked furious.

"There was something wrong with my clip," he shouted loudly at the top.

"Yeah, it had your fat bum in it," shouted up Khalid, unusually bravely, and Struan didn't have the heart to tell him off for it.

"You do it then!" shouted Jimmy. "You'll probably *die*." So Khalid did do it, perfectly and without fuss, and earned a huge round of applause from his classmates.

Then the girls shuttled up, and the remaining boys, until finally it was only Oksana left at the bottom. Struan looked at her.

"Come on now, Oksana," said Mrs. McGinty, busying herself. "Up you pop!"

Denise glanced up. She was used to nervous children like this and was ready to help.

"You're going to be okay," she said calmly.

Oksana sighed and looked at Struan.

"What is it?"

She looked around and they moved somewhere slightly quieter. When she spoke you could hardly hear her voice at all.

"They bombed the house next door," the little girl finally said, very very quietly. She had never spoken about the Donbas. There were groups for Ukrainians in Fort William and Struan knew her mother took her to those in the hope she would express herself in her own language.

"We had to climb over the wall."

This was in a whisper. Struan didn't say anything. He couldn't imagine such horror, especially here where it was so very safe. Then he thought about it. Screw it, the one thing this child did not need after being torn halfway across Europe, running away from a war, was some stupid idea of character-building.

"That's okay," he said, mildly. "Want to head back down? Or we could lift you up. I bet Skellan could. You don't have to do anything you don't want to."

"Oksana Dineko! Come here immediately!" said Mrs. McGinty. "We need to get over our fears."

Oksana and Struan exchanged a look. Struan knew that one of the first rules of teaching was never to publicly disagree with another teacher; it was terribly unprofessional and very bad form. As well as rude. But nonetheless. That rule was superseded by another, more important rule. Never ever humiliate a child. Because children can carry that forever.

"Screw it," he said. "You don't have to go if you don't want to."

Oksana glanced upward.

"You can do it!" shouted Isla, and Bronte joined in.

Oksana frowned. She had been very quiet since she arrived in the UK; understandably, as she didn't speak all that much English, except what her harassed mother had tried to teach her on the long journey through Poland. But she was clever, and it was soon obvious she understood everything. She had still, however, kept herself a little apart from her classmates who had been at first curious, then respectful, and sometimes warm.

Oksana looked at them, then back at Struan, who shrugged and kept his expression completely neutral. Then suddenly, as if giving herself a talking-to, Oksana shook herself, and Struan absolutely hated to see it. But still: she then pulled herself carefully, hand over hand, feet bouncing off the rock, cheered on by her classmates shouting words of encouragement and support. By the time she reached the top her face was absolutely beaming with happiness and pride, as they streamed around in a tight pack, patting her on the back and congratulating her.

Well, well, thought Struan. You didn't get that playing weddings in a band.

He even grinned at Pamela McGinty, before he realized it was his turn. Struan had no problem playing music in public, standing in front of an audience, or any kind of performing really.

But he had quite a few problems climbing up a rope; namely that he was physically very uncoordinated, not terribly brave or athletic, and was actually quite afraid of heights.

Well, there wasn't much to be done about it now. He was being ridiculous, he told himself, even as he found his hands shaking as he approached the rock. It didn't look so small after all, now he was up close to it. Just do what the other kids did he told himself. God, even Anne-Marie had managed it, and she was the size of a fairy. Mind you, being the size of a fairy was probably helpful when it came to hauling your own body weight up a great big piece of smooth stone.

Struan attempted to take to the climbing rope in an urbane manner. Unfortunately he misjudged the pull and ended up scrabbling with his feet in midair as the children laughed hysterically. Khalid took photographs on the disposable camera he had bought exactly for this purpose as phones weren't allowed, but Struan didn't mind. It actually put mean wee Jimmy in a better mood, as he was able to point out loudly that he hadn't been as rubbish as Sir. Struan did his best to remember that Jimmy was the youngest of four fairly feisty boys and an aggressive father, which, even if it didn't make him much more likeable to be around, certainly made him more explicable.

All successfully up the cliff, they found themselves more exposed to the elements, on the ridge. They bundled up, pulled down their hats, and set their wee faces against the wind, trudging on, less talk and chatter now half of them had barely slept a wink from excitement the previous evening.

The route crept round the mountain at one point, and the

north face was exposed and absolutely punishing. The views were remarkable—there was nothing beyond Archland and you felt tiny in the world, clinging to a rock, and not even a very big rock, plonked in the middle of an endless, unfriendly sea. In the far distance was the glimpse of an occasional vast tanker, plowing the routes to Scandinavia, remote in the huge passageway of the northern waters. And to the northeast was the great and beautiful field of windmills, all whirring like crazy in the rising wind. It was beautiful; even lovelier for knowing it was clean, free power, en route to warm homes and keeping people safe. Struan absolutely loved them. Then he remembered that there was going to be no power tonight because they were camping out on a ridiculous mountainside like a bunch of idiots, and that brought him back down to earth a little bit.

Round this side, the wind was too noisy for them even to hear one another, and Skellan beckoned them fiercely, ushering the little bodies onward to the relative calm of the other side of the mountain. An hour later they had made it, more than halfway up, to the sheltered natural little outcrop that had become a famous campsite. White-painted stones marked the edges of the flat, grassy ledge. Birds stayed away, as the regular influxes of humans made them less than keen to build their nests there, but they could be seen shearing up and down to the water nearby.

The tents were already there, all set up and waiting, to Struan's massive relief. Putting tents up was part of the teenagers' trips, not the little ones'. There was a cave there where gear was stored in boxes. It was too low, dripping damp and dark to sleep in though, filled with guano to boot. Struan was tired. Skellan and Denise of course were showing no ill effects at all, and they'd already nipped up that morning to fix the tents. But Struan wouldn't have wanted to start fixing poles to things for any money. It wasn't what he considered one of his core skills. Mind you, as soon as it was made clear to him that he was going to have to explain to the children what a long-drop toilet was, it became clear he had quite a lot to learn.

Denise lit a fire in the fire pit immediately, warning the kids to stay well back, but it's difficult to keep children away from a fire, particularly considering that as soon as they stopped walking, the bitter coldness immediately became apparent. The sun had passed over them on its journey west, and the clearing was in shade. The fire was extremely welcome as it crackled high, and Denise took out a large saucepan that was stored there and started pulling out big packets of sausages from her bag.

The children washed up in the little stream, which turned into a waterfall on its way down the mountain, fretted about sheep poo, and queued up by Struan if they needed medication. Baked potatoes were cooked in their skins in the base of the fire, wrapped in tinfoil, so they were smoky and crunchy on the outside and soft and delicious within, with copious amounts of butter and salt to make them even more tasty. A sausage eaten outside with the drifting smoke of a peat fire, and the sun going down, is a wonderful thing, even if the air is cold. Everyone was wrapped in old blankets from the cave. The children smelled of sheep, and cuddled up in front of the fire, chattering loudly and getting through more sausages than you might consider possible.

Suddenly Anne-Marie yelled loudly and pointed. The birds had been the usual mix of gulls and guillemots coming down the cliff, but down below, heading toward the water, they suddenly saw a group of puffins, tearing down like tiny dive bombers.

"Look, look!" she shouted and the children ran to see them, being called back quite sternly by the organizers before they breached the row of white-painted stones that marked the beginning of the slope of the ridge.

They were a joyous sight, the little seabirds, their tiny comical feet pointing upward as they dived full length to grab the fish out of the water.

Struan poured some fresh hot tea into his flask cup and caught the eye of Denise, who was smiling at him.

"Pretty cool huh?" she said, looking at the excited, engaged children.

"You must get bored of seeing it all the time," said Struan.

"I never do," she said. "Kids . . . they're all the same underneath. All of them. Rich, poor, lucky, unlucky . . . they all need to be out in the fresh air. Using those young limbs they're born with. I love it."

Struan looked at Oksana, who was now in the middle of a group of four girls, all of them pointing excitedly. Khalid, normally so timid and skinny in the class full of farmers' sons, had, by virtue of cleverly packing a camera, become the most important person there. He was now the official recorder of the trip and everyone was begging for pictures of them with the birds in the shot. None of these photos would be at all useful, showing either a bird and half an out-of-focus head, or a head and a gray blur, but Khalid's future popularity was assured. Even Jimmy and his henchmen were enjoying the bird display and, pleasingly, weren't throwing stones at the creatures.

"Yup," he said with a small lump in his throat.

Later, the kids had sung along to every single song Struan knew and he was slightly worried he was going to default to "The Wheels on the Bus."

Then, chilled and worn out, they had turned in with a surprisingly low level of complaints and chitter-chatter, long-drop toilets and all. Struan had found Skellan had made their tent relatively comfortable with a big flashlight and decent mats and realized he was happily exhausted. After no sleep the night before, a long energetic day, lots of fresh air, and about the right number of sausages (i.e., one more than what would generally be considered a disgusting number of sausages) he was more than ready for bed.

He had shepherded the boys into their sleeping bags—no getting changed and no washing went down extremely well, although there was some cursory tooth-brushing. It was notably cold, but they were all more or less dressed for the weather, and bundled up in their tents. Struan reminded them he was just outside, and that under no circumstances were they to get up and wander off in the dark. This wasn't something that seemed likely to happen, even with the made-up story that went around every year about how someone's big brother's friend had been on a trip and got up to go for a pee in the middle of the night and *never came back again*, even though they searched the mountain for months! Sometimes the story involved bones. It never actually involved anyone anybody knew, but it was generally quite useful for the teachers to keep the kids more or less where they had to be.

With the minimal bedtime preparations done, they got back round the campfire, and, for the last time that night, Struan took out his guitar.

Once he'd given them the notes, they'd sung for Skellan and Denise, so soft and gently and beautifully into the flaming sunset that Denise got slightly tearful and even the birds, it seemed, stopped what they were doing to hear, all alone, on top of a mountain in a completely deserted, utterly lonely, cold, and desolate place, the beautiful sound of children singing.

CHAPTER 34

S kellan?" said Morag again into the radio. "Skellan, can you hear me? Over."

There was more crackling whilst, back on Carso, the three looked at each other, worriedly.

"Yes, yes, we're here."

There was a sigh of relief.

"And . . ."

"Not ideal to be honest."

Skellan explained that he had gone out with a flashlight, but hadn't made it a few steps before he declared it absolutely unsafe for children, the wind whipping the snow up into complete white-out conditions. They'd be falling over the edge of the ledge. It was still dark now but if this kept on, there wouldn't be any visibility at dawn either.

All the kids were awake; many had painfully useless cheap sleeping bags that couldn't keep them warm, and the snowstorm meant they couldn't light the fire. They'd moved them all into the cave, but the children were frightened. The staff joined all the sleeping bags together and shepherded them into a large mass, like puppies, half of the unzipped bags below their bodies and half above to try and keep them snug.

Back at control, Morag was staring out into the night.

"How's the forecast?" Skellan asked. His normal laid-back tone sounded more concerned.

"I can't see it shifting," said Morag. "Not for a while."

"It's . . . it's very cold up here."

"Yup," said Morag.

"And I think . . . I think the abseiling cliff. I think that isn't going to work in this. I'm not sure we could get them down it. In zero visibility, this temperature."

"How much food have you got?"

"Two meals. But it's the cold, really. I'm not happy. I'm really not happy, Morag."

"You couldn't have known. Bloody Met Office."

"Yes."

There was a pause. Morag glanced over to where the helicopter normally sat; it was gone.

"Have you spoken to Gavin?"

"I have," said Skellan. "They're way over the other side; there's a woman having a baby on Mure."

"You're kidding," said Morag. "Couldn't she have held it in?"

"Oh, there's always something," Skellan said in a flat tone.

"Yes, but that's one baby; this is loads of children!"

"Even if that were possible and they were in fact willing to dump a woman in labor, which let's just say, they aren't," said Skellan drily, "there's complications. They're picking up, taking to the mainland, then they'll need a new crew. We'd need to do loads of trips . . ."

"And they're miles away," said Morag.

"Aye," said Skellan.

"What about Aberdeen?"

Aberdeen search and rescue was a very very long way away indeed.

"It's been a bad night for everyone," said Pete, glancing up and reading off the monitor.

There was a silence.

"Some of these kids," said Skellan. "They're in trainers and My Little Pony jackets that have barely been outside the shopping center."

"Uh-huh," said Morag.

Morag thought of the children, parked there on the ledge. Freezing cold. So frightened.

"I'll get back to you, Skellan. Over," she said, clicking off and turning round. They needed solutions.

They all thought about the cliff. If that was too windy or buried in snow . . .

She radioed Gregor.

"You could drop them supplies," he said immediately. "Heat packs too. If it clears enough to fly."

Morag had thought that also. "Do you really think it's that bad?" she asked nervously.

"I absolutely do," said Gregor. "And they won't have supplies for more than a night. I mean, that walk is meant to be a gentle stroll, not a life-threatening experience. They're ten!"

"Bloody bloody bloody Met Office," said Morag.

"It's not their fault," said Gregor. "The robots will take over totally and start doing it soon enough."

"Well, that isn't cheering me up."

"And global warming will mean it'll stop happening," said Pete.

"No, it won't!" snapped Morag. "It makes extreme weather events more likely! That's what . . ."

She saw Pete's stricken face.

"Sorry," she said. "I'm just on edge."

"We'll figure it out," said Gregor. There was music just about discernible on the line.

"What's going on with you?" said Morag.

"Oh, they've found the old priests' cellar," said Gregor. "Apparently they used to get very good wine every year from the Vatican. It's all still down there. Well, not anymore."

"Are they behaving themselves?"

"They are not," said Gregor, with commendable restraint, considering he prized a quiet life above almost all things. "They have written me an IOU and I believe there is a reasonable chance that by the time they get back, the happy couple will be divorced."

"Can't you tell Barbara to bite them?"

"Barbara doesn't mind other people getting married. It's only you and me she's worried about."

There was a silence. If they hadn't been surrounded by other people and on an open radio mike being listened to by more or less everyone in the village and surrounding area, Morag would desperately have wanted to know more at this point, even as the snow clouded the window and you couldn't even see a trace of Inchborn in the distance.

"Uhm," said Morag.

They were saved by a loud clatter and a squawk down the mike.

"Oh God," said Gregor. "They're upsetting the chickens. I'd better go."

"Come here, you! I just want an egg sandwich!" came a loud voice in the background, then the line went dead. Morag winced.

Then she patched through to Skellan again.

"Uhm, okay," she said. "I mean, there's no point in us landing if you can't get down, is there?"

"Well, no," said Skellan. But he agreed to the supply drop.

Morag tried to visualize the ledge on the mountain but she couldn't. It was, she was pretty sure, extremely small.

"What would you need?"

Quietly, unobtrusively, Gertie was by her elbow with a notepad and pen. Morag looked up gratefully as Gertie took notes.

"Clothes. Blankets. Hand warmers. A gas stove if you could manage."

"I'm not throwing a gas stove out of an aeroplane."

"You could wrap it up carefully. And fly really low."

"I am not flying really low in a snowstorm across a mountain," said Morag. "And Ranald won't either. Sorry. I can send lots of firelights and matches and some wood if that helps."

"It will," said Skellan. "Just . . . I mean we don't know how long it will take this damn thing to end."

Morag looked out. "Can you wait till first light? That will help with how low I can go," she said.

There was a pause.

"Yes," he said. "But please. Come quick after that."

GERTIE STOOD UP immediately.

"I'll go and round stuff up."

Morag frowned. "What, now?"

It was just 5 a.m.

"What do you think we do at ScotNorth?" said Gertie. "Roll up whenever we like, like we've got our own plane?"

Morag smiled in genuine surprise at her cheek, as Gertie took the list, put on her four layers of clothing, and headed off back out into the night.

Morag sighed and stared out of the window. She'd wait an hour or so before calling Erno and Gramps. It would be all hands on deck then.

She was not a religious person, Morag, certainly not by the fairly cast-iron standards of the local kirk. But she stared out into the swirling dark and said a little prayer.

CHAPTER 35

Sure enough the tiny supermarket was already readying itself for the day; milk and egg deliveries came early, and the bakery was up and running. The newspapers were coming in. They opened at 6:30 a.m., and there was a lot to do before then.

Gertie knocked nervously at the back door. They would barely remember her now, would they? She'd seen the girls on the front, for sure; you could hardly avoid that in this town. But she hadn't seen Mr. Wainwright. Hopefully he wouldn't be in so early.

To her disappointment—they were a bit short-staffed—her old boss was indeed there, looking as craggy and forbidding as ever, helping pull the milk off the float from Johannes. She stopped short.

Mr. Wainwright looked up, and to her total surprise, his face broke into a smile.

"Wee Gertie! I thought you'd left us forever!"

"Uh . . ." she stuttered, feeling pink. "No."

"What are you doing out in *this*?" he said, gesturing to the swirling air. "The milk's practically frozen! Come on, give us a hand to get it inside."

Gertie did so, finding it easier to act than speak.

"No, I mean it though," he persisted, once they were inside the blessedly warm shop, the fluorescent light buzzing in a way Gertie found strangely comforting after all this time. "What on earth are you doing? The planes don't go this early, do they?"

He eyed her sternly.

"Is Morag working you too hard? You're always welcome back here, you know. No questions asked."

He had actually just asked about a billion questions but Gertie politely didn't point this out.

"No," she said, her voice sounding small. Then she remembered. This was important. She cleared her throat. "It's the Archland trip. The kids."

Mr. Wainwright immediately grabbed at his coat. "Oh my God, of course," he said, shaking his head. "I never thought . . . I never thought . . . Mine are grown up," he added, apologetically. "Oh my God. Are they all right?"

"We're going to drop some food and blankets and things," said Gertie, "just to make sure. In case they can't get down for a while."

Mr. Wainwright started nodding immediately. "Yes, yes. Here."

He looked around and started pulling out food. Chocolate biscuits, packet noodles, bottles of water. Babybels.

"Not the Babybels!!!" said Gertie. "They're so expensive!"

"Nobody's paying for these."

Gertie blinked. This was completely unheard of.

"Nothing but the best for those babies."

Gertie nodded in amazement and held out a large bag. He would have filled two if she hadn't told him gently there was a limit to how much they could safely drop, and she still needed as many kindling blocks as she could manage. They were practically out of them, it being May, so the front of the shop was unhelpfully taken up with sunglasses and buckets and spades. Luckily they found kindling blocks and firelighters in the barbecue section, and in fact, added a couple of disposable barbecues, just in case the staff could find enough shelter to light them. It couldn't hurt.

"Okay, that's about all I can carry," said Gertie.

"Oh, we can do better than that," said Mr. Wainwright. "Surely. I walked here—I didn't think the Porsche would manage in this weather . . ."

"Milk float won't make it to the airfield," said the milkman, shaking his head. "I'm amazed she made it this far to be honest."

They looked at the pile on the ground.

"Of course I'll . . ."

He had a considerable stomach, Mr. Wainwright. Gertie wasn't sure she really wanted him out in the storm. She didn't want to find herself responsible for anything else going wrong.

Suddenly there was a commotion at the front of the store—a great banging on the window.

Gertie squinted forward to see who it was.

CHAPTER 36

"Come on then!" Jean was shouting. "It's bloody *freezing* out here!"

Wrapped in twenty layers of knitwear apiece were the KCs. All of them except Elspeth. Majabeen, Jean, the twins, Marian bringing up the rear, all waving frantically.

Instinctively, Gertie put in the code to unlock the door. They hadn't changed it, which they should have.

"We brought knitwear!" announced Jean, loudly and, probably, unnecessarily.

"How did you know?!"

"Someone was listening to the radio channel," said Jean, unwilling to admit that perhaps, occasionally, she and Ranald had chatted on it. Just occasionally. They did Wordle together, over the phone. And in the night sometimes. It was hard to sleep as you got older. And it was perfectly innocent anyway so Gertie could shut up.

She looked at Gertie.

"You're not too cross with us for being interfering old busybodies?"

"We brought blankets for the children," added Majabeen.

Gertie looked at them, smiled, and shook her head.

"Sometimes," she said. "I suppose sometimes the world needs interfering old busybodies."

"Are you kidding?" said Jean, taking her beloved daughter in her arms. "It wouldn't run without them."

Gertie indicated the bags of stuff on the floor.

Marian stepped forward immediately and all the others were right there too. Carrying heavy shopping bags through extremely difficult weather was a school of expertise the middle-aged women of Carso had mastered decades before.

"Okay!" shouted Jean, who was wearing a bright purple knitted coat so was the easiest to spot in the blizzarding, slowly dawning day. "Follow me!"

And so it was with amazement that Morag and Ranald saw the party stagger in, huge misshapen forms loaded with bags and slowly trudging the kilometer-long road, straight into the wind and weather, treading, like King Wenceslas, in each other's footsteps.

"Well," Morag said, as they deposited their bounty on the airport floor. "Well. This is going to cover it."

"Bring the bairns home!" said Jean and Morag glanced at her, and realized she was talking to Ranald, who had arrived unobtrusively half an hour before, and was examining printouts of the weather forecast. He looked back at Jean and nodded, briefly.

CHAPTER 37

Struan wasn't sure what woke him, but the first thing he noticed was that it was cold. Very very cold. And something felt odd. The condensation inside the tent was forming into ice. He grabbed his phone and turned on the flashlight. Skellan—who had, in fact, shaken Struan awake in passing—was no longer there. Struan rubbed his eyes, grabbed the water bottle by his bed, and took a long pull—the water was absolutely freezing. When he unzipped the tent, he couldn't believe his eyes. The wind was roaring, he realized; the flakes were a total white-out. They'd been expecting rain but this was something else altogether. There was a larger, better flashlight there and he swapped out his phone for it; there was no signal anyway.

He grabbed his jacket, put on his gloves, and headed out.

Outside was a maelstrom. Standing up in the full path of the wind was extraordinary; they weren't quite exposed to the northern flank, which was funneling snow straight down from the poles at high speeds, but even so, it was very unnerving. He felt like Captain Scott.

He turned toward the mountainside. Already, the tents were racketing and bucketing in the wind. Struan panicked, wondering if there were children inside, but, as his eyes adjusted, he could make out all the pinpricks of light—they were all huddling in the cave, squeezed in together, with Skellan and Denise.

He made his way over to it and the children's delight turned to dismay as they realized it was just him, rather than someone arrived to get them out of there.

"Hey!" he said. "This isn't a bit of rain!"

There were very weak smiles. He decided to play it up for all he was worth.

"Well," he said. "Maybe it'll blow away my guitar and that will be one good thing."

More weak smiles.

"Are we going to be all right, sir?"

Skellan stood forward. "Of course you are," he said quickly. "I'm going to pile you under all the sleeping bags together."

"I'm no' going near the boys—yuk," said Bronte, and Denise pointed out that that was going to be very chilly otherwise and Bronte asked if they would stop farting and Jimmy Gaskell said he would not, and demonstrated thusly, and Struan was slightly heartened.

". . . and keep us warm, and the snow will stop and then we'll have a big snowball fight and run around and have a great time," finished Skellan.

"Can we maybe just go home?" said Khalid, his voice a little shaky and several people agreed with him.

"Well, let's see," said Skellan. "Now, who wants an energy bar?"

Denise was bringing all the sleeping bags from the tents.

"We'll use them to line the cave," she explained. "Keep the drafts out."

Struan frowned.

"You really think it's going to get that cold?"

Denise shrugged. "Och, just when you think the mountains have thrown all there is to throw at you . . ." Her voice trailed off. "You can never predict it," she said. "That's the mountains for you."

CHAPTER 38

Morning crept painfully slowly through the white-out; you could barely notice. There was a change from black, to navy blue, to dark gray. And the flakes kept coming. Morag stared out ominously, but finally, at around 7 a.m., turned to Ranald. He was less worried about the snow than he was about crosswinds. Heavy, large planes didn't really suffer, but their little twin otter wasn't terribly happy in them.

"Gonne be bumpy."

Morag nodded.

"You know," she said. "When you say you could fly this route blindfolded."

Ranald nodded. "Yup," he said. "Today's sure the day to test it out."

There was no hope of ferries or flights today. The helos weren't there, and in any case wouldn't be able to get a whole clutch off a mountain. Only Dolly 2 could make it. Mackintosh and Pete were already out, shoveling snow off the gritted runway.

The same could not be said of the other end. It would depend on the weather whether they would drop supplies and return, and wait it out for tomorrow, or attempt a landing today if conditions improved.

Morag sat down with Gertie, who would be needed in case they couldn't land and useful if they did, and outlined what they were going to do. Gertie was going to have to be ready. Morag could really do with Nalitha, very familiar with the plane, but Gertie could manage. There was a hatch at the back of the plane. Morag would fly low; Ranald would come back and open the hatch. They'd be as accurate as they could—Ranald started talking about his father's bombing missions again. And they had two parcels, bundled up in bubble wrap, wrapped in wool, so even if one missed they'd still call it a success.

It was going to be difficult flying. Very difficult. Low, in terrible conditions. Morag thought back to her old job: long miles of nothing, copiloting holidaymakers up and down to safe airports in Portugal, Spain, and Greece; happy children, drunken stag nights; safe, repetitive, solid flying.

This . . . this was the real thing. This would take every ounce of her skill and training and experience. She felt nothing but excitement.

Morag caught Ranald looking at her, reading her every thought. He winked, slowly, understanding it all, and this made her even more reassured. Gramps had no doubt at all they could do it. It was what they had trained for, practiced for, after all. He was looking forward to it.

MORAG WENT OUT to walk to the plane. The wind grabbed her breath, shocked her as she went out into the maelstrom. Oh, those babies, she thought suddenly. Those poor babies.

She noticed a commotion in the tin shed. Gertie had already gone forward toward it.

It was, Morag realized, the parents. Word had gotten around. She frowned and looked back at the office, but then realized Gertie was already there, dealing with everything as best she could.

"When are they coming home?" someone was demanding. "Why are you even still here? Why didn't you go last night?"

"Where are the helicopters? Can't the boat go?"

"Are they safe? I want to talk to my kid right now!"

"This isn't a supermarket, Gertrude! Kids could die."

Gertie had her hand up trying to calm the situation but her color was dangerously high. She wanted to tell them everything would be all right, but what if that wasn't true? What if it really was dangerous? Khalid's mum was in floods of tears. Many were shaking. They were right. This wasn't the supermarket.

And perhaps she wasn't the right person to go. Maybe she couldn't do it. The wind was making even louder noises across the rattling tin can of the airport, and she felt the worry build inside her.

Just as Morag was wondering what would be the best thing to do, and if interceding would make it look like she didn't trust Gertie either, suddenly the KCs had materialized, in a line, between Gertie's desk and the families.

"Listen!" Jean was shouting. "Do you not think these guys have been flying here forever? Do you not think those people up in Archland aren't trained?"

"My kid only has an Iron Man sleeping bag," said Jimmy's mum, worried. "I'm not even sure it's suitable for outdoor use. The year I went the sun shone all the time and we were too hot. I thought it was just a joke."

"They'll be getting extra blankets," said Jean, sharply. The other KCs were forming a barrier between Gertie and the mothers.

"Gertie is going to go and help . . . We're going to make sure everything is okay here," Jean said firmly, turning her face toward her daughter, who nodded.

"Magnificent woman!" murmured Ranald to Morag, who looked at him curiously.

"And we're staying here to look after you," said Jean. "Don't worry. They're not going to let you down. Gertie would never let you down."

Gertie felt a lump in her throat.

One of the mothers looked out toward the weather through the heavy doors, which were shaking in place, and she made a tiny sound of anguish.

"Right," said Morag, briskly and calmly. "Let's get going. Come on, Gertie."

CHAPTER 39

The airfield, unprotected from the wind, was a howling abyss. Pete and Mackintosh, normally so relaxed about everything, were out shoveling furiously still. The grit and salt had done their work too; everything around them was white, but the runway was black.

Morag checked her phone and sighed.

"What?"

"Helo is still out. Climbers trapped all over the place; one with a broken leg, exposed. That beats some kids in a cave, I'm afraid."

"Well, it shouldn't," said Ranald.

"They'll be fine," said Morag, once again, trying to make herself believe it.

They looked at one another.

"The pilots won't have any more legal hours left in them," said Morag, saying what she knew Ranald was thinking.

"They'll get some in from the rigs."

"They would," said Morag. "If they didn't stop decommissioning all the bloody rigs. They're miles away."

RANALD CHECKED THEY were full on fuel—it could take them there and back twice if they needed to, or they could circle. Anything flexible. Air traffic control wasn't an issue, given nobody else was flying near them that day; everyone was avoiding the storm. Glasgow wished them well and promised to keep an eye out, and thanked them.

The bags were loaded; they were fuel heavy and weight light, which was useful and something to bear in mind. Morag and Ranald looked at each other once again, and then ahead at the swirling flakes on the runway.

"You do the honors," said Morag. Ranald was due to retire in the next year or two. There wouldn't be many more opportunities like this.

CHAPTER 40

A strange silence had settled on the children, as they huddled under the tiny unzipped sleeping bag tent. Skellan and Denise were trying their hardest to keep the fire going by the entrance to the cave, but it was hard work, with little light and heat coming from it, but a great load of choking smoke, and they were fast getting through their firelights and matches. They were also conferring closely with one another. Finally, Denise nodded and Skellan handed her the radio.

Mrs. McGinty, on the other hand, seemed to have lost her head completely. Instead of doing what she normally did—bark orders at children in a seemingly random fashion—she was sitting, numbly, not responding.

Struan kept telling himself they'd be fine. They were in Britain for goodness' sake. One of the most mild and friendly climates in the world. He thought of the climbers every year who got caught out by unseasonable weather and inappropriate footwear, and were rescued anyway. These kids were in supermarket trainers.

Yes, he told himself again. But that was the odd climber here and there. This was a whole party of schoolchildren. They'd activate the entire RAF if they had to; of course they would. It would be a national scandal. So. There was no point in dwelling. They would be fine. Oksana was on the brink of tears and he didn't want them to become infectious, as these things so often did.

"Come on then," he shouted, putting a snowball over the cave.

"Snowball competition! Let's see who can get it furthest off the ledge!!" and of all people Jimmy came out to join him.

"Me!" he said loudly, and before too long most of the children were venturing out, jumping up and down and gathering snow up in their mittens. Denise narrowed her mouth; she wasn't keen on their hands getting wet in this cold, but on the other hand, they were rushing around and taking their minds off things, and that was the best thing for them. She glanced at Skellan, who nodded, looked at Mrs. McGinty, who was holding her lifeless phone in her hands and staring at it. A look passed between them, then Denise moved toward Struan.

"Uhm," she said. "Okay, I think . . . Skellan is going to climb down."

Struan looked beyond the ridge edge. It was absolutely terrifying out there. "You're kidding. In this?"

"He knows it really well and he'll be very careful." She flushed, proud of her partner.

"Yes, but why??"

"We're worried about the plane. It won't be able to land if the runway is too snowy. He can put out the landing lights. And he wants to take a look at the cliff."

"Why?" said Struan, who hadn't given it much thought at all. As soon as the snow stopped he reckoned they were just heading down the hill again. He hadn't thought about the cliff at all.

"If it's iced over . . ." Denise shrugged. "It can be pretty tough to get down."

"When you say tough?"

She blinked. "The kids couldn't do it."

Struan frowned.

"But what does . . ."

"Skellan's going to take a look," she hissed. "Don't say anything. And don't tell *her*."

She clearly meant Mrs. McGinty. Struan nodded, but suddenly he found himself a little more scared.

"I'm going to focus on the fire," she said. "Try and get a kettle boiling."

This seemed unlikely with the pathetic flickering of the flames, but there didn't seem much else to say.

"Keep them moving and engaged," said Denise. "But maybe . . . not with their fingers out. In case of frostbite."

SKELLAN MOVED CAREFULLY. He had been a professional climbing guide for twenty years.

He knew this mountain like the back of his hand, in every wind and weather. Which is why he knew better than to disrespect it, even for an instant. Without a wink of sleep and no coffee, it was difficult. But not impossible. And down at the base camp there were more firelighters, flasks—everything they'd need. He could fill a rucksack and make his way back, he was sure of it. Plus, he could light the landing lights for the plane. He had a lot of respect for Morag and Ranald, but knew they wouldn't be out on a day like today if there was any choice in the matter at all.

Denise was on the radio. The wind was like a knife on his face, especially when he circuited on the narrow path round the north face. There, the full fury of the snowstorm hit him, over and over again; straight down from the North Pole, to a rock in the middle of the ocean; a wind, screaming, "You don't belong here; you are not part of this! This is not for humans! Leave! LEAVE!" like the wrathful mermaid herself, back from the grave, no longer looking through the telescope for her earthly lover, who would never return.

And Skellan, who respected the elements, bowed his head into the wind and agreed. They should not be there. "But please," he muttered under his breath, "please spare the children."

But the wind was making no promises. And when he saw the cliff, he drew in a sudden intake of breath.

CHAPTER 41

Gertie sat in the first row of the little cabin and she pulled back the curtain. She couldn't understand what Morag and Ranald were doing. She was slightly frightened, but they seemed very calm and capable, so she was trying to follow their lead.

Also she couldn't get out of her mind how funny and joyous the kids had been the day before. How ready for an adventure. The idea of them being up there all by themselves . . . her nerves paled by comparison. She held the bags tightly. They had wrapped the bottles and firelighters carefully in the woolens. The hand warmers were the most useful; you broke them open and they heated you up. Then everything was wrapped in plastic and tied with twine, as carefully and well as she could do, which was actually pretty well, given her experience with knots. Morag had picked it up and glanced at it, nodding briefly, which to Gertie was the highest praise.

"Nah, you do it," said Ranald finally to Morag at the controls. Morag looked at him. "Your eyes are a lot younger than mine," he said finally. "I'm fine, I'm fine. But we want perfect. Not fine."

"You also have thirty-five years more experience than me," said Morag, but nonetheless she took left seat, checked, and rechecked the instruments.

"Okay," said Morag, as Ranald filed the flight plan.

"We're going straight to Archland full northbound. We're going to circle the Mermaid's Spyglass, then bring it down to forty meters, open the rear hatch, and hopefully gently drop onto the ridge . . ."

Morag grinned again. "This is proper *Mission: Impossible!*"

"Don't think you're up to it?"

"Speak for yourself, Gramps."

It comforted Gertie immeasurably to hear them talk like this when she herself was scared rigid. She was terrified all right, but she was going to do it.

". . . then Skellan is on his way down to base to hopefully sort out the runway. If it's clearing, we can wait to land. If it isn't, we'll have to come back. There's no hangar of course: if Dolly gets iced up we're just adding to the problem."

Ranald nodded. "We'll make the decision at the time."

"It'll be short."

"We've plenty of fuel. Don't worry about it. Knowing we're here will give them a shot of adrenaline too. Get them scampering down. They're like mountain goats—children."

Morag nodded.

"Okay," she said. "Throttle back."

SKELLAN STARED AT the cliff in consternation. Not only was it a full sheet of ice from the snow that had landed there and then frozen over; the fixed ropes had also been torn out by the wind. He cursed. They were solid; they had to be. It was wild up here; the rocks had cracked around it. But now it was a flat blank slope of nothing, an eighteen-foot drop of sheer ice.

GERTIE WASN'T AN experienced enough traveler to know, thank God, how difficult that flight was. Even though Morag had once flown without instruments on the little plane, she had done it in full and perfect visibility. This was the opposite of that. Outside was just a maelstrom of flakes and the wind buffeting them every which way. Ranald had his head bent over the flight plan, calculating their speed, as well as checking the instruments every two seconds to make sure they weren't actually plummeting downward into an invisible sea.

"We all right?" said Morag, holding the juddering yoke. Ranald indicated ahead.

What had to be the Larbh lighthouse was sending out its beam, much bent and twisted through the heavy snow, but visible. They both nodded.

The plane bumped and shook as it jiggled in the air. This was more or less how Gertie had always expected flying to be, like being on the back of a horse, so it didn't bother her much. She looked out of the cockpit window ahead; they had propped open the cockpit door so she could see straight into the whirling flakes. She saw the faint lighthouses of Larbh, Inchborn, and Cairn for the first time from above; saw how their lights intertwined when they swung into sync with one another.

"Wow," she said, and Morag glanced at her, pleasantly surprised.

After twenty-five minutes, where they flew by instruments alone, Morag turned around again and was even more surprised when she saw Gertie sitting, knitting away calmly, as if they weren't on a tiny bouncing prop plane in the middle of an unpredictable snowstorm.

"What are you . . . ?"

"It's very calming," said Gertie, somewhat defensively.

"Ha," said Morag warmly. Then: "I approve."

Then two seconds later: "Did we not have the discussion about whether you could have knitting needles in an airline cabin?"

Ranald snorted loudly.

"What?"

"Oh, the KCs had us on that one way before you came."

"All this time Nalitha's been letting knitting needles in the cabin?!"

The plane dropped 12 meters through an air pocket and everyone's stomachs rose. Morag fought harder with the yoke.

"This is what's known as running a local service, Morag."

"Breaking international aviation law?"

Gertie looked up, the clicking stopping temporarily.

"No, you're fine," said Morag, fixing the nose carefully according to Ranald's calculations. They were beyond the reach of the lighthouses now. "Keep knitting. It can be our Very Exciting Scarf. Something to remember today by."

The radio crackled, but nothing new came through. Morag and Ranald glanced at one another. There was nothing lit down on the ground. There was no one at the landing strip. They were flying by sheer experience and instruments alone. Which meant they had no idea whether they could land or not. They didn't even know, beyond scribbles on a piece of paper, that there was land there at all.

Skellan didn't have time to answer his radio; he was scrambling down to the runway as fast as he could; running now. He had abandoned his pack. He could hear, just about, or so he kept imagining, the drone of the plane's engines above the noise of the howling wind. He sprinted on down, desperately hoping he would be in time.

"Doesn't look like they've got anyone down there," grunted Ranald.

Morag nodded. "Well, we can make the drop and go back."

She looked out into the furious winds. The last thing she wanted to do was go back. They had no idea when the helicopter might make it. Going back to the safety of the mainland was against everything Morag wanted.

But the fact was, there could be ice built up on the runway; they could skid, or miss it, or get stuck fast, or it might simply be completely impassable. There was no clear way of knowing.

"Let's do the drop now then," she said, and, craning her face to see it, made a very wide bank around the Mermaid's Spyglass.

DOWN BELOW, THE children heard the plane's engines above and their eyes lit up.

"Someone's coming to rescue us!" shouted Khalid.

"Now, now," said Denise. "Let's not get overexcited. I need you all to stay inside the shelter of the cave."

Morag spiraled the plane down, slower and slower and closer and closer to the needle of the mountain, making sure all the while they were never going to stall; but even so the twin otter always impressed her. It wasn't a complicated piece of machinery—or rather, no more complicated than any aeroplane needed to be—but it was light and responsive in her hands and she knew it better than any plane in the world.

The radio crackled again.

"We have visual."

It was Denise.

"That's great," Morag said. "We have nothing down in the landing zone. Over."

There was a pause.

"Ah," said Denise. "Skellan is on his way . . ."

She didn't finish the sentence. What if he hadn't made it? What if he had slipped and fallen? What if . . .

"We'll deal with that as and when," said Morag. "Is everyone out of the way?"

"Roger."

It was easy to see a plane-shaped shadow looming across the snowy sky; much more difficult to make out a person on a snowy ledge down on the ground. Ranald had the binoculars but even so.

"I'll send up a flare," said Denise. Instantly the side of the mountain exploded in pink light.

"Got you," said Morag.

She and Ranald looked at one another.

"Okay," she said. "I'm going down to 220 meters. Dropping to 220."

Ranald nodded. He didn't really think in metric. This was 700 feet above sea level. It was 50-odd feet off the ledge. It was a *very* close pass. And they had two seconds to drop the parcel properly.

Ranald unbuckled and motioned for Gertie to do the same. Then they pulled up a section of the carpeted flooring toward the back of the aircraft, behind the hold. There was a tiny section inside, with a bolted hatch. With the carpet up the air was suddenly much colder and the rattling a lot louder. Ranald and Morag needed to speak through the radio, even across the small area of the plane, which was still descending, weaving choppily from side to side.

The dying lights of the flare twinkled down, sinisterly pretty in the falling snow, and another one came up. Gertie grabbed the huge soft wrapped parcel, dragging it over. Ranald looked at her and nodded, shouted, "HOLD ON," to her, pointing to one of the plane's struts that came up through the space, then wrenched open the hatch.

The world changed. The noise and terror were immense, blinding. Immediately the snow whooshed up inside the plane. The wind was so loud you couldn't hear another thing, the tug of the gales incredibly strong.

The radio crackled and still they were going down, down.

Gertie glanced out. Now you could see the rock through the snow. It was so terrifyingly close, and whipping past so terrifyingly fast she felt she could reach out and touch it. She swallowed hard. Her heart was pounding in her chest; she mustn't panic. She wouldn't. Those kids needed her.

Morag came in as smooth as she could, but she could still not prevent the plane being rocked from side to side. She could see the landing spot clearly now and counted it down to Ranald. "5 . . . 4 . . . 3 . . . 2 . . ."

"GERTIE!"

Ranald was pulling on her sleeve and Gertie came back from her blind panic, and handed him one corner of the parcel. Together they stretched their hands out into the open air, freezing cold on her fingers, until she heard, "NOW," through the radio and they both let go at the same time, and watched it tumble down to earth, clip the side of the cliff, then, to their utter dismay, bounce slowly over the edge, and crash all the way out of sight down the mountain, far down to the water below.

Gertie closed her eyes.

"Bugger," she said.

"Don't worry," said Morag on the radio, sounding as calm as ever. "That's why we brought two. We'll go around."

Bouncing around the mountain again, this time with the hatch open, was incredibly unpleasant. Ranald didn't strap himself in again and it didn't occur to Gertie to do it either, despite being so much less experienced, so she was hanging on to the struts for dear life. Everything in her was shaking and trembling with the motion of this tiny little fragile piece of metal that felt like absolutely no opponent to the mighty elements.

Ranald glanced at her, and patted her frozen fingers.

"We'll get it this time."

Morag made her tour of the mountain and they reached the passing spot again. They had to be right this time. Gertie crawled over to get the second parcel.

This time Morag did her countdown and banked very slightly to the left, closer to the side of the mountain—extremely close, in fact; a mere three meters separated their port side wing, and the children who saw it nearly fainted in fear that the plane was going to hit the mountain.

This time, when they counted down, Gertie and Ranald let the parcel go as gently as they were able, and were rewarded, just before Morag pulled full back and took the plane straight up into the sky, by seeing it bounce once, twice . . . then come to land, not far at all from the edge. But on the ridge. Safe. Hours bought.

SKELLAN TIED THE new rope on as best he could with frozen fingers. It would hold him; he couldn't for the life of him imagine how they would get the children down it. Well. They would worry about that later. But if they had to spend another night like last night . . .

He couldn't think about it.

Carefully, freezing, he edged himself over the side of the rock. It was a straight drop. The wall was covered in ice. Nevertheless he was trained for this. He tied the rope around his waist and started to feed it out.

The rope wobbled, but just about held, but the wind buffeted him back and forth across the wall, and he had to fight hard to keep his footing. His radio was bleating but he had absolutely no way of getting to it. The rope was nowhere near as secure as a harness or as what he would have liked, if he'd had time to fix up the proper ropes. Skellan was genuinely fighting concern as he battled again and again to stay close to the rock wall. He let a little rope out, then more, faster, his lungs dragging in the cold air, his fingers trembling uncontrollably, his mind, which knew he had to go slowly, fighting his body, which demanded he get down onto terra firma as quickly as it possibly could.

He was closer . . . closer . . . now more than halfway. The knot slipped, and barcly realizing what he was doing, he panicked a little, and pulled it free of the rope, loosening himself. Skellan tried to lightly drop onto the rocky ground below . . .

CHAPTER 42

Back in the air, Morag looked with some concern at her fuel. They had been flying against the wind, not with it, and it had been a battle all the way. They had a little time before they absolutely had no choice but to turn back, but not long. And there was nowhere else to land on the way home; Inchborn's beach was covered in snow; the other islands even further away with exactly the same problems they had here; no runways cleared and no people or time to clear them. This was their only chance. To land and take off again and get back to the mainland . . . well. It was getting very tight.

Morag flew high, happy to be away from the mountain, and wondering if she would be able to see a break in the weather ahead but still the snow fell, sideways, upward, every way, and the wind blew. She could remember snow in May—she could remember snow in June—but she couldn't remember it being quite as sustained a threat as this. And for the Met Office to get it so wrong . . . She tried to cut them some slack; forecasting was a complicated business. But a single degree of error had made the difference between a few people getting a soaking and a full-blown emergency. The Met Office was based in Exeter. Sometimes Morag felt this explained a lot. They wouldn't have expected their children to go out today even in heavy rain. Softy Southerners.

Regardless, this didn't help the problem. She circled once more. Gertie had picked up her needles again; Morag could just make out the click-click over the roar of the weather and the engine, and felt proud of her flatmate, and her calmness. Nalitha had been right from the start.

A FLASH OF pain went through Skellan like an electric shock. He swore mightily, the wind knocked out of him completely. His entire body trembled as he tried to get back on his feet when he realized he had gone over on his ankle. The pain was tremendous—biting and sharp—and he swore furiously. He saw the faintest gray outline of the little plane circle high above him once more and Skellan steeled himself. There was only one way to go, and it was down.

Skellan hobbled, cursing and shouting out loud on the pain of his shattered ankle, hopping and dragging it over the sheer rock and pebbles. If he couldn't get down in time to sort out the lights, the plane would leave, and having seen the condition of some of the children . . . he couldn't let that happen. Hypothermia could kill in hours, particularly kids, who had a different surface area to adults. It was deadly, and it happened in the Scottish mountains. But not on his watch.

The last hundred meters or so were pure, teeth-gritting agony. Thank God, though, he thought when he saw it. The blacktop was relatively new, the surface exposed to the wind, which had stopped the snow from settling deeply. He wouldn't have to sweep it. He couldn't have anyway.

Up the stairs of the little hut, to switch on the lights, Skellan hobbled on his hands and knees, step by grinding, agonizing step; tears in his eyes, until finally he made it to the lever, and pulled it, collapsing in a heap below the level of the window. He didn't even have the energy to watch the plane's approach.

LIKE A MAGICAL alien road, the pathway opened up under them, light after light after light; green on the north side, indicating their safe way to approach, followed by white leading into the short distance.

Morag hadn't realized till she saw them that she'd been holding her breath. Ranald nodded as she took another turn up, explaining her steps to ATC Glasgow. There were no other planes in the vicinity today, apart from a couple of heavyweight transatlantic airbuses out of Edinburgh and Glasgow who didn't care what they flew in, and the whole of ATC was listening in, and, she could sense, wishing her well. Although, as usual, they betrayed not a single note of emotion in their voices.

"Cleared to land TO Dolly 2 permission to land."

"Roger," said Morag.

CHAPTER 43

It was eerie, descending from the plane into a deserted world; snow muffling all sound and, out of the worst of the wind, the sudden silence was odd and slightly unnerving. There was nobody there; Gertie found Skellan in the little hut, looking white. They took a view, supported by Skellan, to strap up his ankle until they could get him back, turned on the electric heater that was attached to the generator, and set him in front of it with paracetamol and a large glass of whisky, precisely the opposite of what the manual said but under the circumstances, and provided he drank lots of water, they figured it was all right.

They radioed up to Denise, who sounded her usual unflustered self, even when she heard about the cliff and Skellan. "But," she broke in, "it would be rather better if we could evacuate now rather than tonight," which, in Denise language meant, "Get us the hell out of here ASAP."

Up on the ridge, Struan was cheerfully unaware of any of this. He was rather enjoying, in fact, huddling everyone together, getting them to jump up and down, and distributing some of the bounty of the packages—neither Denise nor he thought there was any point in rationing; surely they'd be down today, now they knew the plane could drop packages. They had even seen it circling and then vanish, low down, from sight, as opposed to soaring into the sky, which meant the grown-ups were fairly confident they were on their way home pretty soon.

Struan was cheerfully going through the bag like Father Christmas.

There were warm socks and hats and scarves that he immediately bundled the children up in. The removal of wet socks in particular was incredibly useful. Denise was privately worried about how blue the children's feet looked, and very grateful indeed for the foot and hand warmers, particularly for some of the children in trainers.

There was chocolate and water and bananas, bashed from the fall, though that didn't worry anyone. They still couldn't get the fire going outside the cave, but Denise was going to seriously consider doing it inside, choking or no choking. A hot drink would do them all the world of good. The problem was, it is one thing to play out in the snow for a little while, then come back in to hot chocolate and a cozy fire. It is quite another to be out in it all day, with little hope of shelter except a dank, dripping cave. Still there were firelighters, and fuel-burning logs. So Denise would give it a shot. Mrs. McGinty had fully retreated to the cave.

Denise was technically meant to look for Mrs. McGinty with the news from the radio, but took one look at her and told Skellan instead.

They had twelve children to get down an eighteen-foot solid wall of ice. They didn't have the fixed abseiling ropes any more, and Skellan had not been crazy about the fixing hook left on top of the climb. It was very slippery and dangerous, and the children were not particularly fit.

But the longer they stayed up there, the greater the risk of exposure. Frostbite was entirely possible. The temperature was zero degrees Celsius, with the windchill making it considerably colder. Some children were already refusing food, the first sign that the cold was setting deep into their bones. They had four logs for the fire, now spluttering inside the cave, which made it incredibly unpleasant. Each log would burn for an hour. After that they were in serious trouble. The helicopter was just about ready to go out again, but they couldn't get over till midnight, earliest. RAF Lossiemouth was out on the rigs, evacuating men.

On the plus side, the three airline crew were willing to help, and whilst Skellan couldn't come, he could tell them what to do. And there was equipment down the mountain. They just had to get up and get moving.

Denise made her mind up. They were going to make a go of it. She explained her reasoning to Struan, who agreed.

"It has to be a game," she said. "It has to be fun. If they're frightened, it's not going to work."

He nodded, fully on board. Meanwhile, Mrs. McGinty burst into tears.

BACK AT THE base, Skellan was talking through what they had to do, and showing them the ropes.

"Does anyone know knots?" he said.

"We're pilots, not sailors," said Morag, faintly irritated.

"Uhm," said Gertie. "Well, I kind of do."

Skellan beamed. "Oh thank goodness."

Gertie shrugged modestly as he talked them through it. They had a rescue truss, that needed to be tied up in a certain way, with a certain number of people to winch up and down and that would work for the cliff. Morag glanced at Ranald, unsure if the older man would be up to going out in a snowstorm. She immediately realized this was a ridiculous state of mind to be in. His jaw was set like granite. He was delighted by the challenge and obviously very up for it.

They dressed in every mad piece of outdoor gear they could find in the clubhouse, plus large and serious walking boots, and, with full packs on their backs, left behind the comfort and safety of the little hut and set out up the snow-covered terrifying mountain on their own: people with a mission.

It HAD BEEN very hard work to boil the kettle with the melted snow, and mixed with chocolate it was still not very nice, with gritty bits in it, and nobody got very much, but also nobody complained. A worry in itself.

"Now!" said Denise, keeping the same children's TV presenter voice—the best defense she had.

"What we're going to do now is head back down!!"

There was a silence.

"In this?" came Anna-Lise's voice, finally.

"It's fine," said Struan. "It'll be fun! This is part of the bravery challenge."

"I don't want the bravery challenge," said Khalid decisively. "I am fine without the bravery challenge."

"There are medals," said Struan, on a whim.

There was some interest in this and Anne-Marie's face popped up. "For everyone or just some people?"

"For everyone who comes on the bravery challenge," said Struan, crossing his fingers.

"Down the hill in the snow?" said Jimmy. "Nae bother." And for once, Struan was glad of Jimmy's bravado. It was a massive help.

"Yeah, you talk crud though," said Wee Shugs. "We've had that proved."

And then Struan was annoyed he'd called him out on it, about the climbing.

"Is the bravery challenge just walking down the mountain in this snow?" said Oksana finally.

Struan nodded.

Oksana shrugged. "I have done worse," she said.

And nobody argued with that.

THEY EVEN MADE a show of tidying up the camp, partly because Denise was trying to stall, waiting to hear the airline crew were at the cliff edge, and partly because she wanted to make the children think that this was all perfectly normal and nothing out of the ordinary was happening, rather than dash away in a panic. But in the end everyone—including Mrs. McGinty, whom Denise was slightly more worried about than the others—followed Oksana down, while Struan kept them singing, and told them stories of Shackleton, then stopped before he got to the bit about them killing seals and spending a *year* living in the ice and snow.

DENISE WOULDN'T HAVE admitted it in a million years, how relieved she was when the radio crackled and it was Morag, Ranald, and their stewardess, in position at the bottom of the cliff.

Gertie had found the entire thing astonishing. She was a child of the Highlands—familiar with long winters and the cold bite of the windy air—the bending over of the rushes and the thick grass; the bliss of going indoors to the warmth of home and the local fires burning.

But this was new. And strange. Like the weather was happening at a time out of control. Rain or snow or sunshine, the supermarket was always the same. As was the tin shed, to be fair, in that it was always cold. But this was something else. This was the world trying to harm you. Actively, the wind was whipping around the

Mermaid's Spyglass tearing, screaming, "You don't belong here." Even wrapped up properly, two pairs of gloves, goggles, two hats. Even with everything they had, it was still very clearly saying to her: "Go. You have no place here," the wind shrieking like a banshee chorus.

She kept moving, Ranald in the lead, the two women behind. The switchback where they hit the north side was almost unbearable; completely blinded by the white-out, they clung to the rock walls and inched their way around, each thinking, but not saying, how difficult it was going to be to get the children down from there.

One thing at a time though. They plowed on, and up, for ninety minutes, until Gertie's world meant nothing more than snow and roaring; although she had no clear idea how long they'd been out there. The light did not change; the swirling snowflakes bounced and could not settle hither or thither because of the strong winds. Between the soft white of the flakes and the misty gray of the sky it was very difficult to see anything much.

But then, finally, they were there, at the base of the cliff.

Gertie felt the sudden rush of adrenaline as she spied, staring up the icy expanse of cliff, a face carefully peering back at her. It was such a long way down.

Struan was keeping all the children back from the cliff edge, excited though they were. There were a few tears now, and even the perkiest were looking very cold and unhappy.

Morag pulled the harness out of the bag, and they put it together the way they'd been shown. It was effectively a seat winched up on a strong rope by the adults on both ends. Simple, but effective. As long as everyone was calm enough to keep their heads and not panic. Carefully, Gertie got on Ranald's shoulders until she could get high enough to throw it to Denise, leaning downward. It took a while but they managed with a great whoop, Ranald only wincing a little.

Denise, Struan, and Mrs. McGinty topside, then the rest of them below, to gather the children in. Although they would have to be careful turning round the cliff on the way back down, the rest of it they could more or less just clamber down, if they were careful. Once this bit was over. The difficult bit. Just as long as nobody . . .

"I can't do it. I CAN'T!"

AT THE BOTTOM of the cliff, Gertie finalized her knots. They were as neat and tidy as one could wish for and Morag checked them over; they looked exactly like the sketches in the guide card Skellan had given them. She gave her a thumbs-up; it was hard to talk in the howling gale.

UP ON TOP of the cliff, Struan had gone to get Mrs. McGinty. She was standing in a small alcove in the mountain, trying to protect herself from the wind.

"We're going to get the children down the cliff," he'd said. She kept staring at the rock.

"It's not safe," she kept saying. "It's not safe!"

"It'll be fine," said Struan, unwilling to reassure her that it was perfectly safe when it clearly wasn't. "Come on. The children need us. You're upsetting them."

"Can't they send a helicopter?"

"They've sent a plane," said Struan. "Here."

He held up a beautiful rose-colored scarf from the package. "Wrap this around you, keep you warm."

Mrs. McGinty shook her head furiously. "I'm NOT going!"

Struan looked at her, then glanced back at Denise, who had her hands full keeping the children from the cliff edge.

"I'm afraid . . . you're going to have to," he said. Mrs. McGinty shook her head mutinously, like a much younger child than the ones queueing up carefully outside.

Morag and Gertie had successfully managed to send the harness up the ropes that Denise had secured rather more carefully and successfully than Skellan had managed in his rush. They sent down a full rucksack first to make sure it would hold, which it did, quite comfortably, Struan and Denise controlling it from the top; but that was light. Some of the children were on the large side and they had themselves to get down too.

Denise expected to be able to make it down last by climbing herself, so they were keeping the lightest children to the end when one person could feed the rope through. But that wouldn't really help them if Mrs. McGinty was still recalcitrant.

Nonetheless, against the weather, they all tried to keep up the jolliest of veneers to their voices; something children would, of course, have seen through right away, if those children hadn't also been so desperate to believe in the grown-ups; hadn't themselves been so desperate to believe everything was going to be okay that they could be fooled by a lilt in the voice, a singsong twist.

Oksana—bless her—came forward first, again massively cheered on by her classmates, her face set in stone. Struan felt briefly so unhappy that it had to be this way, before being proud of her once again. She put her newly mittened hands on the rope, clasped it hard, and, hearteningly, waved at her classmates.

Gradually and carefully they winched her down, and Morag and Gertie grabbed her at the other end, happy to see her and delighted she was okay.

Everyone was cheery. Except it had taken over six minutes to get her down safely, plus they then had to check the ropes and carefully send them back up again. And there were twelve children. Which meant, at the absolute bare minimum, it would take ninety minutes. They were located on a completely exposed part of the mountain; no caves to shelter in, just the wind whipping past. If Skellan had been there he could have started ushering them down to safety, but he wasn't.

"Stand by the wall," said Morag, but they were chilled themselves and it was clear to see how frozen and exhausted Oksana was. It wasn't ideal.

"Can we hurry it up?" she said into the radio.

Denise and Struan toiled all they could; geeing up the children, carefully strapping them in, getting them to cheer, up or down, even as the cheers grew more ragged and exhausted, and Gertie grew more concerned. It was very tiring up there. Struan was strong but even so, some of the ten- and eleven-year-olds were on the larger side and they had to hold the rope absolutely as straight as they could manage against the wind so it didn't flap about too much. It was hard work and they were getting slower: Gertie did not like the look of the children, all huddled together. They were trembling hard.

"Come ON!" Morag shouted through the radio. "Come on. We have to get them moving."

"Yeah," said Denise. "We've got all the kids. But there's a problem."

Indeed there was. Mrs. McGinty was still refusing to get on the winch.

It was no use. Struan tried gentle persuasion; Denise was rather more forthright. Nothing would fetch her. No way was she getting into the harness. None at all. In vain they tried reason, but she was insistent she would break it; she was too big for it. She couldn't hear them telling her she was fine, not big at all, that it was designed to take down a large man; she simply couldn't listen.

MORAG WAS INCREASINGLY worried about the very cold and still children down below and wanted to take them back alone, but was also concerned about the path and the scree, particularly shepherding them round the north face. It had been hard enough when it was just the three adults doing it themselves. Gertie looked at her, wondering. Then it came to her.

"I'll go up," said Gertie suddenly. "If I go up and help Struan, then Denise can come down. She can lead the children down, with your help. And then we adults can get down on our own."

Morag looked at her, then at the children.

"Are you sure?" she said.

"Yes," said Gertie. "You can get down and sort out the plane and get it ready to take off. I can't do that. We'll be right behind you. I can knot the rope properly and climb down it—you know I can. We'll tether it to the top and I can do it with Struan on the bottom."

This was a very bold claim for Gertie to make.

Morag glanced at Ranald who wouldn't have admitted it in a million years but was also feeling absolutely worn out.

She radioed Denise, who looked at Struan. He hadn't set a foot wrong; he'd been useful and calm and knew exactly what they were doing.

"You get McGinty down from here if you have to throw her," she said quietly.

"She'll be better when we aren't pressuring her," said Struan, which was a compelling argument. And the number-one priority at this point was the children—so much less able to survive in extreme temperatures.

Denise nodded, finally. "Okay."

GERTIE HAD NEVER, in her whole life, thought of herself as brave. She had always felt quite the opposite: cowardly, overlooked. Not an important person in anyone's eyes—barely in the eyes of her own mother. She kept herself safe and lived in her daydreams, which were so much nicer than her real life.

From the moment Morag and Nalitha had burst into her shop, though, nothing had been like that.

She'd tried being brave, she thought. With Calum. And look how that had turned out.

Then it occurred to her that perhaps being brave was something you had to practice. Something, maybe, you got better at. Getting slowly deeper in the water instead of jumping in all at once. Or the first time you tried cabling.

"Okay," she said, her voice barely perceptible above the roar. "Strap me in."

Ranald did so.

"It is an honor," he said as he did so. "To fly with you."

She gave him a half-hearted grin and thumbs-up, as Morag gave the line two tugs and the children did their best to give a half-hearted cheer, even though they were drowsy and confused as to what was happening. Slowly, Gertie lurched up into the freezing air.

She gasped in surprise; as she drew higher, the scale of the whipping snowflakes and harsh ice became broader, stretching out, on every side, into utter darkness, only the far-below flash of the lighthouse and the tiniest gleam of the landing lights to show you which way was even up. She felt, suddenly, even more than she usually did, like the tiniest dot in a vast universe, pressed down by the weight of a huge sky full of snow.

But normally, feeling small in the world was not a good feeling. It made you feel like nothing you did mattered, that you could shout into the void—as, indeed, Gertie could right now—and nobody would hear you; nobody would care. She was a minuscule unimportant speck. And this was not a dream. This was as real as real could be. She froze, staring out into the maelstrom, seriously wondering for a moment if, truly, it mattered. If she disappeared altogether, slipped free from the harness, launched herself into the wind . . . It wasn't a suicidal impulse, more the dreadful thrill that sometimes takes over you on a train platform, that you might suddenly do something ridiculous and step off.

And then she heard a voice above her.

CHAPTER 44

Gertie blinked away the snowflakes from her eyes and felt the tiniest tug on the rope. She looked up through the maelstrom. A confused pair of hazel eyes was looking down at her from over the lip of the cliff, and the owner of the eyes was hauling with some effort on the ropes.

"Sorry, sorry I'm fine, pull me up!" she said, shaking her head to come back to herself.

Back on the ledge Struan, Denise, and Gertie retreated to the side, where it was quiet enough to have a conversation.

Mrs. McGinty was still in the corner of the cave, refusing to engage.

"Hiyah," said Gertie, who had always been as scared of Mrs. McGinty as everyone else.

Mrs. McGinty shook her head fiercely. "I'm not going down," she barked.

Denise was already strapping herself into the harness.

"I have to go," she said severely. "Pamela, you have to manage yourself, or retreat further into the cave until we figure something out and the weather clears."

This had been a bluff to make the woman move, but it failed.

Mrs. McGinty looked defiant as ever.

Denise was exasperated. "I'm sorry," she said. "I'm afraid I have to choose a priority."

"You have to go," said Gertie, quickly. "The children . . ."

"Yes," said Denise, still clearly in bits at leaving someone behind.

Denise glanced down sharply. Struan showed Gertie what to do and, hurrying, they lowered Denise down as quickly as they could manage.

Gertie couldn't think how to persuade the head teacher to follow her. Struan, utterly exhausted from wrestling twelve bonny children down a steep cliff, was out of ideas too, and he glanced back at the cave, then looked at her and oddly, given that they barely knew one another, they each understood what the other was saying straight away. They would have to beat a retreat.

Denise gently landed and disentangled herself from the harness and they hauled it back up, worried about what, exactly, was going to happen next. Would Mrs. McGinty move? And if she didn't, what were their options?

As it happened, she leaped up as soon as Denise disappeared.

"Where's Denise?!" she demanded, eyes and hair completely wild. She had discarded the hat and her head was covered in snowflakes. She looked like a mad witch.

"Uhm, she's gone down," mumbled Gertie.

"Oh my God," said Mrs. McGinty. "You work in the supermarket! Oh my God! Are *you* meant to save us?"

"Denise has gone to take the children back," replied Struan.

"Well, I want . . . I want to be where Denise is!" said Mrs. McGinty, shooting a terrible look at Gertie. "Not with a shopgirl!"

"Well," said Struan boldly, infuriated. "You underestimate Gertie at your own risk!"

Gertie looked at him, surprised. But also, they didn't want to be encouraging Mrs. McGinty to stay where she was.

"No, no," she said, stepping forward toward the woman. "You're quite right. I'm just a shopgirl. I'm useless. You should absolutely go where Denise is."

And she held up the harness.

For a second Mrs. McGinty was caught between them. She paused, her face appearing terrified.

Then she looked again at the two young people.

"DENISE!" she yelled again, and stepped forward and grabbed the harness.

"THIS IS HOW you unstrap yourself at the bottom," Struan was trying to explain, but it was obvious Mrs. McGinty wasn't listening. She kept saying, "Denise will sort me out."

Meanwhile Gertie didn't think Denise would still be there. She'd already be taking the children down to desperately needed safety and warmth.

"I need to hurry up," Mrs. McGinty was saying. Well, she could probably catch them up, just about. Gertie radioed and Ranald said he'd wait at the bottom; Morag and Denise had gone on. Once Mrs. McGinty was down, Struan and Gertie would have to use the knots method. The ropes, Gertie knew, were very strong, and the pulley was holding. It would work.

When Mrs. McGinty heard Denise was already heading back down the mountain she was even more keen to get away. She simply wasn't listening to Struan's repeated instructions, and when they lowered her over the edge she kept hollering at them to go faster, faster. Once suspended, she kicked her legs against the side of the icy rock to try and make it go, giving a lot of strain to the side of the pulley Gertie and Struan were working on together.

"Nightmare," said Struan, rolling his eyes.

"I always knew she was evil, even in Primary 4," chipped in Gertie, and Struan smiled.

"Me too! My mum said I was being daft but . . ."

They shared a look.

When she reached the bottom, Mrs. McGinty had to unclip herself from the line, which could then be hauled back up and used again.

In her panic, and her refusal to listen to reason, she did not do this.

Instead, as soon as she reached the bottom, the head teacher dashed straight off down the hill in pursuit of safe sensible Denise, pulling the harness and rope with her, then, as she realized, desperately pulling herself away from it—whereupon the harness, dumped on the icy ground, simply slid off the other side of the path, and tumbled all the way down the mountain.

CHAPTER 45

Inexperienced Gertie and Struan didn't realize what was happening—the rope had relaxed in their hands when she had reached the ground—until it was too late. It skittered out of their fingers and vanished over the side of the cliff, far down below.

Gertie made a desperate grab for it but it was too late and Struan had to pull her back before she nearly hurtled over the edge too.

Together they stood, looking down in horror.

Mrs. McGinty had made it halfway down the scree before she had realized she was still attached to the gear, and had turned back with a scared expression on her face. Ranald swore mightily into the radio.

"I'm . . . I'm sorry?" came Mrs. McGinty's voice, sounding dazed, but it was too late. Ranald tried a couple of things to throw the rope up, but throwing a rope—even knotted, or tied as a lasso, or with a rock attached—directly upward 18 feet is more or less impossible without a bow and arrow. Gertie told him to stop trying; he had been out there too long and was getting chilled. They had supplies. The others would just have to leave Struan and Gertie behind.

So they watched, from high up and far away, as the mismatched little party, Mrs. McGinty stumbling ahead in front of Ranald, vanished surprisingly quickly into the snowstorm, their feet silent under the roaring wind.

And just like that, Struan and Gertie were completely alone.

* * *

THE FIRST THING to do was get back to the cave. Gertie grabbed the remains of the parcel and took it in. The fire was just about still going, and she took out the paper in the parcel and burned it. It flamed up, just a little.

"There we are," said Gertie cheerfully. "I'll get the water on. See where we're at."

The children had taken all of the chocolate, but there were a couple of packets of biscuits, and some tea bags. Presumably they could melt snow over the fire in the old pot that had been left there. She couldn't imagine how long it would take but they might as well get on with it.

She turned round. Struan was still standing out in the howling gale, staring down the crevasse and the empty road that wound its way down to safety—empty and out of reach. Snow was already covering up the children's footprints.

Gertie blinked for a second, and called his name again but he didn't turn.

That's when she realized what was wrong. Whilst they had been making their way up, in their professional bad weather gear, he'd been standing here, all day and in fact most of the night, in the snow, still helping the children, getting colder and colder and wetter, in his absurd, not at all suitable festival clothing.

Whilst the others had huddled round the fire Struan had been out helping the children play; whilst they had jumped and clambered down the rock, he had stood, steady as a rock, in his ill-fitting and hastily put together outerwear.

Now he wasn't sure what was going on. He was feeling hazy and sleepy and suddenly, to Gertie's absolute horror, he sat down in the snow.

* * *

"STRUAN!" SHE SHOUTED, but he didn't respond. Gertie rushed to him, attempted gently to tug him into the cave.

"I'm sleepy," he muttered. "Just going to have a wee nap."

"You are not!" said Gertie, as sternly as she'd ever said anything.

She began to drag him into the cave. Hypothermia killed in these mountains. If you lived anywhere near them, you couldn't escape it. Every year climbers died. People thought that because Britain had a temperate climate it wasn't dangerous in the way South America or the Himalayas were dangerous. People were so wrong. Normally the amazing Mountain Rescue Team managed to get out in time.

But nobody was coming today.

She knew what to do; everyone got taught it at school. Unfortunately it rather depended on the person who had hypothermia realizing they had it and agreeing to come with you, rather than sitting like a blob and insisting they were going to take a nap in a freezing snowstorm.

Gertie went and put another log on the fire back in the cave and gritted her teeth. The cave was smoky and unpleasant, but it was gradually warming up; it was still cold, but certainly warmer out of the wind. It crackled, at least. Okay. One thing at a time.

"STRUAN," Gertie yelled, raising her voice as she went back out again. No response. She tried again, slightly louder. Still nothing.

Gertie was trembling and not just from the cold. What if she couldn't move him? What if he wouldn't go? What was she going to do? He couldn't possibly survive a night out here and night was coming. It was entirely possible he would make himself so ill he couldn't get down the slope even with a new rope, and then it wouldn't even be worth being picked up at all. It didn't bear thinking about. She had to get him in. But he wasn't listening to her.

Gertie knelt down. And said the words people had been saying to her her whole life.

"Wake up," she whispered. "Wake up now. Stop dreaming. Wake up."

"Huh?"

"Wake up. Wake up. You have to move. This is real. Move."

Struan's head twisted and his eyes cracked. He looked around him as if not realizing where he was.

"That's right," she said. "Stay with me. Wake up. Go toward the fire! Go! Now! Stay awake. Stay awake with me."

Gertie yanked him up, hard, onto his feet and he stumbled a few steps in the right general direction.

"That's it," she said, in a voice growing stronger, even in the noise of the storm. "Stay awake. Stay with me. No dreaming. No more dreaming, Struan. Do you know who I am?"

"I have . . . I have always known who you are," came his voice, low and confused. "I have always known you."

Oh for heaven's sake, thought Gertie. He was delirious. Completely delirious. Frightened suddenly, she sharpened her voice even more. "MOVE!" she screeched, in a voice that would have surprised Jean, if not her fishing ancestors. "Move yourself! Move! This is happening! This is real! And you Have! To! Move!!!"

And suddenly, incredibly, he was obeying. It was working. And he was following, shakily, blindly as she hauled him into the cave and sat him down by the stuttering fire.

GERTIE LOOKED AT Struan. At this stupid face she had mooned at for so long; had dreamed of and longed for. Not as soft now his cheeks; stubble where before they had been smooth and completely hairless; a formed jawline where it had once been unde-fined; and hollows where there had once been plump skin. But still a lovely-looking man. She winced internally, figuring the only way she could get this close to him was when he was semi-comatose from a dangerous illness. Still. There was no other way. She knew what she had to do.

And this was not a fantasy, or a daydream. The time for those was over. This was the real world, and she had to live in it.

She gathered up the sleeping bags the children had left behind and threw some over the entrance to the cave. It was getting very smoky but that didn't matter; she had to warm it up at any cost.

Then she took more of the blankets and, from the box they'd dropped, pulled out fresh socks and blankets and heated them by the fire. She zipped two sleeping bags together and placed them likewise.

Then carefully, she dropped to her knees and started unlacing Struan's boots.

THE FIRE CRACKLED as she dried off his feet with a towel—they were blue and soaked through. Gertie realized immediately his trousers would have to come off too. This was ridiculous. If her thirteen-year-old self could see her now. Well, she wouldn't have a clue what to do, but nonetheless. She told herself this was a medi-cal procedure and she had to be strictly professional.

And there it was, as she leaned forward; just the tiniest hint of the aftershave he used to wear. It wasn't anything expensive; he'd got it for Christmas one year and just stuck with it; a gender-less, watery nineties scent. Gertie had always had terrible trouble around other men who had worn it.

She forced herself to focus on the matter at hand.

"I'm taking off your trousers," she said as sternly as she could manage. "To make you feel better." He tugged his mitts off, slowly, attempted to fumble with his buttons, but couldn't make his fingers bend. They had gone very dark. Gertie looked at them, worried. She pulled off his trousers quickly, then his top and wet fleece. Even the undershirt was wet. His skin was like marble; completely lifeless.

Gertie thought about it. There wasn't much else for it. She was correctly dressed and the smoky cave was heating up. She bundled Struan, only wearing his boxer shorts, into the first sleeping bag.

Then she sighed, rolled her eyes at herself, and at the ridiculousness of everything; she pulled off her outer clothes, and, as the instruction manuals always said, hopped in with him.

CHAPTER 46

Struan was like a block of ice. Gertie had pulled them close to the fire and piled every single sleeping bag she could gather both below and above them, and crammed on mittens, socks, and a hat onto his wet curly hair. His eyes were open only a crack, not really focusing on anything.

Gertie felt absolutely terrible, like she had manifested an awful monkey's paw version of a deep long-suppressed desire. Stupid Struan McGhie who thought he was it. Who didn't even notice her. Who hadn't even recognized her, years later.

But she knew what she had to do. Carefully Gertie wriggled out of her layers, her body still warm underneath. And she pressed herself very carefully against him.

It was odd. She willed her warmth to leach into his body.

Struan muttered something and she leaned closer to hear what it was. His breath was visible in the air.

"Sleepy," he was saying.

"No, you're not," Gertie replied immediately. "No, you aren't. You're not going to sleep."

He blinked, as she took one of his hands between hers and tried vainly to rub some warmth into it. Finally, she gave up and tucked them under her own armpits, desperate to heat him up.

"I . . . what . . ."

He sounded incredibly drowsy and confused.

"Concentrate," she hissed.

"Wee Gertie," he said, blinking in confusion, but sounding a lot more like himself. "Is that you?"

"It is," she said. "Keep talking."

He considered it for a minute. Then, finally: "Did we get really *really* drunk?"

Gertie squeezed his hands under her armpits, harder now. "Ouch."

"You felt that?" she said.

Struan blinked. "I think so . . . argh."

She did it again.

"Why . . . where are we? Why are you torturing me?"

"Because you thought the only way we could end up under a blanket together is if you'd got blind drunk?"

Struan still wasn't quite focused and his face screwed up again. "I don't think that," he said, his voice far away, as if he thought he was in a dream; didn't really know or care what he was saying because he was so distant.

"I would never think that. If this was real . . . it would be . . ." His voice stuttered out.

"Keep talking," said Gertie, urgently, and for more than one reason.

"It would be . . . amazing," he said finally.

Gertrude looked at him.

"Do you even know where you are?" she said.

Struan blinked slowly. "I am not," he said, his words a bit slurred, "exactly sure."

Gertrude reached out of the sleeping bags and, with some difficulty, grabbed the hot flask.

"Drink some of this," she ordered. "Slowly."

He spluttered down the warmish tea, but without, she noticed, seeming to want to let go of her or move away.

Then he settled back down again, his hands tucked around her, and his eyelids fluttered again.

"NO," she said. "No. Wake up. You can't go to sleep."

"But I'm cozy," he said, sounding like a grumpy child. "I don't feel cold anymore. I like being here with you. It's like a dream."

"It isn't a dream," Gertie said firmly, rubbing his arms.

"I would not mind," he said. "To fall asleep in your arms, Gertie. I would be a happy man."

"You would DIE a happy man," replied Gertie, and started rubbing his hands harder than she'd intended.

"Well, yeah." Then: "Ow," he said and "Ow!" again.

"Good," said Gertie firmly. "That means the nerves are waking up."

"I don't . . ." Struan screwed his face up again. "I'm really . . . Am I still up the mountain . . ."

He jerked suddenly, his face showing obvious pain. "Where are the children?" he said in a panic.

"They're fine, they're safe," said Gertie, in a more soothing voice. The fire was dancing shadows on the walls of the cave. "You got them all down, do you remember?"

"Kind of," said Struan. Then: "Owww" again.

"This is good," Gertie said softly. "Where is it sore?"

"Still my hands."

"Not your feet?"

"I wish you'd just . . . I need a little nap."

"I'm afraid not," said Gertie. "Bring your feet up."

It was obvious Struan wasn't sure he could. Somewhat inelegantly, Gertie pulled his knees up.

"This is a very weird one-night stand," complained Struan.

"I am assuming," said Gertie, "you won't remember this tomorrow or if you do, you'll apologize endlessly."

Struan looked suddenly more awake. "I'm sorry, I'm sorry. Am I doing something bad?"

"No," said Gertie. "No, you aren't. But you need to stay awake, and I'm going to have to go and try and save your feet."

"This is a really weird dream," said Struan.

"Keep talking," said Gertie, as she wriggled down inside the sleeping bag. Even with two pairs of her socks on, his feet were still blue and freezing. Not able to think of anything better to do, she hugged them close to her.

"It's a nice dream though," said Struan. "Being here with you I mean. It's very nice. Although I didn't think you'd be hugging my feet."

"I also did not think that," said Gertie.

"But I like that too."

"Go on," said Gertie, massaging them and squeezing them as hard as she could.

"And I know you," he said again.

Gertie pursed her lips. Because he was half out of his mind with the cold. And he didn't know what he was saying.

She changed the subject.

"Tell me . . . tell me about home."

Struan's eyelids fluttered, and she could see the shadows from the dancing flames casting his eyelashes onto his cheeks. She wasn't going to let herself worry. She wasn't. She wasn't going to panic.

He smiled. "Nobody ever lets me talk about home. Everyone says ooh, Struan, go to Aberdeen; oh, Struan, you need to tour more; oh, Struan, don't you have ambition."

Gertie pressed hard, desperately trying to rub life back into his extremities.

"And I want to say . . . I want to say, look. Come down of an evening, when the wind is blowing fresh from the north, and watch where the seas join. Top of the world. Feel the breeze in your face and say hello to the seals and fill your lungs and watch the wee plane take off and wave to the fisher boats go out and I would say, Gertie, wouldn't you, what better place is there in this life? When you come down the Salter's Road and even the coos know you and come over to say hello and there is barely a child who wouldn't ask you for a song, or a place you wouldn't feel welcome, and would have you in to share their hearth, aye?"

"Go on," Gertie urged.

"Everything else is wood on the fire, Gertie. You burn it away. All of it. Money or cars or the world. You burn it away and you're left with your friends and your family and your music and the laughs and what you love and that's all."

Gertie couldn't tell if he was being delirious or totally honest.

"Of course people keep telling me to go out and get all that other stuff," he conceded. "Ouch! My toes!"

"That's good!" said Gertie. "That's really good! If you can feel them!"

"Bugger, I can!! Oh God."

He blinked. The pain seemed to be waking him up; his hands were now a bright red and he was cradling them in pain. He was also shaking uncontrollably.

"Bloody hell."

"Keep talking," said Gertie.

He squinted. Then he did. He told her all about Saskia, and about the audition, and how he had to go and do things, bigger things.

"I think, sometimes," he concluded. "The only time I feel like a failure is when everyone else thinks I'm a failure."

Gertie stopped what she was doing for a second. "I know what you mean," she found herself saying. "I know exactly what you mean."

Suddenly she felt his hands gently on her shoulders.

"This isn't good, is it, Gertie?"

She crawled up to look him in the eye.

"It's going to be fine," she said. "All you have to do is get warm."

"I . . . I can't."

"Come here," she said.

And she held him, and rocked him, and made him sing to her through the pain and when he did she felt herself grow warmer, and decided that that was, on balance, a good thing, even as the fire burned down and she did not know when or how it would go again, or if the snow would stop, or if they would both, in fact, just drift off to sleep; lose themselves in dreams forever.

CHAPTER 47

The children were not at all the happy, bustling crowd Morag had taken out only the previous day. They were teary, tired, and every last one of them desperately wanted their mums. She turned the heat up in the plane as far as it would go without burning through the last of their fuel. Poor old Denise had no choice but to get some new rope, change in the hut, and head out again, heroically.

Unfortunately before they could get to their families, who were quivering and on trigger edge back in the tin shed, there was the small matter of the media who were absolutely slavering at the fact that children had been caught in the storm. It was disgusting but unfortunately there was nothing they could do about it. Nalitha, who had hoofed her way to the airport even though she couldn't fit her uniform, not even nearly, was furious with them and doing her best to look official and clear them out. They were so disappointed when they found out everyone was safe and well, that if Nalitha wasn't trying to protect the integrity of her unborn child, she'd have kicked someone. She found Big Shugs and told him he was the official family bouncer so every time someone sidled up from the paper to try and get a quote from the "distraught Mermaid's Spyglass parents" he could get in between them and bark "no comment" in a menacing tone. Something, it turned out, he rather enjoyed doing.

By 2 p.m., with the snowstorm finally starting to die away a little, although many of the smaller roads were still impassable and people's cars iced in, the tiny tin shed was full of pretty much everyone in the village. Pete's wife, Linda, was making a killing on the revolting coffee and they'd completely run out of shortbread. People were passing around Toblerone. I mean, they were barely an airport but they were still a little bit of an airport. You couldn't call yourself an airport, Nalitha always argued, if you didn't sell Toblerone. It was in the International Laws of Aviation. Morag had said, Well, it wasn't, but as usual Nalitha wasn't listening. Also, she had always argued, you could use them as weapons in case of a hijack.

MORAG RADIOED PETE in the control tower, who let Nalitha know. She had been going to keep it quiet, but unfortunately the entire population of the town had their eyes trained on her face when she put the radio down, and they knew immediately. The children had been found.

They rushed out to line the runway. The local plod was there, along with all the volunteer firefighters in the town, who'd had a very busy night of it digging lambs out of snow holes. Nonetheless they were ready and waiting in case any emergency aid was required.

Very slowly and quietly, at first impossible to hear, or something you might disregard, there came the very lowest of drones. Almost nothing . . . but then, a little louder. And through the clouds, just the tiniest glint of metal against the wide, wide sky. An intake of breath, held, amongst the people watching; the clasp of an arm, the plucking of a sleeve, the squeeze of a hand . . . as Dolly 2, the little prop plane, gradually gained outline and shape and form through the endless clouds, bumping through the stormy air, first this way, then that, descending all the way. People instinctively stood back, but without having to worry, as the little plane buzzed down and down, and settled easily on her two wheels at the end of the runway with a tiny roar, whooshing on forward, but easing up, easing up, until she came to a perfect stop 50 meters from the crowd.

AT FIRST, NOBODY made a sound. Then, pandemonium. The crowd surged forward, and Nalitha and Pete were very glad of the firefighters and Big Shugs hollering at people to keep back. They did settle, eventually, and everyone waited, many with cameras up as slowly the propellers stopped turning, and the plane was completely still. Then, inside the plane Morag stood up and came out. She had whacked the heat up as far as she could and even though it was a short, noisy, rattly flight through the snow, half the kids had already fallen asleep. Mrs. McGinty was propped in a corner, staring out, not looking at anyone.

"Okay," said Morag, as the kids stirred and, when they realized they were about to see their parents, perked up considerably. Ranald was already standing by the door.

"I just wanted to say, you have all done extremely well and been very very brave. You were all heroes. You're all amazing. And you will have a *great* story to tell the Primary 7s!"

The children, remarkably perky now they were home again, cheered weakly.

"Now I want you to follow Captain MacIntyre in an orderly fashion down the steps, okay? Even if you see your mum or dad, even if you want to run, you absolutely can't cross a runway, do you understand?"

They all nodded seriously, not needing to be told twice.

"You'll probably need to be checked out, although you all look pretty strong to me. And I think whatever your favorite tea is, you'll probably get it tonight."

"Pizza!" shouted Khalid.

"Chips!" shouted another.

"NO, ice cream!" shouted Wee Shugs, to widespread laughter.

"Right enough," said Morag. "Seatbelts off. You have all been quite wonderful."

And she stood by the door, and formally shook every one of their hands as they left.

OKSANA'S MOTHER STOOD amongst the crowd, separate and alone, refusing to accept the random cruelties of fate. Her face barely changed as Oksana descended, even as she couldn't avoid noticing that her daughter appeared to be in the center of a group of close-knit girls, all whispering and holding hands.

Likewise, as they reunited, there were no imprecations or tears, as in the other families. They hugged each other formally. Except suddenly, Oksana pulled away, her face distraught.

"Bodhan!" she said, devastated. "I don't have my bear! I didn't notice."

"Perhaps, *Kokhana*. Perhaps you don't need him anymore," said her mother.

CHAPTER 48

Gertie refused. She would not dream. She would not fall asleep. Instead she pulled herself out; she knew she had another log to put on the fire, and she wanted to open the doorway a little to let more smoke out; it was unpleasant and it wasn't doing them any good.

"Do not fall asleep," she said. "I'll be two minutes."

"Come back soon," said Struan. "I like being cozy with you."

"That's not what this is about," said Gertie, and nipped out. It was freezing. But the snow seemed to be whirling past the door with less intensity. She put a handful in the kettle and put the last log on the fire, and picked up Struan's clothes, which they'd thrown hither and thither, to try and dry them out; he'd need to put them on again at some point.

Gertie picked up his mittens and turned them inside out. To her surprise something fell out; a second glove under the first one. It was fingerless and faded and badly frayed and . . .

Gertie marched back to the sleeping bag.

"Hey," she said. "HEY!"

"What? I'm awake, I'm awake," protested Struan. "I'm doing the circle of fifths in my head."

"What's this?" said Gertie, thrusting it in his face. He looked at it.

"Can you come back in here?" he begged. "I'm freezing."

Gertie obliged, trying to warm him whilst also staying as far away from him as she could, which is very difficult in a child's single sleeping bag.

Struan took it in his stiff fingers, blinking.

"It's a fingerless glove," he said finally.

"I know what it is," said Gertie. "I mean, where did you get it?"

"I can't remember," said Struan. "Oh no, I do. I think it was a Valentine's Day thing. Yonks ago. Someone gave it to me."

"Someone?!"

"Yeah, never did find out who. It was back at school. I mean, when I *was* at school, not when I was teaching. God that would have been weird. But anyway, oh my God they've been great. They're perfect for playing because your fingers stay free and . . ."

"I know that, you idiot," said Gertie, cutting him off. "I made them for you."

Struan looked at her. "For Valentine's Day?"

"For Valentine's Day 2005!"

"*What?!* Why didn't you SAY?"

"I thought you all knew! I thought you were all laughing at me! Then, even worse, you forgot all about it."

"Forgot about the best pair of gloves I've ever had in my life??"

He looked up at her, their faces incredibly close in the firelight.

"I knew I knew you," he said, quietly. "I always did."

And, just then, they heard the roar.

CHAPTER 49

The force of the helicopter blades sent the snow piling into a curtain across the opening in the front of the cave.

Gertie scrambled up and back into her clothes, hopping about in a fury of being freezing, and slightly pink from other reasons.

The helicopter had a dazzling light at the front of it and she couldn't see a thing. It only just managed to fit on the ledge. She shielded her eyes and walked forward.

"What?"

The figure that came out from behind the light, once the blades had more or less stopped moving, had its arms stretched wide.

"Gertie!"

Gertie blinked.

"I am here! To rescue the heroes!"

And Calum Frost gracefully bowed. To Gertie's utter astonishment, he was wearing her scarf.

STRUAN WAS ANNOYED because Jim and Gavin made him get in a stretcher, which was embarrassing. Gertie was annoyed because Calum had let a TV journalist come along and try to ask annoying questions about how she felt rescuing all those children. And Calum was annoyed because Gertie was very shy with the journalist, forgot to name-check Calum's airline live on air for picking her up, and was happier sitting at the back of the helo talking quietly to Struan to keep him conscious, even though it was clear the danger was mostly over.

"You okay?" Calum said to Gertie, who nodded.

Then she screwed up her face and asked, "Did they let YOU land the helicopter?" and he had to say no in front of the woman filming.

"Oh!" said the journalist, as they came in to land. "Also the fashion department wants a word about taking some photos— apparently the children were wearing incredibly designed high fashion knitwear?"

CHAPTER 50

After the Easter holidays, with the formidable Mrs. Thompson safely installed as the new headmistress, Struan walked into school, two toes lighter, in fact, but otherwise more or less unscathed, to find a surprise. His Primary 6s were quiet as he walked in, barely saying a hello, waiting with only the occasional giggle from Bronte or Oksana, silenced with a telling-off look from Anna-Lise. And there, on his desk, was a brand-new Gibson acoustic guitar to replace the one the storm had cracked to pieces on the Mermaid's Spyglass. He looked at it, astounded, as the class erupted in happy cheers.

The Mod—the Gaelic music festival—held its heats in various islands around Scotland, and their nearest this year was in Cairn. It was on the same day as the audition for the London tour.

Saskia had been waiting at the hospital.

"Seriously," she had whispered. "You had a near-death experience to get out of going to that audition?"

He had half-smiled at her. "I'm so sorry, Saskia," he said.

"I am too," she said. "I'd say pack up your stuff . . . but I'm not sure you ever unpacked."

"I did warn you that musicians were terrible bets."

"I wanted a musician!" she said, scandalized. "YOU want to be a primary school teacher."

And they parted, not exactly as friends . . . but not as enemies.

RANALD HAD LOOKED so exhausted coming off the plane that Jean—she explained ferociously to the others later—couldn't help it. She had run up and given him a cuddle, which everyone had seen. Jean vehemently hated being a figure of gossip that she hadn't personally instigated.

On the other hand, Ranald had not refused it. Quite on the contrary. It looked like the post box toppers the KCs had planned for the harvest festival might be rather late, without Jean there to up the pace. On the other other hand they had new reinforcements: the door had rung at the Shore End cottages one night, Jean being out yet again with Ranald, and Marian had answered it to a rather sad and penitent-looking Peigi. She had asked, if she didn't bring her dog, would they mind terribly if she came in and did some knitting, seeing as she'd moved in to one of the other cottages just down the close?

And after a moment everyone got a hold of themselves and agreed that they would be delighted.

JEAN LOOKED AROUND the clean but spartan drawing room in Ranald's big drafty house.

"Huh," she said.

"Don't say it needs a woman's touch," said Ranald. "I had one here for ages."

Jean looked at the family photos that lined the walls.

"Do you still miss your wife?"

"All the time," said Ranald honestly.

Jean nodded.

"What about you?"

Jean laughed. "God, no. But I've got Gertie."

It was Ranald's turn to nod. "Girls, eh?"

"Oh yes." Jean smiled. Ranald put out his big, safe, calm hand. "Want to stay for lunch? I'm not much of a cook, I should warn you."

"We could have chips," said Jean, smiling at him and stepping closer. "Later."

And she squeezed his hand and wondered, briefly, if it was the first hand she'd held since slowly, reluctantly Gertie had released her own, and flown free.

She beamed at Ranald and tilted her face up to his.

"Let's not tell the girls just yet," she said.

"Yeah," said Ranald. "News never gets out in Carso anyway."

THE DAY AFTER Struan headed back to school, Morag looked at Gertie over their porridge.

"What?" said Gertie, nervously. "Is it the newspaper?"

Sure enough, the children in her beautiful scarves and hats were plastered all over the lifestyle section, and her blog was somehow getting visitors from everywhere, lovely comments, and emails too.

Morag shook her head. "Nope," she said. "I saw Struan in the hospital. He told me . . . that Valentine's card . . . that was you!"

Gertie colored. "It was ages ago. But you all laughed!!"

"I KNEW what you did to Calum reminded me of something!" said Morag. "And we weren't laughing at you! We didn't know who you were! We were just amazed by how good the gloves were! That was all we were saying. We never connected it with you at all. The running joke was one of the teachers must have done it. Which actually seems a bit ironic nowadays considering his job."

"Huh," said Gertie.

"Do you still . . . ? I mean. He was asking about you."

Gertie looked confused. "Only because I put him in a sleeping bag."

Morag gave her a long look.

"What?"

"I could imagine the two of you together. You have a certain . . . quirkiness."

"I do not!" said Gertie, which would have been more believable if she didn't have a crochet hook in her hair at the time.

"Huh," said Morag.

"Anyway," said Gertie. "He's got a girlfriend. And I . . . I don't want to be like that anymore. Dreaming about people. It's a waste of time. Look at what happened with Calum. And Struan, at school. Nothing but embarrassment. I need to live in the real world, like the KCs keep telling me. Find someone of my own."

"I think you did pretty well in the real world up that mountain," said Morag soberly. "There are people who have trained for years who couldn't have handled it as well as you."

"Thank you," said Gertie, pink.

"Thing is . . ." said Morag, lingering.

"What?"

"Well, Struan needs his flat back. He's broken up with Saskia."

Gertie sat bolt upright. "Oh."

Then she considered it. "I'd better move home."

Morag shook her head. "You don't have to. This is your real life, remember?"

She half-smiled.

"I'm hardly here anyway. And after the rescue, well." Morag flushed and her voice trailed off. "I think it focused Gregor's mind on a few things. He wants to talk about us getting a place together. Just him and me and well, everyone else is up for discussion."

"Right," Gertie mumbled, then realized something. "I'll miss you."

"We'll be working together for a bit though," said Morag. "And anyway. I think . . . I think your mum and my grandfather . . ."

"Oh my God!" said Gertie. "All the times she was out!"

"Looks like it."

Gertie beamed. "Bloody hell," she said.

"I know," said Morag. "I think . . . I mean, if they get married, what would that make us?"

Gertie laughed.

"Oh, and also I have this; the cleaners found it. Could you give it back to Struan to take to school?"

And she tossed Gertie a little moth-eaten bear.

CHAPTER 51

One evening in late April, the KCs traipsed up the stairs, enjoying the opportunity to visit Gertie's flat, and exclaim at how nice it was, with the new rugs and the soft throws everywhere, plus it meant they got to gossip solidly about Jean to her face, so everyone was happy. Even Elspeth had made it up the stairs without too much trouble, and exclaimed at the pretty sea views. Finally, spring had broken; the sun had come out and although the air was still cold, the hedgerows were bursting with fresh growth and tangled outbursts; bluebells carpeted the woodlands, the birds were cacophonous and the nights stretched out, light, ahead of them for months.

"And what about your 'flatmate'?" asked Jean, smiling around at the KCs.

"Mu-um," moaned Gertie, handing round the raisin biscuits she'd made. "Don't be daft. We're just flatmates. Stop saying it in quotation marks."

As if on cue, Struan came in humming and holding his guitar.

"Hiyah," he said absently to everyone, then looked cheerily at the biscuits. Jean passed him one over.

"So how is your new 'flatmate' arrangement working out?" she said.

Struan shrugged. "It's fine, huh, Gertie? I barely see you. I'm busy at school anyway. We've got the Mod coming up."

"Oooh," replied Jean. "What do you think, Gertie?"

"It's fine," said Gertie. "Honestly, Mum. Stop worrying about me. I'm a grown-up. I'm fine."

"There is," said Jean as she stood up later to go, and hugged Gertie tenderly, "no such thing as a grown-up daughter."

"That's true," said Elspeth, quietly.

And Gertie smiled, watching the gaggle of them, with their knitting bags and boxes and needles, walk down the road together, having decided they should go and get chips, seeing as they were out, and well, if Ranald happened to join them, Jean wasn't going to mind a bit, all of them arguing in the familiar ways with the exception of a new topic, which was how incredibly annoying Peigi was. They hadn't been this happy in years. Gertie had chosen not to go; she had an early start at the airport after all, getting back to normal, getting on with things.

STRUAN REENTERED THE lounge, smiling.

"Ah, bless 'em," he said.

He moved toward Gertie, who moved back from the window, in case anyone could see them, and when she realized they were fully alone, she slowly advanced toward him.

"I can't believe you make biscuits too," he said. "I think, Gertie, you are just too talented."

And she replied, "Could you possibly not call me Gertie? I've never liked it."

And he said . . .

He straightened up, carefully not putting weight on his sore toes, and thought about it, scratching his chin. He needed a shave. Gertie loved it.

"Sure. Do you mean it? What would you like?"

"I'm not sure," said Gertie.

"What about Trudie?"

"Ooh," said Gertie. "I like that."

She did, but anything he said she liked.

"I do too. You sound like some kind of sexy . . . well. Just some kind of sexy person. But you are, anyway. Whatever your name. And whatever you do."

Struan's voice changed and deepened, and he put his hand out, again, to gently touch her cheek.

From the second Morag had moved her things out, commiserating all the while with Struan about Saskia, the atmosphere between them had been absolutely charged.

Gertie couldn't quite believe it was happening. But also, to her surprise, it had felt like the most natural thing in the world. From the second he'd turned up at the door with his rucksack, he hadn't been able to stop staring at her, until she'd felt stupid. And she kept stealing glances at him, and blushing like a lunatic whenever he came into the room. And he gave her the old gloves so she could patch them where it was needed. And she'd put them back on his fingers herself, so carefully that they'd had to both immediately go to their own rooms.

Then, on the fifth day, he'd sat down with her at breakfast, limping heavily. She'd looked up at him, concerned.

"I'm not sure," he'd said. "I'm not sure this is going to work."

"What do you mean?"

"Us being flatmates?"

"Why?" she'd said, worried.

And he'd leaned his head on the table, and ruffled up his hair, his eyes squeezing together in embarrassment.

"Because I can't sleep and I can barely eat and . . . oh, Gertie, I have the worst, worst crush on you."

And as if this was a dream, or a film—except she was in Snoopy pajamas, and had just eaten a large bite of toast and marmalade,

and Struan was missing two toes, and although it was now technically nearly June, there was hail blowing against the windows,
and she was going to be late for check-in . . .

In spite of all those things, Gertie had, completely out of character, moved her chair closer, then slipped toward him and sat upon
his knee. And Struan had kissed her, and they had both tasted of
marmalade, and it had been everything she had ever dreamed of.

"WE'LL HAVE TO tell people sometime," said Gertie now. He pulled
her closer.

"I know," he said. "I know but . . ."

"The KCs will start speculating," murmured Gertie.

"And everyone will say it's too soon for me," said Struan, groan-
ing, even as he held her close.

"Is it?"

"It is not."

And he squeezed her so tightly she could have absolutely no
doubt he meant what he said.

"And my mother will go nuts."

"And the kids will all . . ."

"Just a little longer," said Gertie, beyond happy in the little
dreamworld they were building for themselves, their own little
castle in the air.

"And the plane can wait," said Struan, kissing her deeply.
"Truly, Trudie."

CHAPTER 52

Two weeks later, Gertie had a spring in her step as she entered the old tin can, settled her special guest, shared out the coffee she always brought, smiled at Mackintosh and Pete, and hummed Struan's songs to herself as she tidied up the check-in desk.

Calum was in with the helicopter boys, and saw her out of the corner of her eye. Had he really never noticed what fantastic legs she had?

He sidled over.

"I just wanted to say," he said. "I'm sorry . . . I think I was a little hasty."

One of Gertie's scarves was being featured in *Vogue*, just a little bit on a page, with a picture of the children, pink-faced and happy to be rescued, wearing her designs and calling her the hessian heroine, even though she didn't actually knit in hessian—that was stupid. Anyway, it was quite the chat of the knitting circle. Even Tara had considered ordering some wool that wasn't yellow.

"Uh-huh," said Gertie politely, but carrying on.

"I mean, I know I'm rich and always go for women for . . . reasons. But maybe I just want someone to get to know me for myself?" he said. "You know, someone who can be honest with me, maybe? Who gets to know the Real Me?"

"I like the Real You," said Gertie mildly. "I just don't really think it fits with the Real Me."

Calum sighed. She was suddenly as out of his reach as flying a helicopter.

"Can I . . . can I at least have the tie back?" he muttered, despondent.

"Sure," said Gertie, who smiled and turned her attention to the next customer.

THE P6S EN route to the Mod were as full of excitement and cheer as ever, even as the story of their daring night on the mountain had become ever more fanciful and now included the SAS, machine guns, and the occasional dinosaur.

Gertie looked around happily, supporting the very old woman she was bringing along for the ride—Elspeth, on her first trip out of the house together.

"Not you lot again," she said, beaming at them. "What's it going to be this time—shipwreck?"

She didn't look at Struan until she'd fastened Elspeth in securely, front row, window seat.

"Och," said Elspeth peering out. "The people look like ants."

"They are ants," said Gertie. "We haven't left the ground yet."

"I'm still not sure about this," said Elspeth in a small voice.

"You're going to love it," said Gertie. "The plane knits it all together: the earth, the people, the sky, the sea." And she squeezed the old, worn, nimble hand.

Then she nodded up the narrow aisle to Struan at the back. They were still, technically a secret, particularly in front of the children, so she nodded at him and he nodded back and Gertie was fine with that. Love wasn't about grand gestures and showing off; like stories or daydreams. Sometimes love was just about joy, and togetherness, and itself.

She turned back to give the safety announcement she was now qualified to do, and, at the last moment, she opened her bag.

"One last thing," she said, smiling her lovely smile. "MacIntyre Air appears to be carrying a stowaway."

And she pulled out Oksana's bear, now cleaned, stitched up, and wearing a brand-new pullover knitted in MacIntyre Air colors.

Oksana gasped, her eyes wide, and Gertie grinned even more handing it back to the girl, as her new friends exclaimed, and admired it.

That was too much for Struan. He couldn't help himself. He strode on his damaged feet to the front of the plane, grabbed Gertie in full view of everyone, and kissed her full on the mouth, to a loud OOOH from the children.

"I KNEW she was his girlfriend," said Wee Shugs.

"Excuse me, the fasten seatbelt sign is on?" yelled Morag from the cockpit.

"I thought we were taking this slowly," said Gertie.

"Ach well," said Struan.

"It is what it is."

"Listen to the wind upon the hill until the water abates."

"*Èist ri gaoth nam beann gus an traogh na h-uisgeachan.*"

THE CHILDREN HAD just all deplaned when Morag's radio buzzed. She came back to the cabin, where Gertie was unbuckling Elspeth.

"Ah," said Morag. "Not so fast."

Gertie looked up enquiringly.

"Air ambulance wants to know if we can take a job on for them, they're at a road crash. A17 is blocked out of Carso. And a heavily pregnant woman needs a transfer."

"Oh my God!" said Gertie, staring. "Is it Nalitha? Is she okay?"

"She will be, apparently, if we get a move on," said Morag, heading up front.

"Oh, Elspeth," said Gertie. "I was going to take you to the Mod."

"Don't you worry," said Elspeth, settling back. "I haven't had so much fun in years. Now, what color am I knitting for this baby?"

AFTERWORD

My mother taught knitting and sewing, and I don't really remember her ever not knitting something; my grandmother either. My grandmother was a fabulous knitter with terrible taste; she was always sending me purple cardigans with yellow sleeves and whatnot. My mum was very enthusiastic, but adored watching television or talking at the same time. I am the opposite of a hoarder, but even though she died a while ago, I cannot get rid of the cardigans she made for the children, with obvious dropped stitches or unmatched hems when, clearly, a good bit was on, or Robert Redford had just shown up. She could also never quite understand my love for neutrals for babies. I also have fond memories of her staying up to all hours to stitch together my little bits of knitting when I was a child; sewing the pieces together neatly was always my downfall.

I am afraid that I loved knitting for my babies then as they got bigger and bigger got worse at it—but the new school of amazing knitting Instagrammers like @petiteknit and @laerkebagger have truly inspired me to get back into it, and the result is this book.

Lots of love,

Jenny

ACKNOWLEDGMENTS

Thank you to Gavin McVeigh who bid and won to have his name included as part of Business Beats Cancer. I hope you enjoy your helicopter. ☺

Thanks to Vicki Ho for allowing me to use the name of her beloved late sister, Denise Yaternick in this novel; Kirstine Green in Copenhagen, knitter extraordinaire, who planted the seed for this book; Debbie Bliss for the original patterns; Lucy Malagoni, Jo Unwin, Deborah Schneider, Rachel Kahan and all at Little, Brown, Avon, JULA, and Jo Dickinson and team at Hodder Books.

ABOUT THE AUTHOR

Jenny Colgan is the *New York Times* bestselling author of numerous novels, including *The Christmas Bookshop*, *The Bookshop on the Corner*, and *Little Beach Street Bakery*. Jenny, her husband, and their three children live in a genuine castle in Scotland.

READ MORE BY JENNY COLGAN

SCHOOL BY THE SEA SERIES

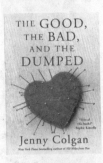

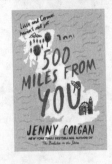

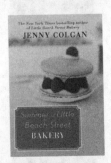

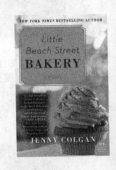

DISCOVER GREAT AUTHORS, EXCLUSIVE OFFERS, AND MORE AT HC.COM